The ANGELS' SHARE

A NOVEL

JAMES MARKERT

THOMAS NELSON
Since 1798

The Angels' Share

© 2017 by James Markert

Published in Nashville, Tennessee, by Thomas Nelson. Thomas Nelson is a registered trademark of HarperCollins Christian Publishing, Inc.

Author is represented by Writers House LLC.

Interior design: Mallory Collins

Thomas Nelson titles may be purchased in bulk for educational, business, fund-raising, or sales promotional use. For information, please e-mail SpecialMarkets@ThomasNelson.com.

Scripture quotations are taken from the Holy Bible, New International Version®, NIV®. Copyright © 1973, 1978, 1984, 2011 by Biblica, Inc.™ Used by permission of Zondervan. All rights reserved worldwide. www.zondervan.com. The "NIV" and "New International Version" are trademarks registered in the United States Patent and Trademark Office by Biblica, Inc.™

Library of Congress Cataloging-in-Publication Data

Names: Markert, James, 1974- author.
Title: The angels' share / James Markert.
Description: Nashville, Tennessee: Thomas Nelson, [2017]
Identifiers: LCCN 2016028403 | ISBN 9780718090227 (softcover)
Subjects: LCSH: City and town life--Fiction. | Family secrets--Fiction. | GSAFD: Christian fiction.
Classification: LCC PS3613.A75379 A85 2017 | DDC 813/.6--dc23 LC record available at https://lccn.loc.gov/2016028403

Printed in the United States of America
17 18 19 20 LSC 5 4 3 2 1

I've witnessed two miracles in my life.
Their names are Ryan and Molly.
They bless my life daily.
This one is for both of you.

Angels' share: the quantity of whiskey lost
to evaporation during the aging process

BEFORE

The house was quiet, even the baby, who'd been crying all evening from teething. His father was on the road and not due back until the weekend. So what were those noises out the window? Hushed voices? He knelt on his bed and eased the drapes apart enough to see his father's fedora below; he was dragging another man across the driveway. Six men walked alongside him. One man led them all: a giant dressed in white, using a baseball bat like a cane.

The man with the bat looked up and the boy quickly closed the drapes. He slid under the covers and squeezed his eyes shut, and he stayed that way until he had to pee. By that time the voices were gone, along with the footsteps. He snuck another look outside. It was only a dream.

But he still had to pee. So he crept downstairs to the bathroom. The garage was visible out the kitchen window. A light was on out there, with shadows moving inside the glow. His mother had left her slippers beside the kitchen table. The boy slid them on his bare feet and opened the back door to a warm summer night.

He walked across the short sidewalk to the garage and climbed on a cinder block to get a look inside.

He hadn't been dreaming after all.

His father was home early, and he'd brought friends with him. One was missing fingers on his left hand. Another was lying in a pool of blood. The man in white had scars on his cheeks. He lifted his baseball bat over his right shoulder and brought it down against the back of the man lying on the floor.

The boy flinched; the man moaned but barely moved. The man in white took another vicious swing that left the child crying. Why didn't his father stop him? Why didn't any of the men stop him?

And now the man on the floor wasn't moving at all.

A bald man as tall as a streetlamp held a sharp knife. The man in white called him Big Bang Tony. "Left or the right, Boss?"

The man in white pointed to his left cheek. Big Bang Tony cut him real slow and careful across the cheekbone, an inch-long gash. That's when the boy lost his bladder and the pain started: a pain in his rib cage, a pain that pulsed like a heartbeat . . .

ONE

OCTOBER 1934

The pews at St. Michael were made of solid walnut, and even the smallest sound bounced off the nave's rib-vaulted ceiling. William McFee, the oldest son of Barley and Samantha, had once dropped a coin during the first gospel and all eyes flashed toward him. But nothing had ever echoed as loudly as Barley's Colt .45 did, just as Father Vincent was consecrating the altar bread. Barley would claim it was the first time he brought a gun to church, but William knew better.

Sunlight hit the stained glass window and cast a prism across the altar. The church smelled of incense, candle wax, and perfume, and the combination made William drowsy. He didn't understand Latin; he stood when he was supposed to stand, knelt when he was supposed to kneel. Mr. Craven was nodding off near the middle pews.

William envied him; he hadn't slept last night. He'd been

thinking about the last words he'd said to his youngest brother. William wanted to write an article, not kick a ball around the yard. He'd told Henry no, not once but five times, until he finally said what he'd said and Henry left the room crying.

He could never take it back, and that's what bothered him the most on this day, the one-year anniversary.

He allowed himself to remember Henry dancing, wearing out the floorboards. He sure could dance: a prodigy, they'd called him. William once believed the talent was God given. But now he wondered if it was only a cruel trick. A four-year loan God snatched in an instant of crushed glass and twisted metal. This was the real reason William let his mind wander, not the Latin—it was his way of turning his back on God. He wasn't going to put in the extra effort anymore.

Typically, the McFees had a pew to themselves in the back— Barley didn't like anyone sitting behind him. He had grown quiet since the accident, and more paranoid. Most everyone in the small town of Twisted Tree, Kentucky, avoided him now. *Lucky to be alive,* they said in whispers. *Too bad about his little boy. Maybe he'll finally reopen the distillery, you know, to cope.* Barley had banged up his leg in the accident, but his real wounds were the kind nobody could see, which was why he was often drunk by lunchtime.

"Some bruises take longer to surface," William had explained to his brother Johnny about their father, *"and some are so deep they never come up."*

Johnny, at fifteen, had already locked lips with dozens of girls while William was still searching for that first kiss. Behind the acne bumps, floppy hair, and shy smile was a boy eager to bloom. He resembled his mother, whom everyone in town considered pretty, with her soft features and wavy hair the color of wheat, but William wasn't so sure he wanted to look like his mother. He wanted that hardened, gruff look Johnny had gotten from Barley. That and an ounce of Johnny's confidence, know-how, and instincts with the babes.

But it was William, though, who'd noticed that their parents no longer held hands in church. Samantha put one of the kids in between them as a buffer, usually six-year-old Annie, the youngest now that Henry was gone. Annie had rickets, which had left her bowlegged.

William glanced at his mother. She was making eye contact with Mr. Bancroft—he of the slick black mustache three pews up and across the aisle. Then Johnny leaned over and whispered in William's ear just as Annie pointed, her quiet way of asking their father to lower the kneeler.

Father Vincent started to consecrate the wine.

Barley bent down to help his daughter, and the latch on his leather shoulder holster came loose. The Colt .45 clunked against the walnut pew and discharged a bullet. Father Vincent jumped and the congregation ducked—especially the war veterans, half of whom were likely praying for food. But it was Mrs. Calloway (whose husband dodged the Great War by claiming a bogus heart defect) who darn near caught a slug in the eye. She hit the floor as Samantha McFee screamed, "Oh my goodness, Barley!" at the top of her lungs.

William was stifling laughter when the gun went off. The joke Johnny had whispered in his ear seconds before—*"A man who trouser coughs in church sits in his own pew"*—was typical Johnny: ill timed and jingle brained.

The bullet punched a hole in the stained glass window on

the south side of the church and then burrowed its way into the door of Mr. Bancroft's blue Model T parked outside.

Had his father also spotted his mother and the *Post* reporter making eye contact? Was that why the bullet lodged in that particular car door? Was it truly an accident?

The entire church was looking at them. William wiped his brow: the sweats had come, and now a nerve attack was inevitable. Like a shell-shocked veteran, he felt his hands tremble and his breath grow short. He felt smothered, dizzy, and light-headed. *Not now!*

Barley made no attempt to hide his gun. He sniffed the barrel before he slid it back into the shoulder harness. Then he went down on the kneeler beside his crippled daughter, closed his eyes, and prayed as the congregation split time watching him and the window's glass splinter.

"We'd better go, Barley," Samantha whispered.

William agreed. He could feel the glares as much as see them, and he was so chilled with sweat that he felt detached from himself, like he was watching from the ceiling beams. While he was up there he noticed Mr. Bancroft hurrying outside to check on his car.

But Barley was deep in prayer, his elbows resting on the pew in front of him, praying, William assumed, for the death of Preston Wildemere, who was doing a banker's bit for vehicular manslaughter. It was the reason their father went to church—to pray for another man's death. Or at least a longer sentence.

Eventually his father stood from the kneeler.

Mrs. Calloway—who had to be wearing five pounds of oyster fruit around her neck—was still on the floor, and people were gathering around to make sure she was breathing.

Barley felt it was a good time to approach Father Vincent at the altar for Communion. The wispy-haired priest eyed him with caution as he approached.

Luckily William's attack hadn't lasted long. He followed his father, not completely trusting what he was about to do. Barley never went for Communion; today he stopped before the altar and opened his mouth.

"Father," William hissed, "he's not even to that part yet. What are you *doing*?"

Barley stood with his mouth open, waiting for Father Vincent to slide a wafer in, which he did after a moment of contemplation.

"Corpus Christi," Father Vincent said—clearly he wanted the McFees to leave.

William wiped his forehead. *Is it really the body of Christ?* By the queer look in Father Vincent's eyes, the priest was thinking the same thing. Barley had fired in the middle of things, bringing a halt to the entire process.

Barley chewed, and instead of the appropriate response of *Amen*, he said, "Thanks."

Thanks? William wanted to sink into the marble steps but instead followed his father down the central aisle. Barley's black-and-white wing tips clicked as he walked. Samantha had already gathered Annie and Johnny near the baptismal font. She slid her fingers into the holy water and motioned the sign of the cross. Barley nodded toward the now-sitting Mrs. Calloway.

William followed his family out into the sunlight, where Barley removed a deck of Lucky Strikes from his coat. Samantha scoffed at this habit, picked up in Europe. In front of the kids she called them "coffin nails," but in secret she smoked them too. William could smell it on her clothes. She'd begun to dress differently of late too, trading in ankle-length dresses for those that showed her knees.

Across the lot Mr. Bancroft knelt beside his car, next to the new bullet hole in the driver's side door. He was pale behind the whiskers and praying, hands folded in a perfect triangle. "Cast the Devil out of Twisted Tree," he shouted when he saw Barley. "Cast him out before the End of Days takes us all, good Lord!"

Barley looked at William. "Can you drive? You're sweating like a horse."

William wiped his face. "I can drive."

It wasn't as new as Mr. Bancroft's, but the McFees had their own Model T. William was the primary driver—Barley had yet to sit behind the wheel since the accident. William started the car as Samantha, Annie, and Johnny crammed themselves into the back. It choked and throttled and spat gray smoke toward the church steps.

Before pulling out William looked over his shoulder to make sure Annie was secure beside their mother, which she was. Samantha was staring across the parking lot at Mr. Bancroft. Her concern gave William the same feeling in his gut he'd had when he'd seen his mother walking with him outside Murphy's Café back in June. And then again when he'd seen them laughing together outside the schoolhouse in August.

William didn't trust the man. He didn't think Bancroft was even Catholic. When he spoke about Christ, he sounded like one of those new Christian fundamentalists. Bancroft had only been attending St. Michael for a few months, and William was convinced it was only to see Samantha.

Barley was oblivious to it all—unless the bullet *had* been intended for that car door.

William slipped the car into gear with unnecessary force, and the Model T lurched toward the winding road flanked by trees turning colors. Barley cracked his window an inch so the smoke from his cigarette filtered out. He squinted as he took a drag. Other than the squeaking of Annie's leg braces, the car was silent.

Before the tragedy their car rides had been anything but silent. Henry liked to dance even in the car. Samantha would join in, clapping, and then Annie would break into made-up song. Back when Barley used to drive with a smile on his face and laughter in his eyes. It would last until Johnny'd pinch Henry or pull his ear, and then the fighting would ensue.

William missed the car noise. He missed the noise around the house too: the dinner table conversations, the day-to-day interaction, Annie chasing Henry in and out of every room until Barley threatened to tan their hides. Although he never would. Not those two. Now it was quiet enough to hear the floorboards creak, and Annie had no one who was willing to be chased.

William noticed his knuckles bone-white on the steering wheel, so he relaxed his grip. Maybe Henry had been the catalyst. The plug that kept the air in their balloon. Ever since they'd buried him, the air had been leaking and the family now moved in slow motion, the car rides palpably tense instead of proudly cherished.

Samantha once told him that time healed all wounds, but he could tell even she didn't believe it.

A mile south of the church and a stone's throw from where a Hooverville of shanties and lean-tos had sprung up on the outskirts of the woods, William pulled the car into the gravel lot of Charlie Pipes's Gas & Taff corner store. Across the street dozens of vagrants warmed their hands over garbage-can fires. Barley called them bums.

"What's a bum?" Annie asked.

"Street clutter," Barley said. He'd already inhaled the cigarette down to a nub. "What are you doing?"

"We need gas," William said. They both knew gas wasn't the reason for his stop. Next to the front door, the newspaper rack was full of dailies. William felt the pull toward the fresh print.

"We're still a quarter wedge to empty." Barley patted the dashboard. "We can make it to Wednesday. Tuesday, at least."

Says the one who never leaves the house anymore. Their bourbon distillery had been shut for fourteen years. Barley had no job, and he did very little other than sit in his chair sipping booze. Yet they somehow had enough money to put food on the table.

William pointed to the sign above the pump: TEN CENTS A GALLON. "It's cheaper than I've seen it since summer." He stepped out of the car and closed the door so he couldn't hear Barley rambling.

Annie yelled from the backseat, "Get me a piece of taffy, William."

Barley rolled down the window another couple of inches. "No taffy, William." He lowered his voice and handed William a ten-dollar bill. "Don't need her with wobbly legs *and* rotten teeth. Get yourself a paper. I know that's why you stopped."

He took the bill from his father.

Barley nodded toward the storefront. A man slept in a bundle of rags next to Gas and Taff's front door. "Don't give that bum any money. He'll spend it on booze."

William knew his father would be three sheets to the wind by dinnertime and four sheets not long after that, passed out in his chair instead of on the sidewalk. *The drunk with money and the drunk without.*

William met Charlie Pipes in the middle of the lot. Charlie was a tall man with leathery skin, coal-black eyes, and a gray beard that he used to keep trimmed. But since the stock market crashed in '29, he'd let himself go. The beard was long and fuzz had taken over part of his neck.

"Fill 'r up, Charlie. And I'll take a newspaper and three pieces of taffy."

Charlie glanced at the car. Barley tipped his fedora.

"Is Barley gonna shoot me?"

"You already heard?"

"Word travels fast in the Tree." Charlie wiped his hands on grease-stained overalls. "Willard and Fanny Mae Patterson left before you pulled in. They were in the church and said it echoed loud enough to crack glass."

"Crack glass and puncture a car door."

"The reporter's?"

William nodded. "Mr. Bancroft's."

"Good. Tired of him snooping 'round here."

"Lucky, though. Could'a been worse." William handed Charlie an extra dollar. "I'll take two papers, Charlie. Keep the rest for yourself."

"Thank you, William. Take an extra piece or two for Annie."

William closed in on the storefront. Truth be told, the down-trodden man sleeping there disgusted him, as did the pungent cloud of stench that hovered. He admired Charlie Pipes for allowing the man the small courtesy of using the storefront as a windbreak. The nights were getting cold. He looked over his shoulder to make sure Barley wasn't watching and then handed the man a dollar.

His voice was a wheeze. "God bless."

God bless? William didn't want to think about God and His so-called blessings. He entered the store to grab four pieces of taffy from the bowl on the counter, catching a whiff of the woodstove churning through pine in the back. Outside again, he dropped two pieces of taffy on the man's lap and moved toward the newspaper rack.

"He moves through you."

"Excuse me?" William stopped. "Who moves through me?"

"The Holy Spirit." The man shifted against the brick wall. "He died for our sins."

William faced the newspaper rack and mumbled, "Yes, so I hear."

"Just yesterday," said the homeless man. "He died for our sins. And now he's coming."

William gave a polite nod and grabbed two papers. One he'd read from front to back, and eventually Barley would use it for kindling. The other he'd carefully add to those he'd been saving since Coolidge took over from Harding in '23.

"It's just the way he was," the man said.

The comment gave William pause. It was what Henry used to say when asked about his dancing. *"It's just the way I am."* William shook it off and perused the headlines on his way back to the car.

Ships tied up in harbors with hulls rotting; freight trains idle; passenger cars empty; eleven million people without work;

the treasury building bursting with gold yet Congress wrestles a deficit mounting into the billions, the result of wild and extravagant spending; granaries overflowing with wheat and corn yet millions begging for food; mines shutting down; oil industries engaged in cutthroat competition; farmers desperate; factories stagnant and industry paralyzed.

It was the same every day. It was why Mr. Bancroft had recently written in the *Post* that the End of Days was near.

William caught a few headlines that struck his fancy. Bruno Hauptmann was indicted for the murder of Charles Lindbergh's son. Adolf Hitler was expanding Germany's army and navy and looked to be creating an air force.

The car horn bleated three times in rapid succession.

One day I'll have a story front page and center. William lowered the paper.

"Read it when you get home," Barley called out the window. "Annie has to pee."

William hustled around to the driver's side and opened the door. He waved to Charlie, started the car, and said to Barley, "Hitler has violated the Treaty of Versailles."

Barley grunted. He didn't care about current events. He didn't care about much of anything anymore. He was the only one in the car who wasn't rattled by the gunshot.

"Is there going to be another war?" Johnny asked from the backseat.

"The last one never really ended," Barley said. "I didn't get around to killing them all."

"There's not going to be another war," Samantha said matter-of-factly. "And there will be no talk of killing. Get us home, William."

William watched his father. At thirty-nine, he still had wavy black hair, although spots of gray had begun to show along the sideburns.

Barley didn't return the look. He never did.

William reached his left hand beside his seat and slid it discreetly alongside the door toward the back, just long enough for Annie to pluck the two pieces of taffy from his palm.

"Street clutter," he heard her whisper. "I'm telling Henry that."

A dented blue jalopy pulled into the lot and stopped in a cloud of rock dust at the second pump. It was the Jeffersons from down the road.

William waved but they didn't wave back.

They glared, though.

Must have heard about Barley's gunshot, a fresh pinprick on an already-festering bruise. Twisted Tree was a town of less than eight hundred people now, several hundred less than the population at the height of the distillery, at the height of Old Sam McFee bourbon. The McFees didn't know everyone, but it seemed the entire town knew the McFees.

Barley especially. Henry, too, as he'd acquired a hint of local fame.

William had seen the glare before, from plenty of people over the years. No one in town blamed Barley for the demise of Old Sam bourbon, not even the faithful who'd stayed behind after Prohibition agents shut it down. And they especially didn't blame Old Sam himself—he was a hero, even if he had stepped away from God long enough to hang himself.

But William sensed an undercurrent of resentment building. The distillery's demise *had* led directly to the death of the town, which, like many other bourbon towns, had started declining a decade before the Great Depression shook the rest of the country. Prohibition plastered its own dark shadow.

But Prohibition was over now. William said, "It's legal to distill spirits and sell booze again, Dad."

"So? Why do you care?" Barley asked.

"Just because I do." William wanted to say more but was unwilling to poke and prod through the garbage.

Because before he died, Grandpa Sam told me I'd run the distillery someday.

The town's resentment wasn't because the distillery had been swallowed up; it stemmed from Barley's utter lack of interest in opening it again. The crowd that showed for the dance marathon a week before Henry's death had assumed it was a party to signal the beginning of things. Why else had the McFees moved back to Twisted Tree? Why return, if not to rekindle Old Sam, to fill the ricks of the aging house to the rafters with full barrels of dark amber bourbon? To hear the familiar rumble of five-hundred-pound barrels rolling across the runs?

But then, after Henry outdanced everyone in town, the beginning of things never happened.

TWO

Not much was said during the four-mile ride home from the gas station. Samantha went quiet whenever she was mad. William had watched her in the rearview mirror as he drove past the town's boarded-up homes and shops. Her jaw never unclenched.

Barley finished another cigarette and flicked it out the window before they turned onto their property, which stretched out like a wagon wheel through the woods of Twisted Tree, their driveway a meandering spoke of dust and gravel leading to their two-story home in the center. They owned twenty acres just south of the Ohio River, where springs and creek beds filtered through an abundance of limestone, making the local water as well known as the spirits produced from it. Barley's father had purchased the land before the turn of the century and started one of the most sought-after bourbons in the region.

William spotted Black-Tail standing on its hind legs in the weeds, sniffing at flakes of peeled white paint on the porch, as he pulled to a puttering stop on the gravel outside their house. "Well, look at that, it's Black-Tail."

Johnny saw the squirrel next. Barley reached for his gun as he shut the car door.

Samantha stood beside Annie. "Barley, put it away. Haven't you done enough today?"

Barley homed in and got as far as closing one eye to shoot before he lowered his gun and handed the Colt across the car's hood to William. "Here, you shoot it."

William kept his hands in his pockets. "I'm not shooting Black-Tail."

The squirrel wasn't born with a black tail. After it had terrorized the McFees' garden, plucking cucumbers and tomatoes from vines and leaving the half-gnawed vegetables on the ground, Barley set a trap. The rodent's life was spared by Johnny's brilliant idea: *"Paint his tail black. That way if he comes back, we'll know if it's the same squirrel."* Barley had jerked a nod like it was the best idea he'd ever heard.

"Daisy," Barley said under his breath but loud enough for Johnny to hear and laugh. It wasn't the first time he'd called his oldest a daisy, or a weak sister. Barley told people at the dance marathon that William liked to "traipse" through the woods with a book instead of the rifle he received for his tenth birthday. Even little Henry, at four, had fired a pistol at a deer.

Barley smirked at Johnny as if to say, "Watch this," and then leveled the gun at Black-Tail. Just when his finger pulled back on the trigger, Annie took a step behind the car. Her leg braces rattled enough to alert Black-Tail, who darted off.

"Quit rustlin', Annie," Barley muttered, never taking his gaze from the escaping squirrel.

He fired, missed, and then fired again, watching Black-Tail disappear into the woods.

Jumpy like the blackbirds now scattering from the trees, William flinched with every pull of the trigger. Then Annie was crying, not because she'd wanted Black-Tail dead, but because her braces had made an untimely noise. Again.

Barley looked off toward the woods, toward the red, orange, and yellow leaves, toward the black-barked white oaks—the whiskey trees—that towered over the old milling barn, cooking tanks, and empty cottages. He breathed deeply, as if he could conjure up the smell of rye, barley, and corn, charred oak and sour mash.

"You need to stop throwing your cigarette butts into the woods, Barley," Samantha blurted, pronouncing it like she'd added an addendum to a contracted list. "It hasn't rained now for weeks. You're apt to burn the entire distillery down."

"What distillery?" Barley asked, monotone, still gazing toward the woods, or perhaps toward the two trees in the distance for which the town was named, where he had found his father, Samuel, hanging the morning after the distillery was raided, his feet dangling two feet above the snowfall.

Samantha walked Annie into the house. She kicked at the same flaked paint Black-Tail had been sniffing and then peeled a white wedge the size of a corncob from one of the porch's four columns. She let it feather to the floorboards. She had her ways of reminding Barley the house hadn't been painted in years.

Fifty yards past the water well, a plow horse driven by a man named Frank pulled a wagon into the tall grass of the neighboring potter's field, carefully navigating the few standing wooden crosses. On the flatbed a burlap sack bounced in cadence with the rickety wheels. William had seen the sacks bounce right off, and he cringed every time they hollow-thudded to the ground. Frank would stop and load them back on like a bushel of apples.

"Another indigent getting planted." Barley straightened his fedora.

Frank waved and Barley tipped his hat.

As Frank began to slide the body from the wagon bed, William's vision clouded and sweat blasted his skin. Death was close; he could feel it in his shrinking lungs. Johnny noticed and hurried over, but William's knees crunched the gravel before Johnny could catch him. Barley looked over his shoulder and pity filled his eyes. William hated him for it.

"You okay?"

Barley's question was obligatory, but William nodded respectfully. He could breathe again. If only he could predict his attacks, then he could prepare. *"It's just who I am."* It was Henry's voice again. William was just an anxious person; Henry's death had made it worse.

"That's two bouts of hysteria today," Barley said. "You had one in church earlier."

"Everything's jake." William shrugged free of Johnny—five years younger but just as tall—and wiped dust from his knees. "Just mind your own."

Barley viewed his son's nerve attacks as weakness, just as the military viewed shell shock. But doctors had recently found credence in the claims. Barley chewed the inside of his cheek and swallowed some pride. "Maybe we should go back to the doctor."

Johnny patted William on the shoulder. "Yeah, William, maybe you should."

"And he'll tell me the same thing as before. It's just something I've got to live with."

William returned his attention to the potter's field, where Frank attacked the soil with his spade and readied the grave.

Who was the deceased? Was it a man or a woman? What had they done in life to have become so irrelevant?

These unattended burials were too commonplace as of late.

Barley, when he was William's age, had asked his father how many bodies were buried in that field. Sam said, *"Hundreds, if not thousands. Probably stacked like bricks in a wall too."* When William, at ten, had asked Barley the same question, Barley gave the same answer, but he'd added, *"Does it really matter?"*

To William it did. *"If they're stacked like bricks, won't they eventually push out of the ground? Won't they eventually grow too high?"*

Barley had shrugged, and those questions went unanswered.

But William grew older and deciphered an explanation—the bodies decomposed, and as more were buried, the older bodies sank deeper into the ground. Or maybe there never were as many bodies in the potter's field as Grandpa Sam had thought.

The McFee family cemetery, however, was easily counted. There were six headstones in two parallel rows. The top row had four while the second had two, the most recent—Grandpa Sam and Henry McFee. William hadn't known any of the top four. One was Grandpa Sam's sister, Jane, who'd died of yellow fever when she was twelve. The other three were cousins who'd played important parts in the formation of the distillery.

The plot was located on the other side of the house, sur-rounded by tall evergreens and much more secluded than the larger potter's field. When Grandpa Sam was asked why he'd decided to build so close to a place where indigents were buried, he'd always said very matter-of-factly that he liked the location. Liked the white oaks—they were perfect for aging bourbon whiskey. He also liked the proximity to limestone-rich creek beds that naturally added calcium to the water and removed the iron. The location was ideal and he knew it would make them money. The neighboring potter's field would add perspective and keep them humble.

William watched as Frank hammered a small wooden cross in the ground and said a quick prayer over the buried. And that was that. He'd be back the next day or the day after with another. Seeing a burial on Henry's anniversary made William melancholy. And talking to that man at the gas station, the more he thought on it, had made him uncomfortable.

He needed to acknowledge Henry's anniversary. Barley was already heading into the house. He nodded to Johnny and they both headed to the family headstones. William sat on the bench opposite his brother, his back to the evergreens that cast a shadow across all six stones.

"Annie still talks about him in the present tense." William cleared his throat; he felt on the verge of tears. "She did it in the car today."

Johnny said, "I heard her."

"When Henry was three, I wasn't paying as close attention as I should have while Mom and Dad were in the city." *Probably the last time they went anywhere together.* "He climbed the dining room table. I'd yet to clear it from supper. He decided to finish off what was left in the glasses. Annie's milk. Mother's tea. The backwash from Father's beer. 'Drinked Daddy's beer, Will'm. Drinked Daddy's beer,' he said when I found him, on his back and belly sloshing. He moved it side to side to listen to it. 'Like bathtub water, Will'm.' I said, 'Get down off that table, Henry!' I told him not to drink after everybody. Well, if you remember, he was just starting to use the toilet about that time. An hour later I saw him *outside* the bathroom, pants around his ankles. I yelled, 'No,

Henry, you can't pee there.' He said, 'I no pee here, Will'm.' And then he pointed across the hall to the crapper *ten feet away*. 'I'm gon' pee way over there.'"

Johnny smiled.

"He made it too. A perfect rainbow. Like the crapper was a pot of gold."

William sighed, looked to the ground, wished for the millionth time that he could redo that last day. Henry had cried a lot, because he was four and, as Barley stated, growing up to be too much like William. William knew Barley didn't know what to think of Henry's dancing. *"Gonna keep you tough, Henry,"* Barley liked to say. And then he'd put a rifle in Henry's hands and lead him into the whiskey trees to shoot something. But Henry never stopped moving, even was always tapping a toe, and he'd end up alerting the deer or rabbit.

Now William looked at the dozen red roses angled against his little brother's headstone. His mother must have been out at sunup. She must have eaten her breakfast here, alone. Or had his father been out too?

The surviving brothers stood and headed back to the house. They knew Barley, half deep into a bottle, was already vegetating in his La-Z-Boy.

Six companies had been allowed to produce legal bourbon for the country's medicinal trade during Prohibition, and four of them were located in Louisville. Barley drank Old Forester because it was quality aged—rare so soon after repeal.

"What are you drawing over there?" Barley called from his

chair, his torso lit by moonlight shining through the bay window. The ledge was decorated with five dust-covered empties of Old Sam McFee, Bottled in Bond. William had grown up hoping to one day fill those bottles with bourbon he distilled but had recently given up on the notion—with Barley's lack of drive, it was a dream even more naive than becoming a journalist.

Startled, William looked up. "I'm drawing you."

He was doodling his father's shadowy profile under the rainbow glow of a stained glass floor lamp. Barley rarely moved from his oddly shaped favorite chair. "Nature's way of relaxing," the magazine had called it. Since Henry died, every morning after he suited himself up from wing tips and spats to suspenders and tie, he'd sit in the La-Z-Boy all day. The wreck had killed both of them. It was just taking Barley longer to stop breathing.

Smoke spiraled upward from a cigar stub wedged between the index and middle fingers of Barley's right hand. He'd removed his fedora after dinner and placed it on the end table beside his chair, right next to the half-eaten bowl of stew Samantha had delivered after the rest of the family had eaten in the dining room without him.

William added another couple of lines to accentuate his father's chiseled jaw and then a few swirls of shade to capture the mystery in his deep-blue eyes. He sketched when he couldn't write. Earlier, he'd attempted to type out some details about his father but didn't get very far.

"Bring it over here." Barley took a drag on his cigar and then smothered the stub in what was left of his stew.

"Did you hear the St. Louis Hawks beat the Detroit Tigers four games to three in the World Series?" He'd memorize things from the paper about baseball as conversation starters.

"It's the Cards, William. Not the Hawks. And I know." Barley gestured for him to come over. The attempts never transformed into anything meaningful.

William's footfalls were heavy across the wood-planked floor. He handed over the sketch.

"Why are your hands shaking?"

William shrugged. He *was* shaking. He never expected Barley to see his picture.

Barley squinted at himself, then handed it back. "What were you so busy typing earlier?"

William rubbed his hands on his pant legs. "I was writing about what happened today," he answered with caution. "At church. Thought maybe a story could be made from it."

"No story I'd want to read." Barley tilted his head back, downed the rest of his Old Forester, and then reached for the bottle next to his Colt .45. "You get to the part where the Calloway broad fainted?"

"I did."

Barley flashed a brief smile. He poured two glasses and nudged one toward William. "Go on, take it. Helps calm the nerves."

William had seen enough drunkards in his life. He'd heard people claim distilleries were arms of the Devil. But his family's distillery had built this town. Still, he felt reluctant: he'd sworn to Mr. Browder next door that his first sip of bourbon would be Old Sam.

"Might be an old man by then," Mr. Browder had said. Along with William, Mr. Browder also dreamed of rekindling the distillery. But Mr. Browder's hair was now as white as his skin was black.

William had seen Fitz Bannion down the road take a sip of some home brew and vomit. But this wasn't bootleg. Old Forester wasn't Old Sam, but it was the real thing, aged and survived. He swirled the amber liquid inside the glass and brought it to his nose to inhale.

"It's not wine, William."

William wrinkled his nose and rubbed emerging moisture from his right eye.

"Don't be so delicate. Breathe in through your mouth—smell the vanilla?" Barley asked. "And caramel?"

"No."

"It's from charring the oak barrels. Brings out the flavors in the wood. By the taste and smell, I'm guessing the mash bill on this is at least seventy percent corn. Twenty and ten, give or take, with rye and barley." Barley poured himself another. "Coat your tongue with it."

William hesitated. Since Henry's death, he'd made a daily promise to himself not to end up a drunk like his father had become. But one drink wouldn't hurt. He tilted his head back. The bourbon slid smoothly across his palate, but then liquid heat went both north and south, burning his chest and sinuses with equal measure. He coughed into his fist and then put the glass on the table.

Barley dumped another two fingers of bourbon down his gullet and eyed the typewriter across the room. "If you insist on being a journalist and not getting a real job, do me a favor."

William's throat felt raw, his voice raspy. "What?"

"Pick a new target. Stories about me will get you nowhere."

"Because you're a vault," William said, understanding for the first time the line his mother used to describe Barley at social gatherings. *It's the whiskey talking.* He did feel calmer and more relaxed.

"A vault. That's a good one." Barley poured more Old Forester. "I'll give you one tidbit then. And you can write this down. For the record. Are you ready?" He leaned forward. "Do you know why my father named me Barley?"

"No," said William, ready for a golden nugget.

"Because if I'd been named Corn or Rye, I would've gotten pasted on the schoolyard." Barley leaned back, proud of himself. After thirty ticks on the grandfather clock, he leaned forward and the recliner closed with a snap. He pointed out the window toward the potter's field, where a lone lantern hovered at a man's height from the ground. "You see that?"

William stepped closer to the window. "I do."

The initial light was followed by another, and a few seconds later three more lantern lights emerged from the whiskey trees, bobbing like fireflies. Barley bumped into the end table on his way closer to the window, nearly spilling everything on top of it. "William, lock the doors."

"What . . . why? What's going on?"

"Lock the door," Barley said. "And get my shotguns from the bedroom."

THREE

Samantha, still sopping wet from the tub, returned upstairs to put Annie to bed, mumbling about paranoia as she climbed the steps. Unconcerned about the crowd in the potter's field, Johnny returned to whatever he'd been doing in his bedroom before he'd rushed down the stairs moments ago. It was just William and his father again, watching the lanterns and torches and all the bums who held them—close to two hundred now. Barley was still convinced they were dangerous.

"Is it the Krauts, Dad?" William had decided to play along.

Barley turned, peered over the window ledge. "Worse."

William faced the window, giving a clear view of his head and shoulders to the shadowy figures outside. None seemed to be paying the McFees' home any attention. The potter's field was rarely used for Twisted Tree residents; the town's deceased were buried on family farms. Most of the indigents out there in the ground came from Louisville. *How far did these people travel?*

"Get down," Barley said. He was tired, his eyes bloodshot. "Get down, Johnny. They're gonna blow your noodle off."

William ignored the command, especially because his father had called him by the wrong name. Outside, many had dropped to their knees, their heads bowed. They prayed in unison—a drone like a swarm of bees. He'd witnessed hundreds of burials in the potter's field, and not once had anyone come to pay respects for the deceased. *Who has drawn such a crowd of mourners?*

They prayed. They cried. They consoled like one great family.

"I can't hear, Johnny . . ." Barley's eyes closed, his fingers limp around the empty bottle of Old Forester. "Where? Where'd . . . his shoes go?"

William let Barley ramble. They'd gone over the mysteries of the accident endlessly. Henry's shoes were never found, the ones he called his dancing shoes. Barley had gone through the windshield first, breaking the glass for Henry's passage. According to the blood trail, Henry had landed in the middle of the road. But when Barley came to, Henry was on the *side* of the road, in the grass, with his hands peacefully crossed atop his chest. Both of his legs had been broken. The only other person there, besides Barley, was wedged between his seat and steering wheel. So if someone had helped Henry off the road, it hadn't been Preston Wildemere.

William patted his father's shoulder, and soon he was snoring —a deep, throaty rumble. He'd be out for the night. Was Mr. Browder witnessing this strange pilgrimage from his cottage? Probably so; Mr. Browder didn't miss much.

William tried another sip, following Barley's directions. He breathed it in through his mouth. Maybe he did catch a hint of vanilla. He sipped enough to cover his tongue, winced as he held the flavors in his mouth. He took another swallow. It burned a trail down his throat, but the finish was crisp and smooth.

One day barrels will roll across the runs again.

William McFee, Master Distiller. He smiled at the thought, then sipped again.

"What's going on out there, William?" His mother was padding across the floor, barefoot and tying the strings of a nightgown around her waist. "I've been watching from the bedroom."

She sat on the other side of Barley. By the looks of her attire, she was home for the night, which gave William comfort. She mourned for Henry deeply, but she also went out of her way to prove her toughness, taking pride in showing she'd overcome the tragedy. He heard her weeping at night with no one to console her, because Barley, if he didn't pass out in his recliner, was sleeping on the couch. Deep down, William knew she blamed Barley for Henry's death.

"A prayer service of some kind," William said.

"This is quite the spectacle." She stared out the window. "Will you need the car in the morning? After you take your brother and sister to the schoolhouse?"

"No, Mother." She was one of only a few women William knew who drove. Barley had been on the road so often during the twenties, she'd felt it necessary to learn. He watched her. "Do you need the car again for groceries? Because we seem to need a lot of groceries of late."

Samantha studied him. "Is there something on your mind, William?"

He wanted to ask her about the glances with Mr. Bancroft during church. The times he'd seen them sharing laughs and walking together. The man was a hack from the *Post*. "No."

"Then quit gumshoeing." She tucked a strand of loose sandy-colored hair behind her ear. "Have you given any more thought to what we discussed yesterday? Father Vincent could hire you at the church to paint and clean the grounds..."

"I doubt the offer is still available after what happened today."

"Yes, you're probably right."

"I want to write." William thought of what the man had said earlier in the day—*"It's just the way he was"*—and said, "I was born to be . . . I wasn't born to be average." And then he added without thinking, "Just like Henry wasn't."

Her glance at Barley spoke volumes. She feared if he didn't find paying work soon, he would turn into his father. Most of the boys—young men—his age had already secured work years ago, mostly hard summertime labor that required sweating in the fields, coal yards, or horse farms. William didn't mind the sweating, but if he was going to do it, he didn't understand why it couldn't be at the distillery. He didn't understand their stubbornness on the matter.

For him, writing filled the void. But if journalism was a realistic option, he'd be writing for pay by now.

His mother must have read his thoughts. "How many rejections is it from the *Courier* now?"

"Eight . . . nine. I don't remember."

"Sure you do," Samantha said, serious.

"Please give me a chance to prove myself."

She reached over Barley's head, squeezed William's hand, and then let go. "Prove yourself then, William. But there comes a time when growing up should come first."

"The *Courier* says I need something more gripping." William ran his hand through his hair. "Breaking news happens, Mother. When it does I need to be ready."

"Going to college is still an option. And don't forget, St. Meinrad is not far—"

"I don't want to be a priest. Why do you and Father all of a sudden think I'd be a good priest?" *I don't even believe anymore. And so what if I'm not as smooth with the broads as Johnny.*

"I'm sorry, I didn't mean to needle you." She watched him. "I don't need the car for groceries tomorrow. I plan to see Mr. Bancroft. I want to give him money for the bullet hole your father put in his car door. If you want, I can talk to him about your writing—"

"No," he said quickly. He'd never take advice from a *Post* reporter. Especially not someone who wrote as sensationally as Bancroft. "Is that all?"

"Is what all?"

"You're just going to see him about the car door?"

"Of course that's all." Her cheeks flushed. "What else would it be?"

She was not a good liar. It roiled him to think she couldn't see through the man. Since the accident, Bancroft had been penning articles hinting that there was more to Barley's part in the wreck than the *Courier* let on. Now he was attending their church, pretending to care about her well-being. He was a leech, taking advantage when Samantha was most vulnerable.

"We'll cover the cost of the church window as well?" He didn't want an argument, and part of him didn't want the truth either.

"I suppose we should." Samantha reached for William's glass of bourbon, downed it in one swallow, and banged it down on the window ledge. Barley snorted but stayed asleep.

There was a low rumble of thunder, and then it started to rain.

"Mother? Tell me about the day Henry was born."

"You remember the storm, don't you?"

"How could I not?" William had been terrified. "I thought

we were going to die." But it wasn't what he was interested in hearing about.

"We all did."

"I mean, it got so quiet in your room. And then Father screamed."

"Your father thought Henry was stillborn." She smiled with the memory. "Because he didn't cry. All babies cry when they come out—you wailed for an hour."

"But not Henry?"

"No, not Henry." This smile was broader. "And then he suddenly opened his eyes and looked around like he'd just awoken. Like he was playing a joke on us all."

"And then what?"

"The midwife snipped the cord, cleaned him off, and passed him around the room. And Henry did what he'd do for the next four years. He left us in awe."

"Made everybody smile."

"Yes," she said. "He made us smile."

⁂

The crowd at the potter's field was gone the next morning, leaving no evidence, other than some trampled grass, that they'd ever been there at all. Perhaps the rain had driven them away. It left William with a hollow feeling in his gut.

Barley snored on the floor beneath the bay window, so William stole a moment in his father's chair, facing the wall where Henry's closed casket had rested for eight long hours before the burial. Sunlight bled through the window just as it had on that day, detailing all the grains in the wood. Annie had knocked on the coffin and said, *"Alright, Henry, come on out now. It's my turn to hide."*

Samantha stormed from the room crying, brushing right past Barley who'd tried halfheartedly to console her. He'd been nearly catatonic as over two hundred Twisted Tree residents funneled into their home to pay respects, filling the dining room and kitchen with homemade casseroles and soups whose wonderful smells made everything feel wrong.

William had wanted everyone out. He hated shaking hands and accepting hugs; all he wanted to do was wallow. Johnny had cried his eyes out the night before and was the only member of the family to have his wits about him. The entire afternoon he stood in suit and tie at the door greeting.

William's heart rate accelerated and the sweats started. He clenched his fists as he remembered walking Annie away from the casket to explain again that Henry was gone.

"Can't we open the box?"

"We can't, Sugar Cakes."

"Then I don't believe he's in there." She went into the dining room to eat a biscuit from Miss Stapansky's basket. William watched her, envious of her ignorance.

But since she'd said it, not a day had gone by that William didn't wonder.

FOUR

o how come Dad had all his shotguns out?" Annie asked as
William steered the car down the driveway. The grass was
covered with red and gold leaves—wet paint strewn across a
green canvas. Johnny was tapping the dashboard to a beat only he
could hear. Annie sat in the back middle seat because she liked to
look at herself in the rearview mirror.

William couldn't wait to drop both of them off at St. Michael
so he could get over to the potter's field and find out who the
deceased was. Frank sometimes painted names on the wooden
crosses; the seeds of a story might be there.

"To clean them," he said. Barley was still asleep on the floor
when they'd left.

"Liar," said Annie, which made Johnny laugh.

William grinned, watching her through the mirror. "How do
you know I'm lying?"

"I just can tell." She shrugged. "You're not as good at it as
Johnny."

Johnny put his fist in the air.

Annie raised her hand. "I've got another memory."

William looked at Johnny. "Let's hear it, Sugar Cakes."

"One day I was in the bathtub with Henry and he passed gas and bubbles came up."

"Good story," said Johnny.

Annie smiled proudly, and so did William. The give-and-take reminded him of the playful banter they'd once shared—evidence that seeds still remained.

Wet, gnarled tree limbs overhung the gravel road. William drove slowly past the abandoned distillery buildings—the shed for storing the grains, the water well, the milling barn and cooking house, the fermentation house and distilling barn, all pitch-roofed and missing shingles. White oak barrels stood empty all over the grounds, home to mice and coons, the bilge hoops rusted around rain-warped staves, some resting horizontally on steel runs that connected the buildings, cross-hatching the property like a train depot.

Life had just stopped here. But the woods still held the smell of mash: the thick aroma of the grains cooking, the yeast turning the sugars into alcohol, the angels' share escaping from aging barrels. William didn't have many memories from when Old Sam was king; he'd only been six. Still, all the good memories of his father and grandfather involved the distillery.

William slowed past one of the barrel runs and noticed Mr. Browder sweeping standing water from the porch of one of the ten vacant employee cottages. Ronald Browder was the only one to stay behind, with his wife and daughter, unwilling to part from his cornfield, which had thrived for decades before the distillery and still thrived after the Volstead Act. He believed the land was blessed. They were one of only a handful of black families left in town. Ronald's wife passed in the winter of 1929, after a three-year battle with tuberculosis at the Waverly Hills Sanatorium. Now it was just Ronald. His daughter, Carly, had married two years ago and moved out.

Mr. Browder took a break from his sweeping, and William stopped the car and rolled the window down.

"Morning, McFees." Mr. Browder approached the idling car. He had two bad knees but refused to use the cane Samantha had gotten him for Christmas. He moved around the front of the hood toward William's side and stuck his head in. He winked at Annie in the back. "Sugar Cakes."

"Snowflake," Annie said to Mr. Browder, laughing. His hair was a white mushroom.

"How them legs, little girl?"

"Better than them knees, old man."

Mr. Browder smiled large, patted William on the elbow. "You talk to Mrs. McFee?"

William sagged in the driver's seat. "Not yet."

"It's okay." He patted William's arm again. He looked back at Annie. "Ain't that right, little girl? Everything's jake."

She nodded, started lightly punching the ceiling.

"Got you a little boxer in the back," said Mr. Browder. "I had another dream, William. About the distillery running."

The door to his cottage opened, and Carly Browder stepped outside in a paisley dress that showed her curves. William had been secretly coveting those curves since his school days. He never voiced his admiration to anyone. She was four years older and black. Neither should matter, and he had convinced himself that his parents would be jake with it—at the distillery's zenith, half of the staff had been colored—but it was irrelevant now. She was happily married. And even curvier than he remembered. *Is she with child?*

Carly Browder—Carly *Charles*—waved from the porch. William jerked a nod; Johnny and Annie waved back.

"Gon' be a granddaddy, McFee family," Mr. Browder confirmed. "My girl and her man are movin' back." He tapped William's elbow again. "It all a sign, Will McFee. And with all dat hubbub in the field las' night, it gon' happen. You watch now. You talk to Mrs. McFee. We gon' get Mr. Barley up outta dat chair and into the houses again." Done talking, he patted the car's roof. "Move along, soldiers."

Mr. Browder stepped back and watched them go. "What was that all about?" Johnny asked. "What do you need to ask Mother about?"

"Nothing."

Johnny looked over his shoulder toward the Browders' cottage. "I would have loved to lock lips with that babe."

"She's nine years older than you."

"I could handle it. I kissed Nadine Swarthwood last week. She's eighteen."

"Nadine Swarthwood has smooched every boy in town."

"Except you, William," Annie said, laughing.

William accelerated toward the main road. "Close your heads, both of you."

The sun parted the clouds, heating the air with humidity William hadn't felt since summer. One of the empty oak barrels moved, breeze-blown, across the run leading away from the distilling house. He followed it toward the potter's field, pretending to kick it along, and then watched it pick up speed as it rolled down the hill and disappeared into the aging house.

William peeled off to the right, where the grass of the field was saturated but not puddled; the hard ground had soaked in the rainfall. The older graves were visible only because he knew what to look for—slight sunken pits in the ground, weed covered and weather beaten. The newer graves were marked by knee-high wooden crosses. He headed straight for the sixth row on the south side, where the shade from the aging house cast a thumb-print against the grass. About twenty paces deep, he found the newest cross and dirt-covered mound. The grass was trampled and muddy around the perimeter. Footprints, big and small, both human and animal, led to and from this grave.

He took his notepad from his pocket and jotted notes about the scene, especially the six deer watching from the woods, the fox spying from the barrel run outside the aging house, and the wood-chuck inching like a wounded soldier up the hill from the whiskey trees. Birds of different sizes circled above—crows, hawks, red-birds, robins, and blackbirds.

A malnourished chocolate Labrador approached, so thin his ribs were visible. His fur was matted with mud and burs, and his tongue lolled lazily. The dog barked three times, deep and throaty but friendly, and continued forward with his tail wag-ging. He rubbed against William's legs much like a cat would and then sat next to the cross. He had no tags or collar. William pet-ted the dog behind the ears and allowed him to lick his hand.

"You need some food, boy?" The dog panted, licked his hand again.

"Go on then." William pointed toward the family's garden. "Grab some off the vines. Get what you need. I'll explain it to Barley."

The dog was reluctant but then barked and ran toward the garden.

William squatted, eye level with the horizontal cross-board. Across the old barrel stave in black paint was written: HERE LIES THE BODY OF ASHER KEATING. And down the vertical stave, his dates: ???–OCT. 19, 1934. Despite the crowd of mourners, no one was close enough to him to know when he was born?

William wrote in his notepad, and by the time he finished the dog returned with a half-gnawed cucumber. He'd never seen a dog eat a cucumber, but if you were hungry enough, you could eat anything. William rubbed the dog's back and felt spine beneath the skin.

"Did you know Asher Keating, boy?"

The dog barked. William then noticed three cats—one gray, one beige, and one black—sneaking in the weeds twenty yards away and realized the dog was barking at the felines, not in response. If Mr. Browder had seen them, he would have claimed it as a sign—the cats had returned to chase the mice away so the distillery could be opened. "I'm not fond of cats either."

The dog finished the cucumber and licked his chops, and then his ears perked toward a coughing noise coming from the aging house, a building that was four stories tall with evenly spaced wood-shuttered windows that opened and closed like doors.

William stood from his crouch. Since it was stripped of the thousands of barrels of bourbon it had once contained, noises echoed off the vaulted ceiling like they did in church. Decades of aging bourbon had left the exterior limestone walls streaked with a sooty black residue, a yeasty-smelling fungus that gave a distilling house character. But now the black streaks looked like shadowy fingers and made him leery.

The man coughed again.

William approached with the strange dog by his side and a pen in his hand. His heart began to palpitate, a precursor to the sweats. He stopped outside the arched wooden door, which was cracked open a foot on rusted hinges.

"Hello. Anybody in there?"

"Come in," a raspy-voiced older woman said. "We mean you no harm."

"We only need shelter," said a man.

The dog barked, trotted inside. A few seconds later the dog opened the door wider, nudging it with the top of his head. A robin flew from the belly of the aging house. William ducked beneath the fluttering wings and stepped inside the building.

One of his earliest memories was entering this very building at six years old, holding his father's and grandfather's hands. *"One . . . two . . . three . . . jump!"* They'd practically swung him all the way across the potter's field, as if he were flying. It was December of 1919. The air was crisp and cold. His father had recently returned from the war, and his grandfather was only two months away from hanging himself.

William had to crane his neck to take in the breadth of the barrels: thousands of white-oak casks stacked on ricks up to the ceiling; nine levels of bourbon whiskey aging for years, turning from clear white to copper and amber, pulling the smells and flavors from the contracting and expanding white oak, filling the house with the pleasant aroma of escaped vapors, heavy with the scents of corn, barley, and rye, vanilla, caramel, and butterscotch.

"You know what that smell is, William?"

"What, Grandpa?"

"A portion of the bourbon evaporates through the stave joints of the barrels. You're smelling what we call the angels' share. Our offering to the angels. We share our bourbon and they protect our distillery from fire."

Now, as William entered, he was met by a gush of cool air and dust motes, a patchwork of sunlight and shadow, vacant wood-planked floors dotted with bird droppings and scratches from dancing shoes. The abandoned ricks and empty barrels were covered with mold. The faint smell of the angels' share still lingered, and William felt like a child again.

The smell had once been their religion.

"Come in, please," a woman said.

A bird flew across the highest pitch of the roof.

William turned to the woman's voice. She was dressed in heavy layers, with thick military-style boots too big for her feet. The laces were untied, and the ends clicked against the wood floor as she stood to face William. Her face was lined and hard lived, her gray hair mostly concealed by a red kerchief, but her eyes were sharp. "We're not here for trouble, I assure you."

Sitting in the shadows were men and women, all white except for two Negroes, outfitted in dresses and suits and coats that were aged and weather beaten.

"What are you doing here?" William foolishly held the pen out as if it were a dagger.

"My name is Beverly," said the older woman. "We came in here last night to escape the rain. Do you live in the main house?"

William nodded. The dog was by his side again. He started to ask them where they lived, but it was clear to him that they lived nowhere. They lived everywhere. They lived inside whatever stronghold they could find each night. He knew enough to be cautious. "You were here last night. Nobody ever visits the potter's field. Where did the rest go?"

A man in a tattered brown suit, mismatched wing tips, and a moth-nibbled derby spoke from his seat atop an empty oak barrel. "They started their walk back to the city."

"Who are you?"

"I'm Clive. I'm happy to be alive." The man, who could have been twenty or forty, it was hard to tell, tipped his hat. "I'm a veteran of the Great War."

"So is my father," said William.

"His name?" asked Clive.

"My name is Barley McFee." He walked through the door of the aging house with a shotgun leveled at the squatters. "And I'm not afraid to shoot. You've got one minute to get your bindles off my property."

"Father . . . don't . . ."

"I've got this under control, William." Barley aimed the gun.

"Father, they're unarmed."

"And how do you know that, son?"

He didn't know. He'd just assumed. And then a tall, bald man in the back removed a pistol from his coat and slowly placed it on the floorboard. Another man two barrels down did the same, except his looked like a Colt. And then a red-haired young woman in a yellow dress slid a shiv from the folds of her faded skirt and dropped it to the floor.

William couldn't believe he hadn't noticed her first. Her eyes were green, as lush as Kentucky grass after a spring rain. She stared directly at him, and the attention made him gulp. She was stunning; feral looking but pretty as a Georgia peach. He shook his head to get his wits about him.

"Anybody else heeled?" Barley eyed the weapons on the floor. "Last chance to show your cards. No?"

They shook their heads.

"Okay, then. Who is Asher Keating?"

William said under his breath, "I was just getting to that."

Beverly stared at Barley, eyes burrowing into him. "Are you a godly man, Mr. McFee?"

"I doubt there is such a thing as a godly man."

"Why didn't you leave with the others last night?" William was afraid his father would tighten the screws on them too quickly and clam them up.

Beverly looked over her shoulder toward the redhead, as if she needed her permission to talk.

It was the redhead who answered. "Perhaps if your father put down his bean-shooter we'd be more inclined to parlay, and everything will be jake." Her voice was sharp enough to cut paper and it took William's breath away. He reached out and slowly lowered Barley's rifle.

"What are you doing, son?"

"I'm trying to have a conversation." William looked back toward the redhead, surprised to discover he wasn't wilting in her presence. "Can you tell us why you all stayed behind?"

"It was agreed by one and all that we"—the redhead motioned to her fellow squatters—"would stay behind."

"What's your name, doll-face?" asked Barley.

"Pauline." She looked at William. "Friends call me Polly."

"And why was it agreed that you all got to stay behind?" asked William.

Beverly answered, "Because we were his closest followers."

"He's our savior," said Clive.

"He made sure we were fed," said a mustached man in a black fedora.

"He made sure we were clothed," said Beverly.

"The Lord God made him our savior," said Pauline, as serious as anyone in the room.

"They've gone off their tracks," Barley whispered to William. "We should take them all to Lakeland Asylum."

William ignored him. "You believe he was a savior?"

"No believing to it," said Clive. "He was. Still is."

"You think Asher Keating was . . . ?"

"Jesus Christ," said Pauline. "Asher Keating was the second coming."

Barley laughed. "Does that explain all the animals outside?"

"It is no coincidence," said Beverly. "Animals are prominent in the Bible. You should—"

"I want you all out of here by sundown," said Barley. "Come on, William."

"We can't." Pauline stopped Barley cold. "I'm sorry, Mr. McFee. But we can't leave yet."

William had never admired someone so instantly.

Barley stepped closer. "And why can't you leave yet, doll-face?"

"Because he is to rise on the third day. We have to wait. A roof over our heads, even for two more nights, would be preferable to the weather."

Barley grinned. "You got rent money?"

"We have nothing," said Pauline. "As you can see."

Barley straightened his white fedora and pointed the shotgun lazily toward Pauline. "Three days. If you're not gone by then I'll bypass the bulls and get rid of you myself. And don't take anything from my garden."

Barley left. William followed, but not before he'd nodded at Pauline and tipped an imaginary hat her way.

"Thank you, Mr. McFee," Pauline said to William.

"You're welcome. But friends call me William."

William hurried to keep up with Barley's pace crossing the potter's field. The dog barked at their heels.

"Where'd the dog come from?"

"I dunno." William shrugged. "He's lost. Maybe he ran away. Can we keep him?"

"No."

"Can we give him a name, at least?"

"You should name him Cat. That would really needle him." Barley patted his leg. "Come here, Cat." The dog obeyed, tongue lolling, which Barley clearly hadn't expected.

"He likes you." William looked over his shoulder toward the aging house in the distance. "What do you make of that back there? Did you count them?"

"No, I didn't count them. Why would I count lunatics?" And then after a few more steps, "How many were there?"

"Twelve. Do you see the significance?"

They'd reached the gravel driveway. Samantha wasn't home from the grocery yet.

Barley stopped at the porch steps. "William, we'll fly to the moon before we have an apostle named Pauline."

"I like the name Cat. I think it's funny, calling a dog Cat." Johnny finished his pork chop and then put down the rest of his Coke. "Come here, Cat. Roll over, Cat. Play dead, Cat."

Samantha wiped her mouth with a cloth napkin and then placed it, folded, next to her empty plate. "Annie, dear, don't play with your food."

Annie stared at the corn she'd smashed between the fork tines, then slid it inside her mouth and swallowed with a sour face. "*Now* may I be excused?"

Samantha sighed, waved her hand dismissively. "Yes, go on."

"Henry is going to love you, Cat!" Annie hustled to the living room and sat by the window overlooking the front porch. The dog had his paws against the window, smudging the glass and steaming it with his breath. William couldn't see his father's chair from where he sat, but Barley was already snoring. Annie put her hands to the window, mirroring the dog's paws.

William watched his little sister. "I wish, for Annie's sake, we could keep him. Haven't seen her this happy in a long while."

Samantha took a sip from her Coke and then studied the bottle. Johnny had brought them Coke to have with dinner for three nights in a row. "How did you come about these again?"

"Coke truck came by after school was out."

"And how did you *pay* for them?"

"I didn't." Johnny shrugged, stood from the table. "He gave

freebies. Advertisements." He grabbed Annie's plate, which was still half full with pork chunks, gravy, and potatoes.

"Your father will eat later, Johnny."

"I'm not gonna feed Father." He laughed. "I'm gonna feed Cat."

"Father said not to," William said. "Then he'll never leave."

"Exactly. And Father's snookered out. He'll never know." Johnny left the room with the leftover food. Samantha didn't stop him.

William swirled his last chunk of bread through the gravy on his plate, still thinking of Pauline and the rest of the followers. Had she felt the same attraction, the same spark? Was it possible to carry a torch for someone he'd just met? The red lipstick on his mother's napkin sang to him. "So how did your meeting with Mr. Bancroft go?"

"He accepted the money." Samantha carried her plate into the kitchen.

"I wasn't worried about the car door." William followed her with his dishes.

She started washing the plates, so he helped by clearing the rest of the table. When he returned to the kitchen, he found her staring out the window above the sink, her hands paused in the suds. Down the hillside, the aging house was aglow with candlelight.

Thinking of Pauline—*"Friends call me Polly"*—gave him sudden courage. "Why hasn't Father started the distillery back up? It was his whole life before the war."

"His and your grandfather's." She resumed with the dishes. "But your father is in no condition now to run a business. He can barely tie his shoes some mornings."

William placed the dirty dishes on the counter. "This morning the wind blew one of the empty barrels across the run. I remember that sound. I'd like to hear it again, on a regular basis."

"William, what are you trying to say?"

"That we should start the distillery again. Old Sam McFee was king. I want it to be again. Mr. Browder—"

"Is a kind old man, but he's also a dreamer."

"Maybe so. He's had dreams of the distillery running again." William sounded more desperate than he wanted to. It was Mr. Browder's fight initially, but William now felt like he had more than one fist in it. "He's been keeping the houses and equipment ready. He's grown barley and rye, as well as the corn."

"He grew rye and barley?"

"Yes. We could have barrels aging on the ricks in weeks."

"But it would be years before our labors could produce fruit. Old Sam ages for at least four years. Some of the batches we'd begun to age for six, seven, eight years—"

"We could sell unaged whiskey while the initial batches are aging. It's what everyone is used to drinking now, anyway."

"William, you know nothing about bourbon—"

"I had my first drink of it last night." *It calmed my nerves.*

She dried her hands on a towel. "I admire your thinking, but too many ghosts have taken root here. And all the workers are long gone."

"I could do the bulk of it! I would gladly help Father out. And Johnny. Carly Browder is with child. She's moved back with her husband. Mr. Browder says they've both agreed to work. Mr. Browder stayed behind because he believed it would begin again."

"I thought you wanted to be a journalist. Distillers don't have time to report current events."

"I wanted to be a journalist because I assumed the distillery was hopeless. But Old Sam's return would be worthy of news. And I could be the one to report it. It could be my first big break."

She returned to the dishes. "Selfishness doesn't become you, William."

"That's not why I support this. Father needs this as badly as the town does—"

"If your father needed it so badly, he wouldn't be cemented to that odd chair of his."

"He just needs to be baited."

"And what of the cost? Do you have any idea how much money it takes to start such a venture? And the taxes. You have no idea. Every time we need to pay for a war, our country taxes the aging houses."

"I'm not addle-brained, Mother. I know we have the bees."

She looked up at him sharply. "And how do you know that?"

"Father doesn't work." William gestured toward the living room. "He doesn't do anything. Not since Prohibition ended. Millions are barely getting by. Hobos are living on the streets"—he pointed out the kitchen window—"and inside our aging house. Yet *we* are well fed. We have money for you to buy new clothes to look pretty for another man."

Samantha slapped him across the face, a snakebite, hard enough to turn his head.

His words and her slap surprised them both.

She was wiping tears when Johnny walked in the kitchen with Annie in his arms. "He licked that plate clean." Johnny noticed his mother's flushed face. "What happened?"

"We were just having a conversation," Samantha said, clouding the truth.

Johnny looked at his older brother. "You a big shot now, William?" He put Annie down. "What'd you do?"

"It doesn't concern you."

"I think it does, palooka." Johnny tapped himself on the chest. "Mother crying makes it my business." He pushed William. "Patsy."

Samantha saw it just as William did—the likeness to their father: the quick temper and unreadable eyes; the handsome face, hard edged and tough.

He pushed William again. "Daisy." He shoved him into the wall. "Weak sister."

"Johnny, stop it!" Samantha cried.

William didn't want to fight back, had never once thrown a punch. But now that he was cornered with both fists clenched, he was comfortable with it. If Johnny poked him one more time, he was going to paste him.

The poke came, so William lifted his right arm, loaded his weight, coiled at the waist, and unleashed a punch that lifted his little brother from the floor.

Samantha screamed. Annie stood in the doorway, crying. "Henry won't like this!" The dog was behind her, barking. And then Barley's voice boomed.

"How'd the dad-blamed dog get in here?" He stood in the doorway behind Annie, staring at Johnny knocked out cold on the floor. Samantha was on her knees, tapping her son's cheeks. William was frozen in his punching stance. Everybody watched him. For a moment William hoped Barley would praise him for his willingness to fight, for doing something worthy of manhood.

"Get out." Barley's eyes bored into him. "And take the dog with you."

FIVE

Candle glow showed through the windows of the aging house. *The twelve apostles.* Maybe they were getting drunk on the lingering angels' share. Now there was a story: HOBO THOUGHT TO BE JESUS CHRIST.

William's first instinct was to walk to Mr. Browder's cottage, but he stopped when he realized he was crying. He muttered a word he'd never imagined coming from his own mouth, the worst word he could think of. One of his father's words. His knuckles were sore from pasting Johnny, and his cheek stung from the impact of his mother's hand. *That* wound had brought about the tears. That slap.

He backtracked through the trees and sat on the barrel run and gazed across the field. He allowed himself to picture Polly's face: her porcelain skin freckled across the nose and cheeks, her eyes like emeralds, her hair so red it appeared aflame. *What would it be like to kiss her? What did she do to end up following a jingle-brained Christ figure?* He should go talk to her.

He stood from the barrel run and cold chills followed by an

intense wave of warmth coated his skin. He clenched his fists and wished it away, but then he started sweating. He kicked a twig across the grass and sat back down on the barrel run. He let the word escape his lips again. And then louder. It felt more familiar each time he said it. "Practicing a new word, William?"

Mr. Browder appeared with a shotgun. He hadn't heard the old man's footsteps. "Oh, hello, Mr. Browder. I'm sorry."

Mr. Browder wore plaid cotton pajamas. Bony wrists and ankles jutted from the arm and leg holes. His leather slippers were scuffed and barely holding together. He dropped the shotgun to the grass and sat with a grunt beside William on the barrel run. In the shadows he looked as black as the bark of the whiskey trees; the whites of his eyes were a stark ivory contrast.

"It's not loaded. Usually I just point it and they run off. The raccoons." He patted William's knee. "I've never heard you curse before. My momma would've cut my tongue out." Mr. Browder stared at the aging house. "But hell, she's long dead."

"I just pasted Johnny. Knocked him out right on the kitchen floor."

"Did he deserve it?"

William thought on it. "Yes."

"Then don't lose time on it. You know how many times I pasted my brothers?"

"How many?"

"Not enough, I'll say that. Just 'cause you love someone don't mean you don't occasionally wanna paste 'em."

"I talked to Mother about the distillery. She said no."

"Ah, that's okay. For now. You planted the seed. Seeds need time to grow. Jus' gotta be patient. You know how many times I asked my wife to marry me?"

"How many?"

"Seven, eight times."

"What changed her mind?"

He shrugged. "Got more handsome as I aged, I guess." He flicked a ladybug off the knee of his pajamas and shot William a confident wink. "And I still haven't stopped."

They sat silent for a moment, the two of them watching shadows move about inside the aging house. "What do you think about them?"

Mr. Browder pursed his lips and blew out some air. "You know me. I've always had an open mind to the mysterious."

"You think that's what this is?"

"I don't know what it is, exactly. Maybe this Asher was just a man. Maybe he wasn't."

"Are you saying he could actually be . . . ?"

"All I'm saying is he obviously touched lives, William. Whether he was what they think or not, he must have had a kind way with people. And wasn't kindness one of Jesus' main messages?"

"I suppose so."

"That man may have been no more of a Jesus than Al Capone, but don't they deserve the right to grieve how they want? What's funny?"

"Nothing. You're just the opposite of my father."

"I respect the dickens out of Mr. Barley, you know that. But no one has ever accused us of being like-minded. Ssshhh." Mr. Browder pointed across the field, toward where three deer had moved silently up toward the door of the aging house, and a fourth walked toward Asher Keating's grave. He moved his arched finger to the north. "There's three more."

William leaned forward, elbows on his knees. "They were here this morning too."

"Do you remember the deer when Henry was born?"

"No."

"The storm? That twister chewed up trees for miles, spitting them out like grass. Tree trunks looked like twigs in that funnel cloud."

"And Henry decided it was the most opportune time to come into the world."

"It jumped, William. I stood there and watched it. Started lifting a couple hundred yards or more before the whiskey trees, roaring like a thousand trains. And then the temperature plummeted. The wind stopped. It got so quiet I could hear your mother screaming inside the house. That funnel lifted and I feared the ground was coming up with it. A loose two-by-four from the old Crawley house across the way came whizzing by and stuck inside the wall of the fermentation house like some giant had hurled a spear. A mailbox flew over the house. A cow from the farm flew across the main road like it had wings.

"And *that's* when the deer came. Dozens of them from the south woods, even more from the whiskey trees. They gathered in a great big cluster across the potter's field and watched, just as I did, while that twister lifted up and jumped right over the distillery, taking nothing more than a few shingles from the main house and a garden rake your father left propped against the downspout. It touched down another couple hundred yards in the distance, echoing like a herd of buffalo for miles.

"The deer, they hung about for a few minutes, stunned like I was, before they retreated back into the trees. One of them looked at me, William. Looked right at me. Then took off in a sprint. It was like they knew it was going to jump the potter's field, and that's why they'd come."

"But twisters jump, don't they?"

"Twisters jump." He nodded. "That's one way to look at it."

"And another?"

"Maybe our famous twisted tree kept it away." He chuckled at the improbability, but Mr. Browder had a way of making anything sound possible. "The twister saw those two trees already coiled in a loving embrace and assumed the damage here'd already been done."

"But twisters don't see—"

"No, they don't. But I once knew a blind man who swore he could drive a tractor. So I bet him five dollars he couldn't."

"And?"

"And I lost five dollars. First he got on and drove about five yards in a straight line. 'Pay up,' he says. I was about to and he brushed my hand away. He was only needling me, you see. He started that tractor back up and drove for twenty minutes like a man with perfect sight. Knew the turns and angles of his acreage by the dips and undulations of the field. Could tell his speed by the sound of the wind against his face."

William worked his sore jaw. What was he missing?

"The moral of the story, William, is don't doubt people until you know some facts." He smiled. "And next time I come face-to-face with a twister, I'm running away, 'cause there ain't no chance it'll jump the distillery twice."

"I spoke to a man yesterday. He said something peculiar that makes sense if you believe twisters can see. He said he died for our sins."

"Who? Jesus?"

"That's what I assumed. But he said 'just yesterday.' He died *just yesterday* for our sins."

Mr. Browder pursed his lips as he gazed out toward Asher Keating's grave, where the four deer nosed the tall grass. "You think that man was in town early, waiting for Asher to be buried?"

"Could'a been. Or he could'a been a lunatic." William made as if to get up but stopped suddenly. "Mr. Browder, was there something special about Henry?"

"Special how?"

"You know. The tornado. The deer. Mother said Henry never cried when he was born. The way he danced left everybody in awe. It was like he was put on earth to make people smile. And you said in your eulogy, at Henry's burial, about his dancing . . ."

"Not everything is learned." Mr. Browder tightened his jaw. "Some things just already are." He used William's leg for leverage to push himself up from the barrel run. "The first time I held Henry, his legs, they just kept moving. Barley, he said, 'Look at'm, Ronald, the boy kicks like an overturned turtle, don't he?' I looked at the boy, watched him close. It wasn't some random kicking, William. There was a rhythm to the way your brother's legs moved, a cadence. I didn't tell Barley, but it looked like dancing to me. And in hindsight I'm sure that it was."

Mr. Browder bent down for his shotgun. "But since you asked, yes, I believe that sometimes God puts a little extra into the recipe."

SIX

The front door opened and Samantha came out with a brown grocery bag in each hand.

"You packed my bags already?"

"No." She put the bags down and stood beside William, hugging his arm. She leaned her head on his shoulder. "I'm sorry, William."

"I am too. I shouldn't have said what I did."

"My open hand is usually reserved for Johnny's backside."

"Is he alive?"

"He's in bed. His ego is hurt more than anything."

"And Father?"

"He'll forget about it all." She let go of his arm and put both hands on the porch railing. "You're not completely wrong in assessing my relationship with Mr. Bancroft."

He didn't want to hear that she was having an affair. The reality would fully crack what Henry's death hadn't.

"We've had a lunch and a dinner, and one evening we went to a picture show. It's nothing as bad as you're imagining."

William's heart slid slowly back down from his throat. He didn't realize how badly he'd needed to hear her say it.

"I needed to get out and have conversations with another adult. He showed me attention that I haven't had in a long while."

"He is snooping for dirt about Father."

"Even *I* thought there may have been more to the wreck. And I was so upset at your father. Mr. Bancroft caught me in a weak moment and I agreed to lunch. And then a dinner. And then—"

"And that's when he started coming to our church?"

"It was foolish, I know. I've become aware that we are not similar at all. He's too extreme in his religious beliefs, and yesterday he spoke down to a poor Negro man simply because of the color of his skin. I despise that hatred. But the man is harder to shake off than a tick. He claims to love me."

"Do you love him?"

"Of course not. I've only ever loved one man." She folded her arms against the nighttime chill and chuckled. "Can you believe the bullet found that exact car, though?"

"Went right into his door. Like it had eyes."

"I don't know what I was thinking." Samantha sighed. "And I don't know what your father did during Prohibition, William. I asked once. He told me not to concern myself, but I had my suspicions. He was on the road too often and his clothes smelled of gunpowder. I laundered enough bloodstains to know he wasn't following the straight and narrow."

William looked at his mother. "So how much cash do we have?"

"Enough." She gave him a sideways glance. "Enough." She indicated the bags she'd carried from the house. "Come on. Let's take our visitors some warm food."

"Father said not to feed them."

"He also said not to feed the dog. And your father doesn't believe in signs. I do."

The twelve squatters devoured the ham sandwiches Samantha had made for them.

As they had crossed the potter's field, William wondered aloud if the group would be fasting while they waited for Asher Keating to rise. Would they eat any food offered to them? The answer was immediately obvious. The joy with which they'd taken the offering proved the Twelve had been fasting unwillingly for too long. Of course they would eat food offered to them.

Samantha graciously accepted their thanks and was set to depart, but William had grown roots into the floorboards. He felt the need to watch them eat, which was rude, but then Polly looked up from her sandwich and smiled at him as she chewed with her mouth closed. The smile was enough. He felt for the pen inside his pocket, uprooted himself, and followed his mother toward the door.

William ambled across the field, so slowly that his mother built a ten-yard distance.

"William."

And there it was, the voice he'd been hoping for. William turned to find Polly standing in the open doorway to the aging house. "Yes?"

She held a pen in her right hand. "You dropped this."

William checked his pockets for show. He walked back

toward the aging house. "It must have slipped through a hole in my pocket." He looked toward Samantha, who'd stopped to wait for him. Thankfully she let him be and returned inside.

Maybe she'd drop the notion of his being a priest now.

Polly handed him the pen and folded her arms against the cold. They stood in a patch of grass highlighted by the three-quarters moon. "What a man carries in his pockets tells the world about him."

"I'm a writer." William averted his glance, but then he locked in on her emerald eyes and felt inadequate. He didn't want to blow it with a rare breed of girl who actually showed interest in him. "I . . . always carry a pen."

"A writer? You seem young to be a writer."

"You seem young to be living on the streets. I'm sorry. That was awful." Now that he'd pasted his brother, he was starting to act like him! He stared at his shoes. "Forgive me."

"Of course. I'm sorry if I offended you."

"You didn't. It's what the people at the *Courier* tell me too." William briefly met her gaze. "I've failed to find my way into print. Despite many attempts. I need the right story."

"That's why you brought us food? To butter us up for a story?"

"I . . . no!"

Polly playfully punched William in the arm. "I'm only needling you. We know the offering was one of kindness."

They locked gazes for longer this time, but then she looked away. "I saw you walking alone in the woods earlier. I think it's noble for men to cry."

"I wasn't—"

"Yes, you were. It's okay. As you were saying?"

He hadn't been saying anything, not anything he could recall.

"I had an argument with my mother. And then I pasted my little brother after he got involved. Knocked him clean out. I know it wasn't a very Christian thing to do. I've never punched anyone before."

"I'm sure if you pray on it, all will be forgiven."

William glanced toward Asher Keating's grave, ten yards away. "What is it?"

Can she really believe it? She appears too intelligent for such nonsense. He started to ask her about Asher but stopped. *She is, after all, waiting for a man to rise from the dead.*

They smiled at each other until the moment became bashfully awkward. "I should get back inside and see how my brother is doing."

"Thank you for the food, William."

"We're happy to do it."

"And your father? Was he happy to do it?"

"He's passed out in his chair."

Polly lowered her head. "We'll pray for him then. And for your family."

William didn't know how to respond. *She says it like she knows about Henry.* "If you need anything else, just let me know. Good night, Polly."

"Good night, William."

He walked five paces toward the house before her voice stopped him again.

"William."

He turned. "Yes?"

"I, too, am a lover of words. It's been some time since I've been able to read something other than my Bible. You wouldn't happen to have a novel that I could borrow?"

William scoured the bookshelf as Barley snored from his chair. He ran his finger over dozens of spines. It was one thing to feel an immediate emotional connection, and even a physical attraction—but to learn that she was also a lover of words!

The knowledge validated his feelings for her. And as odd as it seemed, he thought of her in the same breath as Henry. She'd arrived on the one-year anniversary. He'd met her in the very place he'd last seen Henry. After writing that stupid article, he'd gone outside to apologize to his baby brother. But Henry was dancing, and William simply watched him through the window.

Henry had no idea about the angels' share or the thousands of barrels that used to fill the ricks to the ceiling; he had never known Grandpa Sam. To him, the aging house was a dance hall and he liked the way his footsteps echoed. William watched him jitterbug for twenty minutes before he decided to apologize in the morning . . . He tore himself from the memories and focused on finding the perfect book.

In between *The Little Red Hen* and *Little Black Sambo* and some German books Barley had stolen from Kraut trenches during the war, he found *The Great Gatsby* by F. Scott Fitzgerald. It was the American dream incarnate, a story that showed that anyone could achieve anything. The Seelbach Hotel in Louisville had been used as a backdrop for Tom and Daisy Buchanan's wedding. *Has she already read it?* He didn't want to give her a book she'd already read. She'd be too polite to tell him so and would probably take the book anyway.

He shelved it and removed *Babbitt* by Sinclair Lewis. *A*

satirical look at small-town life? William had loved *The Sun Also Rises* but wondered if there was too much sexual freedom in the novel. He didn't want to seem too obvious. But then his eyes caught *The Age of Innocence* by Edith Wharton, right next to Eugene O'Neill's *Strange Interlude,* and his decision was made. He'd yet to read Wharton's novel, but it was a Pulitzer Prize winner and she was the first woman ever to win the award. Polly would surely appreciate that. In a sense, Wharton was a pioneer, just like Polly.

The Age of Innocence it would be.

The next morning they waited until Barley drifted into his post-lunch nap, and then William and Samantha took a plate of biscuits and jam to the aging house. More deer spied from the trees.

"It's like they're waiting for something," Samantha said of the deer, knocking on the wooden door to the aging house before she entered. Cat was with them. Perhaps it was an illusion, but it appeared as if the dog had already gained weight. He seemed healthier, his fur now clean from the bath Samantha had given him inside the milling barn, away from the house so Barley wouldn't know about it.

William checked to make sure the book was still tucked away inside his belt. He'd concealed it behind a wool sweater that was too hot, and now he'd begun to sweat.

As she had the night before, Samantha smiled as she stepped inside. She missed the distillery, William could tell. The air in the aging house was less musty than the night before. The floors had been swept, the cobwebs pulled down from wooden beams, and the ricks were now positioned in neat rows. Empty oak barrels lined the walls. The twelve followers of Asher Keating sat in a circle in the middle of the floor, laughing about something the squatty black man on the far side had said.

"Are we interrupting?" Samantha placed a china plate stacked with biscuits on one of the barrels. "I brought lunch."

Polly wore a worn white sweater over her faded dress. She waved them in. She was the youngest of the group but seemed a leader of sorts. "Come sit." Polly scooted over to make room beside her. "We're sharing stories of Asher."

William hadn't noticed it the day before, but they all had bindles within arm's reach. A thirteenth bindle rested against one of the barrels. He assumed it was Asher's and was immediately curious about what was in there. He sat next to Polly, then scooted close enough to leave a gap for his mother to sit beside him. He crossed his legs because that was how Polly was sitting. His elbow accidentally touched hers, and she didn't seem to mind. In fact, she smiled, and the gesture radiated kindness.

It was quiet for a minute. A sense of reverence crept over the room as sunlight bled through the windows. While his mother appeared to be in deep reflection, William's only thought was how to get Polly the book without his mother seeing the exchange.

The black man who'd been the source of laughter moments earlier broke the silence by clearing his throat. He was big boned and wide, but his skin was loose in places, as if he'd once been bigger and had lost weight. "Three years ago," he said, pausing to look directly at William and Samantha, "I was forced to the streets. Lost my job and couldn't pay the rent. Turned into a boozehound on what I could beg from the Speaks. Slept in a box by the Fourteenth Street Bridge. I developed a cough. A heavy loose rattle in my chest. When I started spitting up blood, I knew what it was. The white death took my wife and kids. It was preparing to take me too. I had a fever every night, chilled 'til I was delirious. I thought I'd been called one night. Felt a warmth that could have only been heaven. Heard the laughter of my kids and the sweet voice of my wife. She said, 'You ain't done yet, Thomas. You ain't done yet.'"

The man reached into his raggedy clothing and pulled a black-and-white picture from his coat pocket. He placed it on the floor facing William and Samantha. "This is Asher Keating."

In the picture, a man with closely cropped hair, a kind smile, and in full military uniform leaned against a tree, staring at the camera. He had a wide, flat nose, full lips, and a hue to his skin that showed he'd spent some time in the sun. Three pairs of boots, tied together by the laces, hung from his neck, along with a necklace and small cross. Smoke spiraled from a cigarette in his right hand. In relation to the rusted jalopy parked on the street behind him, William guessed Asher Keating was six and a half feet tall and looked to be in his midtwenties. The picture was probably taken soon after the war; Asher's look was one of having survived something.

"I opened my eyes that night and saw Asher leaning above me. He said, 'Relax, my son.' He was bearded, had taken on the wear of the streets, but his voice soothed me right quick. At first I had doubt."

Doubting Thomas.

"He told me to be still. And I stopped trembling. He put his hands on my neck. I stopped coughing. He put his hands on my chest, told me to feel the warmth. The cold chills left me. He told me to close my eyes and rest. I slept for two days."

William had no need to ask Thomas how the tale ended. The man was alive and showed no signs of tuberculosis. Thomas picked up the picture, slid it back into the folds of his coat, and closed his eyes in reflection. William didn't know what to say, and Samantha looked speechless.

"Thank you, Thomas." Polly discreetly gripped William's hand for a squeeze and then let go. "Would anyone else like to offer their story?"

William's hand tingled from Polly's touch. He wanted another story because he wanted her to grip his hand again. Her sweater had side pockets. When she turned slightly, a small whiskey flask revealed itself, the cap protruding like a baby chick rooting for food. Polly slid the flask deeper into her pocket.

Beverly removed a photograph and positioned it on the floor, another black-and-white picture. Beverly started to tell her story when they heard tires skidding on gravel outside and the high-pitched wail of a police siren. Everyone ran to the window. Up the hillside, past the potter's field, two officers approached the McFee house. Barley met them on the front porch, his rifle poised and ready to shoot if they took another step away from their black Ford Model T.

"Barley, don't," Samantha said softly. "Please, go back in the house."

William got a better look. It wasn't a rifle in Barley's hands. It was his tommy gun.

"Oh no, Mother, he's got the Chopper out."

Samantha had to hike up her purple skirt in both hands as she ran with William to the house. "Barley, put the gun down!"

Barley had his fedora tilted against the sun and a cigar dangling from his mouth. He stood confident and poised, without a hint of fear in his expressionless face. William didn't trust him not to fire. The chubby cop wiped sweat from his brow. His partner, one of Twisted Tree's own, had known Barley for years and looked less worried. Or at least he did a better job of hiding it.

Samantha stopped at the driveway. "Barley, put the gun down. Let's hear them out."

"I can listen just fine with the Chopper in my hands." The cigar bounced in his lips. He looked to the shorter cop. "Hey, Baby Bear, you know why I call it the Chopper?"

"I've got an idea—"

Barley unloaded a series of bullets toward the gravel, spraying rock dust in every direction. Pebbles pinged off the windshield of the Ford. The officers hunkered down, covered their eyes, as did Samantha and William.

When all was quiet, the taller officer pulled his pistol. "Come on now, Barley. What are you on about?"

Barley pulled the cigar from his mouth. "Put your little bean-shooter back in the holster, Luke. You got some nerve coming here flashing Louisville tin. State your beef and breeze off."

Baby Bear cleared his throat. "We're here for your son."

Barley looked at Luke. "Is Chubby here jingle-brained? Looks like he's about to soil himself. Which son you talking about?"

William took a step forward, ready to offer himself up.

"Johnny," said Officer Luke. "We've come to take Johnny."

"You're not taking Johnny," Barley said matter-of-factly, implying that perhaps they could take William.

"We have reason to believe he robbed a Coca-Cola truck three days ago," said Luke. "Flashed a pistol. Made off with two cases."

So they hadn't been freebies from the driver. Samantha covered her mouth and looked at Barley as if it were his fault.

"What evidence you got to finger my boy?" Barley asked, gun in both hands again.

"Seems he did some bragging at school about what he'd done," said Officer Luke. "We have ten kids heard his story."

Barley looked at William. "Go in and get Johnny."

William started toward the porch but stopped when the screen door opened.

Johnny came out carrying a case of full bottles. He didn't look at either of his parents. He rested the case on the porch. "Here's what's left. I used the rest." Johnny looked at his mother. "The gun wasn't loaded. It was a prank."

"Walk to the car," Barley snarled at Johnny. And to his wife he said, "Go in and get some money to pay for what was stolen."

Samantha hurried inside.

"I'm sorry, Father."

Barley ignored Johnny. "Put the bracelets on him, Luke."

Luke nodded, took the handcuffs from his belt, and then latched them on Johnny's wrists.

Barley walked down the steps, leaned in, and spoke quietly to the officer. They each jerked a few nods and then Barley stepped back.

"Do your bit, Johnny. Quit crying, do your bit, and everything will be jake."

Samantha returned from the house with a stack of cash bound by a rubber band. Barley took it from her and then handed it to Luke. "See that the Coca-Cola driver is compensated. And take a pair of Cs for your trouble." He looked at the second officer. "Even you, Tin Can."

The police force had implemented a 20 percent pay cut due to the Depression. Now that it was legal to produce and move alcohol again, bribes were no longer rampant. Both officers looked genuinely thankful for the tip.

William loaded the bottles in the trunk, and when he closed it, he noticed a handful of Asher Keating's followers praying around the grave. Polly was with them. *Don't judge me on this. I can't help it if some of my family is jingle-brained.* He tried not to look at Johnny but did anyway. They waved limply at each other, and then William stood next to his father to watch the officers pull away.

Samantha was on the porch behind them, fighting back tears with Annie in her arms.

"Where's Johnny going?" the girl asked.

"To jail." Samantha scowled at Barley and then went inside.

Cat showed up, and Barley reached down and stroked the fur atop Cat's back, then stopped when William saw him being affectionate and instead reached into his shirt pocket for a small flask. He uncapped it, took a swallow, and then handed it to William, who was repositioning *The Age of Innocence* inside his belt. William downed a wince-inducing gulp of Old Forester and then handed it back. Seeing the flask inside Polly's sweater had been jarring. Not so much that she could be a drinker; he was now a drinker, after all.

But it was a piece to the puzzle that didn't seem to fit.

Inside Johnny's room they found two small wooden vats next to the bed and dozens of empty Coca-Cola bottles lined under the window. Ten bottles of carbonated water rested in neat rows on the floor in between the two vats, along with a satchel of ingredients, bags and jars labeled sugar cane, phosphoric acid, lime juice, vanilla, and caramel. Three empty jars were unlabeled. A dark, syrupy substance and a large wooden spoon sat in one of the vats.

Barley stirred it, bent down for a whiff. "He was trying to make cola."

William spotted a bottle that had already been mixed. He sniffed it, took a sip. "He got pretty dang close."

Barley grabbed the bottle. He tasted it and nodded approvingly. "Good thing they took cocaine out of the ingredients."

"I've heard wonderful things about Edith Wharton's writing. Thank you." Polly fanned through the pages as they stood outside the aging house. "So what happened with your brother earlier today?"

William scratched his head. "My brother held up a Coca-Cola truck."

Polly covered her mouth with the book.

"The gun was unloaded. It was a prank. He wanted to make his own cola." William eyed the flask bulge in her sweater pocket. "At least that's what we've surmised."

"Your brother sounds like quite the character."

"Yes," William said. "Unfortunately he is."

"Why unfortunately?"

"It's just that Johnny often does things to get attention and it works. For him, it works."

"And for you it doesn't?"

"I don't go out of my way to do anything that garners attention."

"Perhaps you should."

"Like what?"

She shook her head as if he'd disappointed her somehow. "Oh, William. You're quite the character yourself." They watched each other for a moment. Their breath mingled in a wispy cloud between them.

"Do you *really* think Asher Keating will rise from the dead? Do you *really* think . . . I mean . . ."

Her face had gone slack. "The fact that you added the word *really* implies you think I'm a lunatic."

"What? No, no, not at all . . ."

"And don't think I haven't noticed you look at the flask in my pocket. You're judging me."

"Possibly, a bit. But not in that way. Why do you have the flask?"

"Why does anyone carry a flask, William McFee?" She folded her arms under her breasts. "Learn to ask questions in a way that doesn't offend. Ask me again without that word."

"Do you think Asher Keating will rise from the dead?"

"You see, now that's a strong question." She tucked a strand of red hair behind her ear. "Is this on or off the record?"

My lands, she is pretty. "Off. On. I don't know. What do you want it to be?"

"Off, or I wouldn't have asked."

"Okay, it's off the record then."

"Then yes, I believe he will rise from the dead." She watched him closely. "You look disappointed. Why?"

"You're just so . . . well spoken. And intelligent."

"Implying I should be jingle-brained and dumb?"

"No." *It's as if she can read my mind.*

"Do I think Asher Keating will emerge from the soil and walk away? No, I don't. Not in the physical sense. But I do believe we will witness some kind of spiritual awakening. It is his spirit that will rise. Does that make you feel more comfortable?"

"Yes," he said softly, not confident it was the proper response. He wanted to ask her more questions, but he'd already unintentionally questioned her intelligence and implied that she was a drunk. It was exactly why he had yet to have a first kiss. He was a buffoon. And now he was beading up as if it were a hundred degrees outside.

"You're sweating." She stated the obvious.

"No, I'm not."

"You most certainly are. Profusely."

She grinned, and for a moment he hated her for it.

"And your face is red as an apple." Then she surprised him. She tiptoed and sweetly pecked his right cheek. "Thanks again for the book." She winked. "Good night, William."

William smiled dumbly. "Good night, Polly."

His right cheek was wet from her touch. He would sleep on his left cheek that night so as not to wipe it off.

SEVEN

Breakfast was quiet the next morning. Barley was passed out in his chair, and Samantha was overly melancholy. She placed William and Annie's bacon and eggs on the table and left them alone to eat while she did dishes in the kitchen.

William ate with Annie as sunlight carved the dining room table in half. Neither spoke; only the sound of their chewing filled the void. William finished his last piece of bacon and wiped his mouth on the top of his hand, something he wouldn't have done had Samantha been in the room, and Annie did the same thing. If anything good could come from tragedy, it was this: he and Annie had bonded. He'd decided that any mistakes he'd made with Henry would be made right with Annie.

They heard someone singing; an angelic voice was coming from the woods. It was too beautiful to be real. William hurried to the window with Annie beside him. Beyond the potter's field Polly sat with her back to one of the whiskey trees, her head tilted upward as if singing to the birds. The timbre of her voice gave him chills.

"'Conservati fedele.'" Awed, Samantha joined William and Annie.

William looked over his shoulder. "You know it?"

"It's a Mozart aria. He composed it when he was nine. What a lovely soprano voice."

Johnny spent one night in the Twisted Tree jailhouse. He did his time with "three drunkards, a dope fiend, a dip, and a boob who'd taken a hammer to his wife." He'd had his own cell, but it was right across from the wife-beater, who'd spent all night spitting his fingernails to the floor and asking Johnny if he was Barley McFee's boy.

The charges had been dropped with cash payment and return of the stolen bottles, but Johnny was still clammy looking as he sat next to William on the barrel run that next afternoon. Leaves skittered across the bricked walkways. The air carried a touch of the angels' share. The twelve squatters had been in and out of the aging house all morning, paying visits to the outhouse, taking in the beauty of the whiskey trees and the influx of deer gathering beneath the boughs, but mostly they went out to pray at the grave site.

"Do you believe it?" Johnny asked.

William had just finished telling him the story of Asher Keating healing Thomas of his tuberculosis. "I shouldn't, but I think I do."

"Because of her?" He meant Polly; William had confided in his brother that he'd smelled corn whiskey on her breath.

William paused at the truth of it. The touch of her lips had faded from his cheek but not from his memory.

"So she has a voice like an angel?" Johnny prodded.

William nodded. "But she seemed bashful once she saw us watching."

"And she kissed *you* on the cheek? She could carry a torch for you, brother."

"You think?"

"Are you too jingle-brained to know when a bee wants to sting?"

William glowed in the sunlight. He'd hoped as much, but hearing Johnny say it made it more concrete, more achievable.

"I can't remember what he looked like."

"What who looked like?" asked William.

"Henry. Once a day I go into his bedroom to look at the picture on his dresser. You know, just to remind myself. I saw him every day of his life and I can't remember what he looked like without seeing his picture." Johnny had his eyes closed, like he was trying to remember Henry's smile and dimples. "I think it's my punishment for needling him so much. God made him blur."

"He knows you loved him, Johnny."

He bit his lip to fight the quiver. "But not like he loved you."

One of the Twelve stood in the middle of the potter's field, gazing up toward the sky as a couple dozen blackbirds circled.

Johnny said, "You know how Henry went through that spell with the nightmares? Crying to get into Mom and Dad's room? After they locked their door, he snuck into *my* room at night. Slept in *my* bed. Did that for a good ten months. Flopped around like a fish out of water."

"Did he tell you what his nightmares were about?"

"The Hash Man?"

William nodded. "That's what Henry called him. Had

crisscrossing scars on his face, like hash marks. I was surprised Henry knew what a hash mark was."

"Nothing surprised me about Henry. You know? There was just something about him. Like everything was jake even when it wasn't. He said something odd one night, after his nightmare. His nose was an inch from mine and it was clogged. 'Sometimes the bad stuff gets in, Johnny.' That's what he said about the Hash Man. The way he looked at me, it was like he believed the Hash Man was real. I said, 'What do you mean, Henry? Sometimes the bad stuff gets into your dreams? Makes them nightmares?' He said, 'No, Johnny, it's just who we are. Sometimes it's just right. Sometimes there's a little extra. Sometimes there's not enough.' He stared at me for the longest time without blinking," Johnny said. "And then he said, 'And sometimes the bad stuff gets in.'"

William remembered the intensity of Henry's nightmares. They'd started several months before his death and occurred often enough to become an issue.

Johnny wasn't finished. "I asked Henry how he knew about all that, you know, and he said something I've never been able to shake. He said, '*He* tells me.'"

"Who? The Hash Man?"

"I don't know." Johnny shrugged. "He didn't say. But he smiled when he said that. And he was always scared of the Hash Man."

They sat for a minute in the sun, watching the breeze blow crinkled leaves. Black-Tail made an appearance and then hustled away. William said, "You really thought you could make your own Coca-Cola?"

"Jeffrey Oppingham, up at school—"

"Jeffrey Oppingham is a boob."

"Yeah, I know that now, but he swore to me that Coca-Cola was next."

"Next for what?"

"Prohibition," Johnny said, serious. "They took away liquor. He said now that it's legal again, the government is gonna take away America's second-favorite drink."

"Real dumb, Johnny. But I've got to hand it to you. We tasted it. You got pretty darn close."

"If they came down on cola, I wanted to be ready. I would'a made a fortune." Johnny looked at the house. "You know, just like Dad."

The *click-clack*ing of William's typewriter masked Barley's snoring. He had paused in his writing when Barley mumbled something about Roosevelt's New Deal, but that had only lasted thirty seconds before the snoring took over again. The sleep-talking was a behavior his father had brought back from the war. They'd become used to it, just as they'd been conditioned to his occasional zone-outs and his diving under the car every time fireworks started on the Fourth of July. William resumed typing notes about the arrival of Asher Keating and Thomas's story. He could see through the bay window that the lights were on inside the aging house.

Annie's leg braces scratched against the hardwood floor. She was playing with a nested set of Matryoshka dolls taken from France. Barley liked to say that Germany fought to control the world, Britain to control the seas, France to save their beautiful country, and the Americans for souvenirs. She carefully placed the baby doll inside the next size up.

William watched for a moment and then typed, Do they really believe that Asher Keating will rise from the dead tomorrow?

After rereading the question, he quickly went back to x out the word *really*. He was a slow learner.

Could Asher cure that man's tuberculosis simply by putting his hands on him? According to the Bible, Jesus did similar things. At one time, were those stories not told in much the same way as Thomas's story? All it requires is belief.

William stopped typing. *God couldn't have that much power. If He did, why did He let Henry die?*

They all heard Johnny before they saw him. He had a way of running down the stairs as if the attic were on fire, then he slowed once he hit the first floor.

"It's dark out," Samantha said. "Where do you think you're going?"

"Outside." He held a lantern in his hand.

"To do what?"

He looked guilty, William thought, about something he'd done or was about to do.

"I dunno, get some fresh air."

"Can I go with him?" Annie asked.

Barley grunted in his seat. "Rose Island," he mumbled, slurring. "Don't play with Teddy Roosevelt. Don't bother the big black bear. Cross at the Devil's Backbone . . ."

Johnny stepped outside and closed the door behind him.

William stared at his sleeping father. "What's he talking about?" he asked his mother. "Rose Island and the Devil's Backbone?"

Samantha helped Annie to her feet. "Come on, honey. Let's go get cleaned up for bed." And to William: "Keep an eye on your brother."

William waited until they'd made it upstairs before walking outside to the porch. He didn't need a light to see what Johnny was doing out in the middle of the potter's field. The moonlight was shining directly on Asher Keating's grave, as if it had been fired down in a beam from the purple sky.

Johnny was on his knees, hands folded in a triangle, praying.

⸻

At midnight Polly knocked on the glass panes of the back door. Barley was still asleep in his chair, and the shot of Old Forester William had downed after everyone else had gone to bed had left him light-headed. He was a little worried that each shot went down smoother than the one before it.

He unlocked the bolt and Polly slipped inside, brushing rainwater from the stiff sleeves of a black velvet coat that was too big for her. He'd been so focused on writing he hadn't heard the rain.

"What's that sound?" Polly removed her coat and handed it to William as if she'd been invited over for tea. "It sounds like a bear hibernating."

"It's my father snoring."

She playfully slapped his arm.

She's drunk. "Polly, is something the matter?"

"I refuse to go into that outhouse again." She traipsed past William into the dining room, where she ran her index finger along the tabletop on her way into the living room. Barley coughed but never opened his eyes. His snoring resumed, louder now, which

Polly thought humorous. She put her hand to her mouth to stymie her laughter.

"The bathroom." William urged her along. "It's just this way. Down the hall."

Polly didn't immediately follow. She picked up Barley's fedora from the side table and placed it slanted on her disheveled red hair. She posed seductively with one hand on her hip. "How do I look, William?"

Like a babe. He reached for the fedora and placed it back on the table. She grabbed Barley's booze for a quick nip. It was downright sexy the way she drank directly from the bottle, the way her pink lips puckered against the opening, the way her throat massaged the gulp.

William took the bottle from her as she stared at Barley as if he were an exotic zoo animal. He placed it next to the hat and clutched Polly by the elbow. The last thing he needed was for one of his parents to wake up and find her drunk inside the house.

Polly followed William to the restroom, where she stumbled giggling against the sink, attempted to kick the door closed with her heel, and then noisily sat down. She'd failed to close the door all the way, and for a moment William wrangled with the idea of closing it for her. Her clothes rustled and then she relieved herself for the longest time. *How much liquid has she consumed?* But then she flushed. Water ran in the sink. The towel rack squeaked on the wall as she rehung the towel, and then the door opened.

She looked more composed standing in the threshold, straightening her weathered dress. "I can't tell you how long it's been since I've used a toilet that nice. I almost didn't want to get up from the seat."

How long did it take for booze to leave the body? Maybe she'd emptied her bladder of it?

Polly brushed past William. Instead of moving back through the living room, she stopped at the stairwell. "Is your room up there? Which one is it?"

"Yes . . . the end of the hallway on the right, I suppose."

"You suppose? Don't you sleep in it?" Halfway up the stairwell she looked over her shoulder. "I'd like to see your room, William . . ." Her voice trailed away as she turned the corner.

He hurried up the stairs and turned right. Polly swerved toward his bedroom door and fumbled with the knob, making too much noise for his liking. He helped her inside and closed the door behind them. She turned on the floor lamp, took her coat from William, and hung it on the bedpost, making herself at home. William's heart pounded like a drum.

She sat on his bed, ladylike with hands folded on the lap of her dress. But that pose didn't last long. She yawned and then stood to begin her survey of the room: the reading chair in the corner next to the window; his four pairs of shoes lining the far wall; the small table next to the bed atop which he emptied the contents of his pockets every evening before going to sleep—mostly change. "It's so orderly in here, William." Polly stopped beside his desk, on which were stacked papers and rows of pencils and pens. "I must say I'm impressed." There was a vacant spot in the middle of the desk and she pointed.

"I sometimes carry my typewriter downstairs to write."

"And how is your story going?"

"Well, I don't have much as of yet." He took a chance. "You could help with that."

"You want to know about Asher?"

I want to know about you. "I do."

She looked disappointed. "The world will learn about Asher Keating soon enough." She ran an index finger across William's desk and the tip came back with dust on it. She blew it off, and at that moment he nearly leaned in to kiss her on the lips.

And then Polly said, "I'm nineteen. And you're twenty. And you've never been kissed."

How does she know that?

"Your little sister is adorable. She stopped by this afternoon and told me all about you."

It was silent for a moment. *Maybe Annie and I have bonded too well.*

"It's a shame about her legs."

"The doctor says there is hope for her. That she'll walk like normal someday."

"I'd be more inclined to put faith in the Lord for that," Polly said. "I saw your brother praying at Asher's grave earlier. Perhaps you should do more of the same." She yawned again, covered her mouth.

"We heard you singing this morning. You have a beautiful voice."

"Thank you. So Annie also told me you have a newspaper collection that dates back to the Middle Ages?"

"Not quite that far back." William moved to the closet, showed her the stacked boxes of newspapers he'd collected since the end of the Great War. Thousands of papers neatly stored in fifteen boxes stacked high in three rows. He spoke with his back to her. "I've separated them by year, but some boxes are more specific. Anything to do with the war is in this one here. Oh, and this box is for anything to do with Prohibition." He lowered his voice. "My father, he's never told us what he did during the twenties, but . . ."

William turned around to find Polly asleep on his bed. *Have I bored her so quickly?*

She'd fallen asleep atop the bedcovers, but there was a folded quilt at the foot of the bed, so William covered her up to the waist. She rolled to her side, snoring softly. He tiptoed around the bed, turned off the lamp, and stood in the darkness, contemplating, before he ultimately decided to sit at his desk. He was tired enough to doze off there. He'd done it before.

He watched her as she slept, watched the roundness of her shoulder rise and fall with each breath, watched her eyebrows twitch as she viewed some secret dream.

If she truly believes Asher Keating is the second coming of Jesus Christ, why isn't she with the rest of the followers, sacrificing herself to the cold night?

He closed his eyes and was on the verge of sleep when her voice carried across the void.

"There's room here for two."

He hesitated but then walked to the bed. She'd scooted over to make room for him. He lay down beside her, on his back, his head to the side, staring at her red hair splayed outward on his pillow, hair that smelled vaguely of dry leaves. Her back faced him. He hadn't noticed it before, but in such close proximity it was apparent that she hadn't had the luxury of clean water for some time. The perfume of the streets wasn't enough to change his feelings.

She gripped his arm, felt down to his right hand. She gently pulled his arm across her body and he rolled with it until he was on his side and facing her back, two spoons in a drawer.

They fell asleep that way, the rise and fall of her back touching his chest with every intake of breath and his hand in hers only inches from her heart.

⁂

The morning began with birdsong.

William awoke with a smile that quickly melted. Polly was gone.

His bedroom window was open. Sunlight warmed his pillow. He sat up, put his bare feet on the floor, and rubbed his eyes. His head was heavy from the bourbon he'd had before Polly arrived, but the achy feeling was worth it. Sipping while typing had been magical.

"It's a miracle!" Johnny yelled, his voice like a stiff cup of morning coffee. "It's a miracle!"

The dog barked. Samantha showed herself in William's open doorway, tying her nightgown. "What is Johnny going on about?"

William yawned on the way to the window. *Who knows? Why is Johnny always so loud?* He leaned forward, hands on the windowsill. He blinked a few times to make sure what he was seeing was real. Samantha stood behind him, looking over his shoulder, and then she gripped his arm to steady herself.

Giddy, Johnny was running through the sunlit grass. Annie ran through the grass chasing after the dog. Not nearly as fast as Johnny, but running all the same. Her legs no longer looked bowed. They were as straight as any six-year-old girl's getaway sticks should be.

William yelled out the window, "Run, Annie, run!" He wiped his eyes.

It was a miracle. Did Polly have something to do with it? Was this the evidence of Asher Keating's rising that she'd spoken of: *"He won't rise in the physical sense . . ."*?

It *was* the morning of the third day.

EIGHT

Barley managed to sleep through all of the shouting. When Annie's shaking didn't rouse him, Johnny backed up to the front door to get a good lead and then ran at his father.

"Johnny, this isn't a good idea," Samantha said, watching through splayed fingers.

But it was too late. Johnny was airborne, and he landed full force atop Barley, who awoke, flailing his arms and legs to a sudden upright position.

"Holy Moses!" Barley looked his family over. "What the hell, Johnny?"

Annie spun in a circle. "I don't squeak anymore."

Barley stared at his daughter's legs, and Johnny said, "I did it, Father. I went out to that grave last night. And I prayed." Johnny pointed out the window toward the potter's field. "I prayed for Annie's legs to work."

Barley knelt in front of his daughter. He touched Annie's thighs, knees, calves, and then ankles. "Does that hurt?"

She shook her head. "No, Father."

Barley wiped his right eye. "Come here," he said to his girl, and she did with open arms.

Barley didn't let go for a good minute. Then he stood, placed his hand atop Samantha's shoulder, and headed out to the porch, without his hat, an unpredictable gleam in his eyes.

William followed along with the rest of the family. Barley bounded down the porch steps, across the gravel driveway, and took to the bricked sidewalk. It was strange to see him outside without his fedora. His steps only became longer when he reached the potter's field, his arms swinging like pendulums as he bypassed rows of crosses. Annie ran to catch him and then grabbed his swaying right hand as they closed in on the aging house.

The door swayed open in the breeze. Barley and Annie stepped inside. William hurried past Johnny and Samantha so he would be the next in, but what he saw made his heart skip.

"What are we looking at?" Annie asked. "Where'd the people go?"

Barley let go of her hand and approached the lone bindle in the middle of the floor.

"They moved on, Sugar Cakes." William's tone had lost its luster.

"But what about Polly? She said she'd be my sister."

William felt betrayed. She'd known all along that she would be leaving. Across the airy sunlit room, where dust motes floated and the unwashed smell lingered, Barley nudged the bindle with the toe of his spatted wing tips, as if approaching a Kraut land mine. Beside it was a note, a triangular piece of paper ripped from a magazine—there was an advertisement for what looked like half of a telephone. On the border was writing:

Thank you for the shelter, William. And for the novel. It's time
for us to move on and spread the word. And yes, I felt it too.
Polly.

William lowered the note, grinning. *She felt it too?*

Barley's harsh voice brought him back to the present.
"Open it."

The faded red-cloth bindle, bundled by twine and attached to
a thick wooden stick, was heavier than it looked. William untied
the twine. The sides fell away like wilted rose petals, revealing
a toothbrush, a deck of playing cards, and a picture of Asher.
But what grabbed his attention were the shoes. Three different
pairs—a man's brown-and-white wing tips, narrow blue women's
heels, and a beige pair of boy's shoes.

William recalled Thomas's picture of Asher and the boots
that had hung from his neck. It appeared that Asher wore shoes
around his neck as a habit, for whatever reason.

Barley's face turned ashen. He fell on both knees. He lifted
the child-sized shoes and reeled them in to his chest. Looking as
if the life had been sucked from him, he collapsed.

"Barley!" Samantha ran toward him, touched his back.
"Barley!"

He was breathing, but he was stone faced and unresponsive.

William slid the shoes out from beneath Barley's right arm.
His mother always wrote their initials on their shoes, in black pen
on the heel. At Sunday school the kids took their shoes off, and
she didn't want theirs getting lost. The pair bore the initials *HFM*.
Henry Ford McFee.

"Henry's missing shoes."

Samantha checked the heel and wept.

Whoever Asher Keating was, or had been, he'd returned Henry's missing shoes.

"Is Henry finally coming back now?" Annie asked.

———

"Watch me, Will'm!" Henry slid to his right, clapped his hands, and let loose a flurry of fancy feet. Moonlight found the windows, and the ricks echoed.

"What is it, Will'm? Why you smilin'?"

"No reason." William moved his feet in tempo but he couldn't keep up, not the way Henry moved and grooved, shuffled and spun. He was smiling, large, and it felt good.

"Go on then."

"Go on where?"

"Go on gettin' while the gettin's good." Henry never broke stride. "Check for yourself."

William walked from the aging house across the potter's field. He still heard Henry's shuffling, even into the house, as if magnified. There it was, resting on the stand right under the window: the closed casket. Henry's voice again. "Go on." William did.

He opened the coffin real slow and found darkness inside.

William's eyes snapped open and he sat up in bed, feeling a thread of hope where there should be none.

NINE

Henry's shoes rested in the middle of the table. That was where William put them after they'd returned from the aging house, plopped them next to the salt and pepper shakers like they belonged there. Today he stared at the shoes like a coon would an open garbage can. Samantha cried every time she even glanced at them, and so had taken to staring at the kitchen floor.

William looked at Barley. "Could he have been there that night?"

"Who?" asked Annie. "Are you talking about Henry?"

William looked across the table at his brother. "Johnny, take Annie in the other room."

"I'm not leaving," Johnny said.

Barley spoke, eyes glued on the shoes. "Johnny, do as your brother says."

Samantha stood. "Come on, Annie."

"No, Sam," Barley said to his wife. It had been many months since William had heard Barley refer to Samantha as Sam. "You need to stay."

She inched her way back down.

Johnny didn't argue. "Annie, let's go." He took Annie by the hand and walked with her into the living room, close enough for him to listen in. William could hear Annie saying, "He's coming home soon, isn't he?"

Barley removed a gold-embossed cigarette case from his jacket, pulled out a Lucky, and lit it. He exhaled and then looked at his wife. He closed the case and slid it across the table. Next he slid his lighter. Samantha caught both with hands that trembled less after she inhaled one of Barley's coffin nails. William had never seen his mother smoke before.

"We all know the facts of that night," Barley said.

"Not all of them," Samantha said under her breath.

Barley tapped ashes into his palm and then shook them through his fingers to the tabletop. He didn't look up.

William said, "I've always questioned how Henry ended up alongside the road. Somebody moved him. And now we know that Asher Keating was possibly there—"

"No possibly to it." Barley pointed to the shoes. "He *was* there."

"Did you know?" Samantha asked.

"No, I didn't know." Barley flicked ashes across the table and then reeled them back in with his palm. "If I'd known I would have told you."

"You said he had a look of peace," said Samantha. "When you found our baby alongside the road, you said he had a look of peace on his face."

"And that hasn't changed, Sam. The boy looked of peace."

Her expression was one of steely resolve, the hardened exterior the family had seen for the past twelve months. Her cigarette was growing long with ash. "So we're agreeing he carried our son to the grass?"

William said, "Preston Wildemere was trapped in his car. It had to be Asher."

"Why was Asher Keating even there?"

Barley said, "He wouldn't be the first bum to wander along that stretch of road."

"But it has to be more than coincidence!" William insisted. "Annie is *walking*. He brought Henry *home* to us. Left his shoes in the very spot Henry loved dancing the most."

"Those bums left them there, not Asher." Barley pointed at William with his cigarette. "The 'why he was there' doesn't concern me as much as what could'a been said . . ." Barley trailed off, anxiously took a drag on the cigarette. "Or why he took my boy's shoes."

Samantha stood from the table. She placed a hand on Barley's shoulder and patted it twice. After she'd gone, Barley took a gander at where his wife had just touched him. Then he focused on William. "We need to find those bums. They'll have real answers."

"If we can find them."

"I can find a needle in a haystack." Barley exhaled toward the ceiling.

"A minute ago you said you weren't concerned with *why* Asher was there . . ."

"And?"

"With what's happened here, with Annie's legs and Henry's shoes, I believe *why* is the only question we should be asking."

Before bedtime, William sneaked Annie out to take a couple of pictures with his Kodak Brownie. He'd found a shot from a few months earlier with her leg braces on to compare. He'd also taken pictures of Asher's grave and inside the aging house, where the Twelve had stayed. Times were dire all over the country. People needed a heartwarming story. They needed hope, and he could write a story that would deliver it.

William readied his camera, but Annie interrupted him.

"Do you think those shoes will still fit Henry?"

"Annie . . ."

"If Mommy gets Henry a new pair, I hope I get a new pair too." She twirled just as William was getting ready to snap the picture.

"Annie, stand still. I've got to get this article written."

"I can't wait to show Henry my new legs. I bet I can beat him now in a race. I bet—"

"Annie, *stop!*"

She froze, big eyed.

"Henry's—" William caught himself. He took a deep breath, forced a smile. Annie's face softened and William's heart melted. "Just smile for the camera, Annie."

She smiled wide, then curtsied after he took the shot. "How'd I do?"

"Did great, Sugar Cakes." William put his arm around his sister. "Did great."

He sat at his bedroom desk. He'd yet to touch the tousled covers or move the pillow that had cradled the side of Polly's face. His fingers flew effortlessly over the keys. The typewriter clacked so quickly the carriage shook. Warmed by the bourbon he'd stolen from Barley's bottle, he let the last several days swim back into focus, starting with Barley's gun discharging in church, moving on to the arrival of Asher's body to the potter's field, and ending with Annie's miraculous recovery. The mystery of Henry's shoes he left out. It was too personal to share.

All things happen for a reason . . .

That's how his article started. The gunshot finding Mr. Bancroft's door had been the first sign that something strange was happening in Twisted Tree. He could have been more specific—a random bullet found a specific target—but there was no need to call the town's attention to his mother and Bancroft. He was hitting on all eight—he'd typed three full pages and needed a worthy closing. If only the dog would shut up barking. He'd been at it for ten minutes. Probably spotted a raccoon, or Black-Tail, or maybe the deer guarding the woods had ventured close to the porch.

"Stop barking, Cat. Barley will shoot you," he mumbled. "He'll put you down for the big one. The dirt nap. He'll . . ."

The dog stopped barking.

But it wasn't a gradual quieting; it was too sudden for William's liking, so he stepped out to the hallway. He walked down the steps and peered around the corner toward the living room.

Barley had moved from his chair to the couch. On the floor beside him lay the dog. Barley's right fingers were gently combing through the dog's fur behind the ears.

The ending to his story came to him.

Hope can change even the most stubborn of men.

TEN

By the time William parked in Louisville—with the front left wheel half tilted on the Liberty Street curb—the sun had risen over the downtown buildings. He sat there and closed his eyes until his headache waned and the uneasiness in his stomach settled. If this was the result of drinking too much bourbon, he promised himself never to do it again. Fighting nausea, he drove slowly, and the short ride left him rattled.

He braced his hands on the steering wheel, closed his eyes for three deep breaths.

Standing outside Harper's Beauty Salon, he took a moment to tuck the rest of his shirt in and comb his hair with his free hand. This was his big chance and he shouldn't blow it on appearance. Dozens of cars—beat-up jalopies, Model Ts, Model Bs, a Studebaker truck, and a Rolls-Royce—lined the street at parallel angles outside a dentist's and a doctor's office, a loan building, and an advertisement firm. Car horns bleated. Floppy-hatted boys shouted the morning's news as they waved copies of the *Courier-Journal*: 35 MILLION ACRES OF FARMLAND DESTROYED BY DRAUGHT. DUST BOWL IN OKLAHOMA RAGES ON! LINDBERGH

BABY KIDNAPPER, BRUNO HAUPTMANN, MOVES TOWARD A TRIAL! And her intracity rival, the *Post*: LOCH NESS MONSTER SPOTTED IN SCOTLAND WATERS. Read all about it!

William bought two copies of the *Journal* for six cents and tossed them into the car.

The sidewalk was crowded. Street vendors sold fresh fruit and vegetables that didn't appear all that fresh. A man in tattered beige pants and suspenders swept dust from his livery barn. A tall man in a butterscotch suit and matching boater hat hurried along with a briefcase. He entered a bank and waited as a plain-dressed woman stepped outside, crying on her husband's arm. Miller's Bakery had its front door propped open and the smell of freshly baked bread wafted out. *A loaf for eight cents!* The window displayed a meager assortment of pastries and biscuits and jams, and the sight of it made William's stomach growl.

He promised himself he'd splurge for a bite on the way back home. If he tried to eat now, he'd get sick—the roiling in his stomach quickened as he moved past Threadbare Theatre and Nice Guy's Restaurant, which appeared as if it had sold its last Hot Brown. The windows were boarded and a nest of birds was in the doorjamb.

Dozens of suited men filled the sidewalk looking for work—William bumped into one who called him a wise guy. Then over the sea of bobbing hats and pomade-slicked hair loomed the high mansard roof of the *Courier-Journal* building—Victorian Gothic, with a dark-red and black brick façade trimmed in stone and cast iron. He focused on it, sidestepping and veering as he neared the home of the city's largest newspaper.

"Spare'm some change," said a man at the corner of Liberty and Third. "So a man can eat."

The man, eyes rimmed in red, rested in a heap of rags that smelled of local brew. His face was dirty, his hair long and disheveled.

"Spare'm some change," he said again. It was a croak more than a voice, like something was lodged inside his windpipe. "So a man can eat."

William hurried across the road to purchase two apples. He squatted and handed the homeless man the fruit. The man stared at the red apples with caution, then took a heavy bite that squirted juice into his beard. "A man thanks you, boy."

"Do you know a woman named Pauline? Some call her Polly."

The homeless man shook his head. "No, you're tooting the wrong ringer."

"What about a man named Asher Keating?"

"A man knows of him. A man seen him walk on water. Across the Ohio to save a fisherman from drowning." The man burst into a phlegm-throttled laugh. William couldn't read if he was levelheaded or a lunatic. The man craned his neck toward the next passerby. "Spare'm some change? So a man can drink."

William continued toward the *Courier-Journal* building. Once inside the double doors and high-ceilinged lobby, he approached the front desk as he'd already done nine times prior. The stout, rosy-cheeked woman, who today wore a rounded pink hat, looked up from her paperwork and eyed him behind small glasses.

"Hello, Mr. McFee."

"Hi, Miss Kraven. I've got another story for Mr. Bingham."

She winked. "I'll be back in the time it'll take you to correctly button that shirt."

William looked to his shirt. By the time he'd fixed it, Miss

Kraven had returned with Sylvester Crone in tow, he of the pince-nez glasses and carefully parted hair, the very editor who'd delivered the sour news of his nine rejections.

Mr. Crone scanned the story. "Is this true?"

"Every bit of it, sir." William reached into his jacket pocket and pulled out the picture of Asher they'd found in his bindle, along with the pictures he'd taken yesterday.

"Have you gone to the *Post* with this?"

William seized the opportunity to apply pressure. "I thought I'd give you the first chance."

"Wait here a moment, Mr. McFee."

Mr. Crone scurried toward another office door, knocked, and entered. Only once had Mr. Crone taken one of William's stories into Mr. Bingham's office, and that one—about President Roosevelt's repeal of Prohibition—had ended with a pat on the back for a good effort. William turned toward the front window and street traffic, clenching his fists so tight his nails cut crescents into his palms.

"Mr. McFee."

William spun around. "Yes."

"Mr. Bingham is impressed," said Mr. Crone. "But I'm afraid it won't make tomorrow morning's *Courier*."

William's heart sank. Why was Crone smiling?

Crone put his hand on William's shoulder and looked him in the eyes. "This goes against procedure, Mr. McFee, but I am pleased to inform you that Mr. Bingham has requested your story go directly to the *Times*. Today."

William braced himself on the front desk. Miss Kraven was eyeing him as she typed. The Louisville *Times*! His story was getting published. In a matter of hours it would be news.

He waved to Carly Browder—Carly *Charles*—as she read a book on the steps of her cottage. Published journalists didn't shyly nod to babes. The three biscuits with apricot jam he'd bought from Miller's Bakery with a portion of the seventy-five cents Mr. Crone had given him had settled his stomach.

She waved back with a smile. The sun felt good on his arms; arms that, now when he looked at them, appeared stronger and more roped with sinew and muscle from all the typing he'd been doing. He pulled the car to a stop, got out, and found Barley standing on the porch in a cream suit and fedora, peeling a sliver of dried paint from one of the columns. "What bird got you to rise so early this morning? We needed the car."

"Sorry." William shrugged. "Figured you'd be in your chair all day."

"Figured wrong." Barley looked at the car. "So where've you been?"

"Bread was on sale at Miller's." William retrieved the loaf he'd bought as cover.

"You drove all the way to the city for a loaf?"

"Reckon so." William headed inside.

Barley caught his arm. "You're not a very good liar."

"Not nearly as good as Johnny, I've been told. Where do you want me to take you?"

"To the doctor," said Barley. "I want a scientist's opinion on Annie's legs."

Dr. Nedry Lewis was a busy man. Samantha was told on the telephone that the doctor's slate was full for the day; but after his secretary was informed of the possible miracle, the doctor was on the other end of the line in seconds, encouraging them to hurry to his office. Judging by his expression as they entered, he hadn't expected the entire McFee family.

Dr. Lewis shook Barley's hand and gave Samantha a quick nod before focusing on Annie, who stood in the middle of the office in a pink dress. He knelt beside her and felt her legs, first the left from the knee to the ankle and then the right.

"The braces have done their job, Annie."

Samantha scoffed but then quieted herself. Dr. Lewis heard her but didn't comment. He was a strict man of science. A framed picture of Mendi the Chimpanzee, dressed in a suit and hat, hung on the wall behind his desk. William imagined it served as a reminder of the Scopes "Monkey Trial" in 1925 and the sensational argument between evolution and creationism that had captivated the nation. Clearly, Dr. Lewis favored science, and he wasn't afraid to punch holes in anything religious.

His mother was more of a modernist. She believed that science and religion were two different truths that need not contradict each other. *"Go ahead and learn the story of Adam and Eve in Sunday school,"* she had said to William once, *"but we should honor the rights of those who believe in Darwinism as well. Not everything is black and white."*

William was proud that she'd bitten her tongue in front of the doctor. William was unable to disguise his emotion as he stood with a goofy grin. He was still on a high from having his story accepted—it wasn't his secret dream of rekindling the distillery, but it was a close second—and now Annie was walking without braces.

"The braces actually hurt," Annie said. "It was Johnny who healed me, Dr. Lewis."

He smiled, half genuine. "And how did Johnny heal you, Annie?"

"He prayed for me. At that man's grave." She twirled in a circle and her dress clipped Dr. Lewis in the face.

He stood as if searching for a rational head in the room. "What man?"

"The bum in our potter's field. Johnny prayed for my legs to work and the next morning they did. Henry is—"

Barley held up his hand. "It's a long story. Can you look her over and—?"

"But it's true," Johnny said. "I prayed like I've never prayed before, Dr. Lewis."

Barley said, "Hush up, boy."

Samantha said, "He has a right to his words, Barley."

Dr. Lewis clenched his jaw. Then he put his hands on Annie's shoulders and looked into her eyes. "Now, Annie," he said condescendingly. "We've put years of work into making you better. We crafted braces specifically to fit your legs. You wore them so they would help you walk normally. Do you understand?"

William wasn't about to let the doctor spoil Annie's belief, and his confidence was soaring. "So *you* healed my sister?"

Dr. Lewis looked at William. "Yes. Or I might say we did it together."

"That's mighty lofty of you."

"It was the reason you brought her to me." He looked directly at Samantha. "Did you not ask me to help your daughter?"

"I did. And I appreciate everything you've done," Samantha said. "But as you can see, she's fine now." She took Annie by the hand. "Come on, Sugar."

Dr. Lewis ran a hand through his thinning silver hair. "What was the point of this visit, exactly?"

"Barley needs answers to things," Samantha said. "Because he's as stubborn as you are."

"This is preposterous. I'm thrilled for Annie's improvement, but—"

"You are a fine doctor," she said. "No one denies that. But you've been quite blunt with me and Annie, and for that I hold no qualms about being blunt as well."

"Mother, we should go."

"Wait, William." She spoke to Dr. Lewis again. "Your wife has tuberculosis. How long has she been at the Waverly Sanatorium— three years? And science has yet to cure her?"

Dr. Lewis tightened his jaw. "I have confidence she will defeat it."

"As do I," said Samantha. "As do I. But there was once a doctor at Waverly who lost faith in science and turned to healing his patients with music. It's believed he saved many."

"What is your point, Mrs. McFee?"

"My point is that there are multiple roads, Dr. Lewis. And there can be unexplainable powers. Good day, Doctor. I will pray tonight for your good wife."

"Good day," he said softly, staring at the floor.

The doctor's visit was a bad idea; not so much the visit, but the way in which they'd gone about it. William pulled to a stop in the driveway, and Samantha moved like she couldn't wait for fresh air. After the rest of the family disappeared into the house, Barley lit a

Lucky Strike. "Take me to see Wildemere." He took a drag. "And why were you smiling so much this morning? I don't see that a lot. You smiling." Barley exhaled. "You finally get with a woman?"

"No. Better."

"Better? How would you know what's better than a woman?"

William looked at the house and slipped the car into gear. "How would you?"

Barley didn't paste him for having a smart lip. Some chin music, he would have called it. Instead, he sat quiet all the way to the jailhouse, which was fine with William. Barley was still fidgety; he got anxious whenever he returned to the city. They'd had a house there for years—it was where William grew up— before Barley suddenly moved the family to Twisted Tree. Up until then, the distillery had been a weekend getaway, a private vacation spot, somewhere Barley refused to live full-time.

His father had been trained to become the next master distiller of Old Sam McFee. But the war derailed him. That much of Barley's story William knew, just as he knew his grandfather jumped from three stacked, empty barrels to snap his neck.

But as William drove through the crowded downtown streets, watching his father fidget with the creases in his pants, his knuckles bone-white, he wondered what else had happened in the fourteen years after Old Sam was locked up. Why, as soon as Roosevelt repealed the Volstead Act, did Barley suddenly move the family back to a place that had ghosts made of painful history?

"Park there." Barley pointed to a vacant spot on Armory Street. "Follow me and don't talk unless I tell you to."

They headed toward the brick-and-stone jailhouse, a progressive institution according to the papers, the design an elaborate series of corridors and cell blocks meant to segregate the five hundred prisoners into four groups: men and women, white and colored.

Barley McFee had a way of walking into a room, a straight-backed swagger that made him appear a foot taller than his six-foot frame. Necks turned, eyes followed, and William found himself enjoying the attention as he followed in his father's wake.

The administration wing was built in a castellated style, like a battlement, the entryway arched and bordered by turrets and a parapet. The armed guards jerked nods as Barley strolled into the jailhouse unquestioned. A fat man with a bushel of curls patted him down, and his pudgy hand came out of Barley's coat with the Colt .45 they both knew he had. From there a guard whisked them down a poorly lit hallway, where Barley spoke to a plain-clothed man who patted his back and laughed at something Barley whispered into his ear.

There was some kind of exchange after the handshake, and William felt certain he'd seen cabbage. The last time they were there, the warden had banned Barley from the visitation room. Told him that he could never see Preston Wildemere under any condition, not after threatening his life in front of ten other prisoners, four guards, and a dozen visitors. Yet here they were.

William followed Barley through a set of double doors and into the visitors' room. Amid a cluster of occupied tables, where prisoners and visitors leaned forward in hush-hush conversations under the hawkish gaze of five guards, was an empty table with two chairs on one side and one on the other. William and Barley took their seats, and a guard led a shackled Preston Wildemere into the room.

Wildemere was a small man, barely over five feet tall and 140 pounds. But his size hadn't mattered in the accident. What mattered was the size of the vehicle and how fast his Studebaker had been going, and how sloshed he'd been behind the wheel.

Wildemere was the type of man who got chewed up inside the big house, and his disheveled appearance and dark eyes showed that he'd been through the wringer. He finally looked up from the floor just before sitting at the table, and when he saw Barley he immediately attempted to flee. But the guard easily put Preston Wildemere in his seat.

"I'm sorry, Mr. McFee. So sorry. I told you that last time. If I could take back—"

"Close your head," Barley said.

Wildemere stopped talking right away.

"I'm not going to kill you." Barley leaned forward, hushed his voice. "Not today."

Wildemere had a wife and three kids. How much did they miss him?

"Then what do you need from me?"

"I need you to remember that night."

"That won't be hard. It keeps me up every night."

"Good," said Barley. "I hope you never sleep again."

"Father . . ."

"Hush, boy." Barley leaned on the tabletop, staring Wildemere down. "When I came to, I saw you behind the wheel with your head smashed." A white scar scratched a lightning bolt below Wildemere's hairline. "My boy was in the grass. I need to know how he got there."

Wildemere folded his hands on the table, fingers interlocked to fight a tremor.

"Was there another man there?"

He nodded.

"What did he look like?" Barley asked.

"He was tall. Six and a half feet, at least."

Barley seemed at a loss for words.

"Did he have a beard?" William asked.

"He had a beard, yes!" Wildemere looked more comfortable talking to William. "And long hair. Broad shouldered." Tears welled in his eyes. "I'm sorry about your brother."

"Did you see him carry my brother to the grass? Mr. Wildemere? Did you actually—?"

"Yes. Like a giant holding a flower. That's the thought I had while I watched him. That's how delicately he held the boy. My first notion was that . . ."

"What?" William asked.

"That they knew each other. There was a familiarity between them."

"There's no way my boy knew that man," Barley said. "We've never seen him before."

William wasn't so sure. At the dance marathon, a couple hundred folks had gathered inside the aging house. It wasn't out of the question that Asher had been one of them. William recalled his conversation with Johnny on the barrel run, the talk they'd had about the Hash Man. Johnny had asked Henry about how he knew certain things, and he'd said, "He *told me.*" Could the "he" have been Asher Keating?

"Asher placed Henry on the side of the road. What happened next, Mr. Wildemere?"

"I blacked out."

Barley abruptly stood from the table. He kicked his chair to the floor and left the room. William waited for the commotion to settle. "Why didn't you tell this to the newspapers?"

"To be honest, I thought I'd dreamed it." Wildemere massaged his forehead with two fingers. "I wasn't certain he was real—"

"What about his shoes? Did he have my brother's shoes? Did Asher have shoes around his neck?"

"Who is Asher?"

"The man who carried my brother. The drifter you saw."

"I *maybe* saw." Wildemere turned on William. "Your father? Why did he have the boy in the car? With all that booze? At that hour of the night? Bottles of Old Sam all across the road—"

"He was taking Henry to the doctor. Henry had trouble breathing after a hard dance—"

"So he was a hoofer?" Wildemere sounded like his father. He started to say something, then stopped. He touched his temples and shook his head. "All those bottles."

"I don't know what you're talking about. There were no bottles. Nothing about bottles was in the newspapers. Tell me about Asher. Where did he go?"

"Walked off to the trees. But was he really there? The police covered it up for your father."

"What did the police cover up?"

"The coppers cleaned up the bottles before any reporters got there." He gave an ugly grin, like a man who'd discovered every ill-treatment a prison could offer. "Because he's Barley McFee. And I wasn't the only one drinking that night."

⁂

Barley was ready to go as soon as William left the visitors' room. He was outside pacing the sidewalk with his hands against his ears to protect them from the street noise.

"Get in the car, Father." That was how William said it, and Barley obeyed.

William's knuckles were bone-white against the wheel. *"I wasn't the only one drinking that night."* He couldn't look at his father. Barley McFee and Preston Wildemere were no different. "Why was Henry in the car?"

"I was taking him to the doc—"

"Stop it."

"Watch your tone, son. You're not too old to see the back side of my hand."

"Was there booze in the car? Wildemere says there was booze all over the street. And that he wasn't the only one drinking."

"You can believe a murderer or you can believe your blood." Barley smoked for a few seconds. "That choice is up to you."

William pictured Henry. Saw him swaying from the tire swing as sunlight found holes in the whiskey trees. Heard him laughing at the sounds Johnny made under his armpits. Remembered him peeing a rainbow across the hallway into the toilet. Saw him dancing grooves into the hardwood floor of the aging house while the town urged him on with applause. Slowly, mile by mile, his anger turned inward.

William pulled the car to a stop outside their house. Fall leaves spun around the darkened tree trunks. Barley stopped at the porch steps. An empty barrel rolled from the distilling house. Someone was sweeping inside, swift bristles across hardwood.

"What's your mother up to?" Barley followed several paces behind William.

Inside, they found Mr. Browder up on a ladder with a wrench in his hand and sweat dripping from his hairline, working on the first column distiller. His daughter swept the floor in a flowery dress that accentuated the small mound at her belly. Carly's husband hoisted an empty barrel above his head and muscles bulged from a white cotton shirt. Max jerked a nod at William on his way out the door and didn't stop his momentum with the barrel.

William's heart swelled. *Is this really happening?*

Samantha was on the second-floor balcony with Annie, doing some cleanup work on the pipes that led from the neighboring fermentation house. They must have gotten to work as soon as he and Barley left for the jailhouse.

Barley stepped inside. "What nonsense is this?"

Mr. Browder laughed from the ladder's highest rung. "Mrs. McFee say it's a sign, Mr. Barley. And I cain't help but agree. With what happened with your girl and all. And I heard about that shot fired in church too. They all signs." Mr. Browder grinned like a child at Christmas. "Been waitin' for this day for years. *Years,* Mr. Barley."

"I didn't agree to this," Barley said. Max lowered the barrel and kicked it on down the run, where it disappeared through the wall and rumbled along the track outside. Barley pointed to Max. "Who's he?"

Carly laughed. "That's my husband, Mr. McFee. Remember? Max."

Samantha spoke from the loft. "Barley passed out the day of your wedding, Carly."

Johnny entered next, sidestepped Barley, and called up to Samantha. "Mom, there's a family of possum living in one of the fermentation vats. And birds in the other."

"I didn't agree to this," Barley said, louder this time, pausing as Max walked forward with his massive hand out for a shake. Barley shook it tentatively.

"Here to help, Mr. Barley." Max pumped Barley's hand and let go.

"Was this your idea?" Barley asked William as Max moved toward the corner of the house for another barrel.

"No," William said, and then thought on it, unable to hide a smile. "Well, maybe, yes."

"I didn't agree to this!" Barley shouted and everyone froze. Even the dog froze, having just entered through the barrel run. "How dare you all. I didn't give my permission on this."

Johnny handed Barley the Louisville *Times*. "Mr. Browder picked it up in town."

Mr. Browder spoke from the ladder. "Went in for some apples and came back with that." He looked at William. "Good work, boy."

From above, Samantha said, "We're proud of you, William."

William had been so rattled leaving the jailhouse that he'd forgotten, and now the ink still looked wet across the headline. MIRACLE AT TWISTED TREE. And the subtitle beneath: DRIFTER BELIEVED TO BE JESUS CHRIST.

Barley's eyes flicked side to side as he skimmed.

William waited proudly. Any moment the praise would begin.

Barley lowered the paper. "You wrote this?" His tone was bitter.

"Yes . . . Father, I wrote it. What do you think?"

Barley told him what he thought with a right hand to the left cheekbone, a knuckle-cracking punch that lifted William from the floor and turned his vision black.

ELEVEN

Dusk came as a smear of purple and gold. Samantha sat bedside on William's wooden desk chair. She dipped the sponge into the bucket of cold water, wrung it out, and held it to William's swollen face. He didn't push away as he had the first time. His nose and cheek were numb now. "One child is healed, so your father maims another."

"It's not as bad as that," said William. "So what about the distillery? Do we stop?"

"We'll move right along. Mr. Browder knows enough to get started."

"But knowing enough . . ." William sat up in bed. "Old Sam was built on quality. It has to be perfection. We need Father—"

"Once your father sees us doing it wrong, he'll join. I don't know him completely anymore, but I know him that much. He has too much passion for Old Sam to see it made incorrectly." She winked. "Watch, you'll see."

"And if he forces us to stop?"

Samantha kissed William's forehead. "Your father doesn't *force* me to do anything."

The bedroom door opened. Barley stood in the threshold with a folded newspaper in one hand and a full bottle of Old Forester in the other.

"Sam, I need to conversate with the boy, alone."

She glared at Barley and then brushed past him into the hallway. Barley kicked the door closed with his heel and sat in the chair his wife had just vacated. "How's your head?"

"Still attached."

Barley leaned back in the seat, scratched his slick hair. "I may have gone overboard." He pulled two small glasses from the deep wells of his pants pockets and handed one to William. "I should have gone for the ribs. Those bruises don't show."

"Is this a peace offering?"

"It's just a glass. Hold it still and I'll fill it up."

He poured William's and then his own and placed the bottle on the floor between his black-and-white shoes. William nosed the glass for the vanilla and caramel notes. He sipped enough to wet his tongue, and then the next tilt went down smooth. A warm, oaky finish spread out through his chest and helped him relax, and he realized for the first time that he'd gone a full day or more without having an attack of the cold sweats. Barley unfolded the newspaper, placed it on William's blanket-covered legs, and tapped the main headline. "Read."

GANGSTER ESCAPES HIGH-SECURITY PRISON IN EDDYVILLE. The newspaper was five months old, dated May 6, 1934. William had seen the article before. Probably had a copy of it tucked away in his closet. Tommy Borduchi, also known as Tommy the Bat—he killed using Louisville Sluggers—had escaped from the state penitentiary at Eddyville, Kentucky, after serving only seven years of a life sentence. He killed three guards before exiting by a second-story window. He'd gained allies among the inmates by supplying the prison with heroin, smuggled in by a woman named Eva Carcolli.

Tommy the Bat had a face chiseled from granite, cheeks crisscrossed with scars, and a jawline hard enough to chew rocks. His eyes were dark marbles under a shock of black hair.

A rush of sweat came upon William. He was looking at Henry's Hash Man. He was sure of it.

"Did Henry ever see this article?"

Barley looked at the date. "It was published after his death, so no."

"But it *is* possible Borduchi was in the newspaper before Henry died?"

"Yes. He's wanted in six states. Why?"

Then that's all it was. Henry saw the picture and it gave him nightmares. But William had a feeling of déjà vu that made no sense. He pushed the article away. "Why are you showing me this?"

"He made a shiv out of a toothbrush. Killed his bunkmate. Stabbed him because he snored." Barley lifted his glass. The bourbon slid through his parted lips. "He beat one of the guards to death with a bed slat. Slit another's throat with that toothbrush. Word is he prayed over the bodies. He's a self-proclaimed born-again Christian."

"Stop."

"This man wants me dead, William. He's wanted me dead for years. I had dealings with him in the midtwenties. Things went sour. I was one of the reasons he went to jail."

"Does it have something to do with Rose Island?"

Barley poured himself more Old Forester. "What do you know about Rose Island?"

"I've overheard you talk about it."

Barley sat quiet for a moment. "Tommy the Bat. He didn't know me as Barley McFee. He knew me as Dooly McDowell. A name born of necessity. I had three other partners: Tad McVain, Fop McDougal, and Gio McShane. We were known as the Micks. I was the only one with enough foresight to use a fake name. The other three Micks are dead."

"How?" William remembered meeting the Micks when he was younger. He'd forgotten them until now.

"McVain died the white death. Borduchi sunk Fop McDougal's feet in concrete, then threw him overboard. Into the Ohio while he was still alive. Gio McShane was strangled with barbed wire two years ago in Cincinnati. Borduchi's been looking for me since he busted out."

"How do you know?"

"Our old house in Portland burned to the ground last month."

"Is that why you moved us out here? You were afraid he'd come? That's why you're always looking out the windows? It's not the Krauts? Was our Portland house under your other name?"

"Yes." Barley drank, wiped his mouth as he yawned. "I thought we'd be safe here for a while." Barley reached into his pocket for a cigarette and lit up.

"Maybe he already knows where you are, and the house was just a message."

Barley shrugged, exhaled. "Wouldn't put it past him to give me extra time. Just to watch me sweat. He's like a cat who likes to toy with a ball of yarn." He took another drag on the cigarette, sucking his cheeks inward. "But I don't think so."

"How can you be so sure?"

"Because I know how badly he wants me dead. If he knew where I was, he'd already have me resting in the Chicago overcoat."

William watched his father. Smoke spiraled to the ceiling.

"A coffin, William. Relax. I've had a couple men in the woods for months. Just in case he shows."

"What men? I haven't noticed any men."

"Because they're good." Barley pointed with the cigarette. "But that story you wrote . . . People are going to come now. Crowds searching for Christ. Looking for answers. Watch and see."

William lowered his head.

Barley waved, the cigarette glowing like a meteorite. "It's time for Dooly McDowell to die anyway. Like the rest of the Micks. I need to get Tommy Borduchi off my scent."

"Father, what did you do during Prohibition?"

Fidgety, Barley took a deep drag, exhaled smoke toward the ceiling. "I ran booze. Part of a bootlegging system that rivaled Remus up in Cincy. I was actually one of his runners."

Barley stood and paced around the bedroom. For a moment father and son listened to the sound of creaking floorboards.

"Tommy the Bat and Eva Carcolli. They're dangerous. That moll would walk right into the prison with a balloon of heroin tucked where no one would find it."

William felt like an adult; Barley was talking like he was one of the boys. Not one of *his* boys, but one of *the* boys!

"They'd pat her down, look inside her mouth, and then she'd ask to use the restroom. That's when she'd retrieve it and slide it into her mouth, where they'd already checked. When she kissed Tommy, that's when they'd transfer the heroin."

Barley returned to the chair and poured more Old Forester. "Your grandfather hung himself the day after Prohibition agents locked our houses. They confiscated what we had bottled so the bootleggers wouldn't raid. Which they did—half the agents were corrupt. One twitchy palooka named Royce, he took any bribe he could get. Paced like a caged lion with his tommy gun, smoking nonstop. Had evil in his heart."

William didn't move; he didn't want to disturb this flow of information.

"First night he smashed a full barrel of Old Sam with a sledge-hammer and made your grandfather watch as bourbon spread across the grass. That's what ultimately broke him—watching all his work and sweat seep into the ground. Royce dared me to stop him. I said, 'Don't worry, I will.'"

Barley took a final pull on his Lucky before he put it out on his palm and flicked it in a wastebasket beside the bed. He yawned again, rubbed his red eyes with the pad of his palm.

"I told him to stop smoking around the aging house too. Aging-house fires can't be put out. They burn until dust. 'Appropriate ending,' Royce told me. I hated him. And then I blamed him for my father's death. He kept on smoking on our property. One night I waited until he exhaled, until his eyes were squinted just so, and then I pulled my Luger and blew the ciga-rette from his hand. Part of his thumb along with it.

"He fumbled for his chopper, but I had him on the ground with my gun on his forehead. He was a boy playing with toys, and I was a man who'd crawled through enough quicksand not to care. I pointed the Luger to the ground, an inch below his left ear, and I fired. I did the same to the other side and by that time he couldn't hear. He ran to his car and never reported back for duty. The next agent had a better heart. He was even apologetic when his bosses came to take our entire inventory to a safe house."

"Safe house?"

"The government moved all the whiskey and bourbon to concentration houses so it could be more easily guarded. There were ten of them, four in Louisville. All the Old Sam was stored in the Sunny Brook warehouse. Whiskey was still sold during Prohibition, William, for those lucky enough, and rich enough, to get their doctors to prescribe it for 'medicinal purposes,' which they did nonstop. They'd take those scripts to their druggist and go home with legal bourbon, legal whiskey made from Samuel McFee's sweat, my sweat, and the sweat of others like me. Old Sam was the heart of this town, and it was siphoned out through phony drugstores and bogus pharmacies."

He stared out the window. "It was Tad McVain's idea to get involved. He had contacts in Chicago who were in with Giovanni Torrio and Al Capone. They were making millions controlling bootlegging and alcohol distribution."

"You knew Capone? And Johnny Torrio? Johnny the Fox?"

"Met them a few times, yes. Met a lot of men. Joe Masseria, Lucky Luciano, Bugs Moran, George Remus . . ."

"The King of the Bootleggers."

"Arnold Rothstein."

"The Brain Rothstein? Did he really fix the World Series? The Black Sox Scandal?"

"Never heard you correctly refer to baseball before." Barley grinned, leaned back in the chair with his eyes closed.

"It was all over the newspapers. Who else? Did you ever go to one of Remus's parties?"

It was almost too much for William to stomach. He'd take another punch to the face for more conversation like this with his father.

He looked again at the picture of Tommy "The Bat" Borduchi. William had met the Micks; had he ever met Tommy? A memory like an itch wanted to surface and then came upon him in a flash. *A Louisville Slugger, blood coated, rolled across a garage floor. Hard faces. Tough guys. Dad was one of them. Was he crying?*

William snapped back into the present and swung his legs from the bed. Barley had dozed off in the chair, the bottle of Old Forester resting in his lap. William grabbed it, helped his father to the bed, covered him with the blanket, and turned the light off. He tiptoed from the bedroom and down the steps to the first floor.

It was close to midnight and the house was quiet. William made sure the doors were locked, then stood looking out the bay window. What his father confided in him . . . Tommy the Bat . . . Would his story about Keating bring enemies to their doorstep?

TWELVE

William awoke the next morning to the smell of hotcakes. He sat up in his father's recliner, snapped the footrest down, and squinted out the sunlit window. Out by the hammer mill, Annie walked through the grass with an armful of sticks, and next to her Johnny carried a toolbox from the grain mill. On the end table next to the recliner was a note from his mother:

> You'll have to explain to me why you and your father switched beds last night? Enjoy your hotcakes.
>
> Mother

William felt like there was quicksilver sloshing around in his head instead of a brain. He touched his cheekbone and winced; it was tender to the touch. He hurried through the plate of hotcakes she'd left beside the note. They were still warm because they'd been sitting in the sun, but there was no telling how long they'd been there. The melted butter had turned them spongy, but they did the trick, and by the time he stood from the chair he was more awake, and the throb where Barley had pasted him was more manageable.

According to the clock on the far wall, it was twenty minutes past ten. He never slept that late. *What is that scraping sound?* He opened the front door and found Barley on the porch wearing a white tank top and old trousers. He looked up but never stopped scraping the porch column. Old paint flaked like snowfall, collecting in his arm hair like dandruff.

"You snore, son."

William squinted in the sunlight. "No, I don't."

"How would you know? I'm telling you, you do."

William spotted three paint cans next to the first step. "What are you doing?"

Barley wiped sweat from his face. "What's it look like I'm doing?"

"You're gonna finally paint the porch?"

Barley shook his head, resumed scraping and smoothing with his hand. He rarely showed his arms, but they were corded with muscle. "Did the Old Fo dumb you up?" Barley looked out across the gravel driveway as Samantha, wearing clothes she normally used for the garden, exited the fermentation house and entered the grain mill. Max followed behind her, carrying a heavy box of something clunky. "Like an ant farm."

"What's like an ant farm?"

Barley pointed. "Your mother and her friends. Somebody slip you a Mickey?"

"No . . . what?"

"A Mickey Finn." Barley bent down to pry one of the paint tops with a pocketknife. "It's when somebody puts knockout drops in your drink. You look like you've had a few."

William pointed across the way. "Somebody's coming, Dad."

A green convertible Rolls-Royce approached through the trees, slowing over the barrel run, then picking up speed again as it rounded the bend in the driveway toward the house. A woman with orange-blonde hair, elbow-length gloves, and shaded glasses sat in the passenger's seat holding a young boy in a floppy herringbone hat. The driver was a mustached man dressed in a white suit. The Rolls skidded to a halt a few yards from the McFees' Model T, and the man, whose orange hair was parted and combed down toward his ears with so much pomade that the wind didn't move it, quickly jumped from the car without closing the door.

Barley's gun belt was on the far side of the porch next to the hanging swing. Before the man took his next step, Barley stopped him with an outstretched hand. "That's far enough."

"Is this the McFee Distillery?"

"And what if it is?"

"Then I've found myself in the right place. I'm Roddrick Fancannon." He motioned toward the car behind him. "This is my wife, LuAnne, and my son, Lucas." He looked to his left as Johnny and Annie approached from the mill, at Annie in particular. "Is that her?"

Johnny protectively put an arm around his little sister. "What do you want?"

"Is that the girl?" asked Fancannon, on the verge of tears as he faced Barley. "I beg you. I'll pay."

"We don't want your money," said Barley.

"That story got picked up in our Nashville papers. I drove through the night to get here. To Twisted Tree."

William looked to the man's wife in the passenger's seat. "Why? Because of your boy?"

Fancannon nodded. "He's had a fever for well over a week now. We chill him in baths of ice, and it works, but it spikes again. The doctors are befuddled. We're desperate, Mr. McFee."

"I'm no doctor," said Barley.

"Is that it?" Fancannon gazed toward the potter's field. "Is that where he's buried? The man believed to be Christ?"

William said, "You've come to visit the grave?"

Fancannon nodded. "And I'll pay."

"Cabbage won't improve your chance of a miracle," Barley said. "Jesus wasn't dressed to the nines, if I remember my Bible correctly. Nor did He wear gold around His wrist."

Fancannon glanced at his fancy watch and looked up. "Please . . . you can have it . . ."

"I don't want your watch, Mr. Fancannon."

"Go on." William nodded toward the potter's field. "Go ahead and take your boy. Do what you need to do and move along."

"God bless you," the wife said from the car. Fancannon hurried around to the other side of his Rolls-Royce and opened the door for her. He took the young boy and the three of them hurried toward the field.

Barley watched them go. Then went back to scraping paint.

———

The Fancannons prayed at the grave in the sun while deer spied from the whiskey trees. Barley watched them as he scraped and Cat panted beside him. William got to work inside the grain mill with Max and Carly, replacing rotted boards on the bins, which were set high in the barn, accessible from the second-floor balcony so gravity could help the grain into the mill. Every so often he looked out the window to check on Barley. After the Fancannons drove off, Barley went inside to clean up. He returned to the porch thirty minutes later in a white suit and hat that resembled Fancannon's, then leaned against the Model T, smoking a cigar.

"What's your father doing?" Samantha asked over William's shoulder.

William turned. "Looks ready to go somewhere."

"What did the two of you talk about all night?"

"Grandpa Sam." William sidestepped his mother to grab a broom. "And the distillery."

"Oh . . . what did he say?"

"Not much," said William. Barley had *confided* in him. "What do you have there, Mother? A sample of the corn?" William inhaled. It smelled sweet. "Do we have enough to be milled?"

"Mr. Browder is checking the grains for quality. Making sure they're free of mold. Johnny is examining for cracked kernels." She was upbeat. "You were right. Mr. Browder has also been dabbling with malted barley and rye. We used to buy those from other farms." She handed William the bucket of corn. "Here, take this to your father. Maybe the smell will bring him to his senses."

William took the bucket from her. "Thanks, Mother."

"For what?"

He surveyed the grain mill. "For this."

She didn't answer verbally, but the moisture in her eyes showed her thanks to him, for planting that seed, as Mr. Browder would have said it. Samantha never pinpointed her change of heart concerning the distillery, but William felt certain it had everything to do with Annie.

He nosed the bucket of corn on his way out the door.

Barley's cigar was down to a nub by the time William approached with the bucket. "Go on in and change." Barley nodded at William's hands. "What do you have there?"

"Corn. Mom said to give it to you." He noticed Henry's shoes draped around his father's neck. "Where we going?"

"To the city to look for those bums."

William left the bucket on the gravel and went inside. He put on a clean white shirt and trousers, then replaced his boots with more comfortable brown shoes. He would have liked to have worn a hat like Barley's; he needed something to make him look like a man, something to match the half-raccoon bruise around his left eye. He settled for a small scoop of pomade from his father's tin and ran it through his hair. Checking himself in the mirror, he was convinced it made a subtle difference.

William returned downstairs, and when he opened the front door, he caught Barley squatting next to the bucket of corn, nosing it heavily. But as soon as he'd been caught, his father walked to the passenger's side of the car.

"What took you so long?"

William ignored the question. "Doesn't it smell good?"

"Smells like corn." Barley closed his door. "What's with the hair?"

William parked the car in a vacant spot at Fifth and Main, within view of the Ohio River, where most of the homeless seemed to congregate. Louisville had instituted employment programs after the crash, odd jobs and temp work that paid thirty-two cents an hour, but only one thousand spots were available to the eleven thousand showing up with lunch pails every morning, and the crowded river thoroughfare teemed with those turned away.

The riverfront boasted dozens of taverns and can houses full of wayward customers purchasing liquor with sketchy credit and pocket change. A slow-moving coal barge ducked under the new Second Street Bridge, cutting a frothy V through the waves. The riverbank crawled with bicycles, honking cars, and horse-pulled wagons. William noticed how many of the men he passed smoked cigarettes; tobacco was the only industry in the city unharmed by the Depression. Men smoked more when they were tense. They bought simple pleasures when everything else was unaffordable.

William and Barley moved east along the river and found pockets of drifters to question. Many were too smoked on giggle juice or dope to give any pertinent information. Several claimed they'd heard of Asher Keating—"The man who walked on water," said one; "The preacher," said another. "Is it true? Did he really heal that little girl's legs?"

"It's true," Barley had mumbled, touching Henry's shoes periodically, like a rosary.

"I know those." A wrinkle-faced woman under the awning of a closed dry goods store pointed to the dangling shoes. Her smell was repulsive.

Barley squatted next to her, but not too close. "Do you know the man who wore these?" He touched Henry's shoes. "He wore them around his neck, like this."

The lady nodded, wide eyed, her lips parted. A peaceful smile spread across her face. Barley snapped to get her attention, but she'd drifted back into her own world. Barley snapped again. "Hey, have you seen him? Have you seen the man who wore these shoes?"

William touched Barley's shoulder, encouraging him to move on. He did after one more snap. They continued east, with no luck after an hour of looking.

A Negro-only breadline stretched around the corner of Third Street—at least three dozen blacks, men and women with empty bags in their hands, hoping to get enough to stretch through the week.

Barley pointed. "Look at the billboard."

The advertisement above the line showed a picture of a happy white family driving in a car. "Even got a dog in there. Sticking his head right out the window." Barley removed another Lucky from his jacket, shielded the flame until it lit, and read the billboard's caption. "World's Highest Standard of Living."

William finished it for him. "There's no way like the American way."

"Don't look up," Barley said, although not loud enough for anyone in line to hear. Then he reached inside his jacket and removed a wad of cash. He walked down the breadline and gave each person a bill. They stared at him, one after the next, stunned. And then he crossed the street toward the river.

William hurried to catch up. "What was that about?"

"Nothing. Close your head."

William followed Barley in admiration. Down the bank they spotted a man with a young boy who couldn't be older than ten. They were fishing at the waterline under the bridge with poles rigged from tree branches. The father and son watched with caution as William and Barley navigated the slope of wet rocks. Wind whipped across the water, and Barley had to hold his hat on. By the time he balanced out on level dirt again, he was agitated and spoke tersely.

"Asher Keating. Do you know him?"

The fisherman pulled in his empty line and rested the pole beside him. His brown suit was dirty and faded. His face was stubbly with graying hair matching the tuft atop his head. "Does it look like I should know him?"

"Figured there was a good chance of it, pal."

"Why, 'cause I live on the streets?" The fisherman stood. He was taller than Barley and William. He eyed the shoes around Barley's neck. "Where'd you get those?" And then he facetiously added, *"Pal."*

"None of your business."

"Asher used to wear those around his neck," said the man.

Barley's tone changed immediately. "These shoes? Are you sure?"

"I don't know if they were those shoes or President Roosevelt's. I just know he wore them around his neck like some wise guy."

The boy hadn't looked up since they'd arrived. William thought he looked hungry and scared, two feelings a boy should never have.

"What happened to your eye?" the man asked William.

"Got in a fight. So you know Asher Keating?"

"I *knew* him," said the fisherman. "Papers say he's dead. Which is just ripe by me."

William looked at Barley but spoke to the man. "How so?"

The boy finally spoke. "Because that man killed my mother."

The fisherman cast his line into the water. "I'm John Swell. This is my boy, Peter. He had a twin, Simon, who passed two years ago."

Barley now spoke with compassion. "And your wife?"

"She passed ten months ago." John the fisherman moved his

line in the water. "Without a roof over her head. In the middle of a rainstorm. Right here where we stand."

"I'm sorry."

"Why? You didn't know her."

"I have a wife of my own."

"She's still alive, I presume?"

The edge returned to Barley's voice. "You presume correctly."

John Swell looked back to the water. "And I assume this is your son?"

"I am." William offered his hand for a shake. The fisherman shook it, but the grip was untrusting. "Might I ask why your son believes Asher killed his mother?"

"He came too late." John propped the pole between two logs and sat down heavily on the embankment. "Not that it would have mattered. Whole thing was cruel. A farce. My dear wife got caught up in it."

"You are not a believer?" William asked.

John huffed. "What God would allow a world to dwindle to this? I'm not a believer in God. And I'm certainly not a believer in Asher Keating."

William said, "We've heard stories of healing—"

"He was a magician," John Swell said. "An illusionist, with fans."

Barley sat on a slanted rock. "Tell us about your wife, Mr. Swell."

"Her name was Amanda." John catered to his fishing line for half a minute. "Answered phones at the National Bank. Lost her job when it closed and I had all our money tied up in stocks. Lost everything in the crash. We lasted for months, scraping by doing odd jobs, but those ran dry and we had to move from our home. Amanda never got over Simon's death."

John looked at the shoes around Barley's neck.

"She was depressed. Started getting the cough. Neither of us spoke about it, but we knew. Sounded like Simon's cough. She liked the river. We heard that wind was good for the lungs, and there's a lot of it here. We were walking the riverbank one morning and saw a crowd. Asher stood ankle-deep in the water, with another man in his arms, lowering him into the river. It was a baptism. Asher preached about God's forgiveness. Talked about right and wrong. Told the newly baptized to be good and kind and honest. Amanda was a very religious woman. She was enthralled. It was the first time in months I'd seen her smile."

John Swell wiped his eyes. "She walked toward the crowd, and it parted for her." His hands shook. "Asher called her by name even though he didn't know her. 'Amanda Swell,' he said. 'Child of Christ. Be cleansed in the water and seek God's forgiveness.' I've seen magicians do such things. Surprise people by calling their names. I'm certain one of the people on the riverbank whispered it."

"And she did?" William asked. "She went into the water?"

John nodded, watched his boy pluck a worm from the mud. "She was different after that. Her cough worsened and she lost weight, but the depression was gone. She became one of his loyal followers. I tried to talk her out of it. And she dwindled away."

John pointed to Peter. "He witnessed Asher putting his hands on a woman who claimed to have lost her sight. Asher touched her eyes and the next day she could supposedly see. Another trick of the mind, but Peter begged Asher to put his hands on his mother. Begged him to fix her." John stood from the embankment, pulled his line from the water. "Asher told us that God had His own plan for Amanda, and that her future was not in his hands, but in God the Father's. Which was fine by me. I didn't want that man's hands on my wife."

A fish had stolen his worm. John put the pole down, dejected. "The day she died, Peter sent for Asher. He didn't make it in time. Peter blames him. I don't. I allowed Asher to say a prayer when he arrived. He told us that Amanda had returned to God."

To be with Simon, thought William.

"Me and Peter never saw Asher Keating again."

"Why did he wear the shoes around his neck?" William asked.

John Swell looked at Barley. "Why do you wear *those*?"

"They're my son's."

John hooked another worm on his line. "Don't know why. Heard some say it started in the war, though. Do you know how he died?"

"We don't."

"I don't either." John tried his line in the water again. "Some say he was insane. Part of me wonders . . ."

"Wonders what, Mr. Swell?"

"Amanda spent more time with him than I did. She said he healed a boy of polio and afterward forgot how to walk. Saved a woman from consumption and took on her cough. The lady he healed from blindness: supposedly he couldn't see for hours." John chewed on the inside of his cheek. "Maybe he just took too much of the bad stuff in."

Barley stood with a grunt; Henry's words came back to William in a flash. He asked, "Do you remember a young red-haired woman who followed Asher named Pauline? Polly, to some."

"She lives at the old coke ovens and coal yards. Why do you want to know?"

"Because we'd like to find her."

"Are you reporters? Was it you who wrote the article? The one in the paper?"

William nodded proudly. "But we're not here as reporters, Mr. Swell. We're just chinning here—"

"Should have told me your true business before taking my time."

Barley gripped William's arm. "Come on. Leave them be."

"We need answers too," William said. "You're not the only ones suffering loss."

Barley held out a bill to John. "Get you and your boy some food. Please."

"I don't take handouts."

Barley slipped the end of the bill beneath a rock.

"Leave it there and it'll end up in the river."

Barley left the bill anyway. "Good day, Mr. Swell."

The fisherman watched them for a moment. "Find a man named Solomon Kane. Asher saw him often."

"Is he one of the Twelve?" asked William.

"No." The fisherman jerked his line from the water: he'd caught a glass bottle filled with slime. "He's who Asher got his dope from."

THIRTEEN

William felt oddly betrayed by the news that Asher Keating was an opium addict. But he couldn't condemn the man. If nothing else, it humanized him—a reminder that Asher, a war veteran, a man like any other, was not immune to the temptations of vice. *Let he who has not sinned cast that first stone.*

"I want to see our old house," said William, making a turn.

"It's burned down. I told you that."

"I want to see it."

"Suit yourself." Barley relaxed in his seat. "Your mother refuses to."

She knows? William found Portland Avenue, bordered on both sides by narrow brick homes, clipped yards, driveways with parked cars, and porches festooned with hanging baskets and wind chimes. And then he saw it: a huge gap, a missing tooth in a line full of strong ones. He coasted past the blackened brick wall and charred half chimney surrounded by ash and rubble. Saplings had already sprouted from the tarry heap. Only the unattached garage in the back of the property had been spared.

Seeing the burned house where he'd lived for much of his childhood didn't sadden him as much as he thought it might. But now that they were there, Barley insisted on idling while he smoked a cigarette.

"This wasn't in the newspapers," William said.

"I didn't want it to be."

Just like Wildemere said about the booze on the road.

William stared at the garage they had never used except for storage. "Did you ever bring Tommy Borduchi here? You know, when I was little?"

"He may have been around a time or two." Barley pointed toward the road, and William gave the house one last look before pulling out. He drove toward Clayton Street, slowed over the railroad crossing at Fulton, and parked atop a hill overlooking the coal yards—a sea of blackish rock and dust splayed out before the river. To the right stood the old coke ovens, a row of fifty brick beehive domes standing roughly ten feet high and sharing common walls.

"You should have seen these ovens when they burned all in a row." Barley held on to his hat as they descended. He was being careful not to get gray dust and mud on his white suit. "From a distance it looked like the city was burning. The fires raged day and night. Blackened the sky to soot."

Now they'd become convenient dwellings.

A woman sat against one bricked dome; her bright red hair was unmistakable. William took off toward her. She turned and his heart sank. She was in her forties, not her late teens. She was not Polly. And she had a devious smirk.

"Can I help you lads?" the redhead asked as Barley joined up. "You're not the first father to bring a virgin down to sweet Delia. A dollar and I'll take you into my hive. Ten and I'll marry you."

Barley made as if to retrieve money from his jacket.

William's face turned hot pink to the neckline. He had no hat to hide behind, so he took off running up the hill, and he didn't look back until he reached the car. He got in the driver's seat, slammed the door, and started the engine, hoping the sound of it idling would hurry his father up the hillside. But it didn't.

Barley's fedora was easy to follow as he stopped to question one person after another. Five minutes passed, then ten, and then three cop cars drove in from the west, bleating their sirens. Dozens of squatters hurried off toward the river, but many stayed, unfazed. Barley sprinted as if chased, holding his hat and grinning as if enjoying a sudden thrill.

William backed the car up as soon as his father took a seat.

"Hold your horses, pal." Barley slammed his door. William started forward, then immediately hit the brakes. A squatty man stood in front of the car with his hands up.

Barley rolled down his window. "You want to die today?"

The man had ferret eyes. Hands still up, he approached the window. The cuffs of his suit were so long, only his fingers were visible. "Let me in. There's coppers!"

"Run him over," Barley said.

William drove around him, but the man grabbed Barley's open window and ran along with the car. "Stop. I'm Kane. Solomon Kane."

William hit the brakes, and Barley opened his door and jumped out. "Get in."

Solomon Kane slid into the passenger's seat beside William, and Barley jumped into the back so he could point his Colt .45 at Kane's head.

"What do you want?" Barley asked.

"You're the ones looking for me," Solomon said.

He reeked: a mixture of body odor, opium, and beer.

William didn't know whether to stay parked or drive, so he moved at a slow roll.

Solomon said, "What are you waiting for? Go. I can't afford to be arrested again."

"Find the first alleyway and park, William," Barley said. "He's smelling up my car."

Solomon lifted his arm as if to smell himself. William navigated a few street corners and spotted an alleyway he'd rather not go into, but Barley said, "Perfect," so he pulled in, sidling up next to trash and a light post decorated with a woman's deep-cupped brassiere.

"So how much do you want?" Solomon asked. "I have A-bombs, opium, dope, heroin."

"Tell us about Asher Keating," William said hastily.

Solomon started out of the car, but Barley pressed the gun to the back of his head.

"Asher, he owes me money—"

"Good luck with that," Barley said. "He's decomposing right now."

Solomon nibbled his fingernails. "It doesn't change the fact—"

"How did he pay you?" William asked. "He was a drifter."

"Doesn't always mean no money. Just a matter of what they spend it on."

"Vulture," Barley said.

"Kidnapper."

Barley smacked Solomon in the back of the head. "You asked to get into this car."

"He didn't pay, okay?" He combed his hair down in a slope

toward his brow. "He paid me in prayers. Baptized me in the river. I had a bum knee and he put his hands on it."

"Then why does he owe you money?"

"Because he went off and died on me."

"How did he die?" Barley asked.

"I heard he was murdered. Also heard he had a heart attack. After he healed someone who had a heart attack. Then I heard he was walking across the Ohio and he slipped under."

"Close your head," Barley said.

"That's what I heard." Solomon looked at Barley. "What's with the shoes? I've seen those before. Around Asher's neck."

"Why did he wear them?"

Solomon bit the index fingernail on his left hand. "Assumed it was because he didn't have a scarf."

Barley hit Solomon on the back of the head again.

"Cripes. I don't know! Asher wasn't proud of his habits. He prayed for forgiveness before he took the pipe. He tried to quit but he couldn't. He smoked opium to forget."

"To forget what?"

"To forget what he'd seen."

"In the war?"

"In the war. On the streets. Smoked to forget who he was. What he was. Can I go now?"

Barley said, "Get out."

Solomon opened the door and stepped out into the alleyway. Barley got out of the car to return to the front seat.

"He owed me money." Solomon held out his palm as if he expected Barley to pay.

"How much?" Barley asked.

"Thousands." Solomon ran his chubby hand over his hair again. "Thereabouts."

Barley reached a hand into his pocket and left it there. "You holding out on us?"

Solomon watched Barley's buried hand. After thinking on it he said, "There's a man who'll know more than me. They were in the war together. Oliver Sanscrit. He'll know about the shoes. Had something to do with the war."

"Where do we find this man?" Barley asked.

Solomon smiled. "You don't find Oliver. He finds you."

"Is he a bum?"

"I don't know what he is. But he's always dressed in full military gear. Whenever Asher needed to talk to someone, that's who he went to."

Barley removed the hand from his pocket and flipped Solomon Kane a penny.

Solomon caught it and then threw it back at the car as William and Barley pulled away.

Barley cackled. "William, your cheeks got red as tomatoes back there. Imagine if she'd opened her blouse."

William hit the gas hard in the direction of Twisted Tree.

"The Twelve have moved on. Man, it stinks in here now." Barley pulled a cigarette from his pocket, lit it, and rolled down the window. "Your apostles moved on. At least that's what the whore said. Said they are traveling to spread the word of Jesus Christ." He took a drag, exhaled. "The word of Asher. She actually said that. The word of Asher."

William drove on in silence.

"Oh, come on, William. I was only needling you."

"Needle someone else."

Barley took a drag, exhaled toward the cracked window. "Did you get that guy's name?"

"Oliver Sanscrit. I got it."

The best place to find a war veteran was at the local post of the American Legion in Germantown. It was an eyesore on the corner of a dusty intersection littered with hogshead barrels: squatty and narrow, gloomy from the overgrown grass around the stoop to the American flag swaying at half-mast.

"They opened it after the war," Barley said as William parked. "Your mother talked me into going. Thought it might be good for my nightmares to talk to other vets. It's where I met the other Micks. McVain was a former pianist. He was missing three fingers on his left hand and still angry about it. Blown off at Chateau-Thierry. Red hair. Hard face. I asked if the seat beside him was taken."

William followed Barley across the near-empty lot. "What did he say?"

"'Does it look like it's taken?' Called me a blind baboon. I didn't trust the meanness in his eyes, so when he told me his name, I surprised even myself; I don't know where 'Dooly McDowell' came from. Two weeks later he introduced me to Gio McShane. He liked to smoke two cigarettes at a time, one for each hand. Four weeks later Fop McDougal came into the fold. For a time, our only relationship was the Legion Post, drinking . . ."

"Until Prohibition?"

"Yeah, and then things changed in a hurry." Barley opened

the creaky door. The building was poorly lit and smelled of stale beer and cigar smoke. American flags festooned the walls, and around them hung framed pictures and old military uniforms from different wars. Including the bartender there were only six men inside, a table of three and a table of two. They all had beers. Barley breathed in the smoky air like he missed it. He claimed he hadn't been to the post in years, but the bartender called him by name and the patrons watched as if they not only knew Barley McFee but feared him.

"Where is everybody, Skip?" Barley asked the barkeep.

Skip's yellow hair was thinning up the middle. He wiped crumbs from the bar top. A sign behind him caught William's attention:

What We Hated from the War

1. The composer who wrote the reveille song;
2. The contractor who made the field shoes;
3. The packer who concocted the "Canned Willy";
4. The underwear manufacturer who left the sheep burrs in those pants;
5. The outfitter who tied those knots in the toes of the socks;
6. The rubber dealer who used a sieve instead of a sole for those boots;
7. The uniform buttons.

To William, Barley said, "Buttons were made of pasteboard."

Skip said, "And sewn with invisible thread."

A man yelled from the back of the room, "Don't forget the

girl who told us we'd never stand a chance unless we enlisted. We hate her too."

Another man: "Yeah, Skip, you were supposed to add that one months ago."

Skip stared at the shoes around Barley's neck. "What do you want, Dooly?"

William looked at his father to see if he'd waver upon mention of his alias.

Barley didn't skip a beat. "I'm looking for a vet named Oliver Sanscrit."

Skip spoke to the tables of men across the room. "Gentlemen? Oliver Sanscrit?"

They all resumed drinking.

"What do you want with Sanscrit?" asked Skip. "You in trouble?"

"Does it matter?" Barley asked.

"If you're in trouble it does. You need a lawyer?"

"No. Is Sanscrit a lawyer?"

"Of sorts."

"Either he is or he isn't."

"Not sure if he's fully fledged." Skip poured Barley a beer even though he'd declined. "He represents veterans who need help in court. That's why I asked if you were in trouble."

Barley took the mug and downed half the beer. "I just need to speak to the man."

"Regarding?"

"Not sure it's any of your business, Skip. Are you his secretary?"

"Of sorts."

"Then can I see him?"

"He's not here."

"Where is he? Does he have an office somewhere?"

"No." Skip wiped the bar again. "Just shows up in here from time to time."

A white-haired gentleman in glasses spoke from the far table. "You don't go to Oliver Sanscrit. He comes to you."

William jumped to the heart of the matter; Barley was getting nowhere. "I'm the reporter who wrote the article. Did anyone here know Asher Keating? We were told that Mr. Sanscrit was his friend. From the war."

By their reactions William surmised they at least knew *of* Asher. A man with thick hair spoke from the table of two. "Are you going to write more nonsense in the papers?"

"This isn't for the papers."

"Then I met Asher Keating once. He had issues. They didn't need to be wrote about."

"This isn't for the papers," Barley repeated.

"Then what's it about?" asked another man from the table of three.

Barley touched the shoes around his neck. "It's about finding out why Asher Keating is buried in my backyard. And why he had my baby boy's shoes in his bindle."

For a moment it seemed the air had been sucked from the room.

The first man said, "I'm sorry, McDowell. We all are. Apologies. We didn't mean nothing by it. But Sanscrit . . . he's been back from the war for a long time, but he's not really *back*. You know what I mean? And it's true that you don't go to him. He'll find you."

Barley downed the rest of the beer and touched Henry's shoes—a nervous tick he was no longer aware of.

The man had more to say. "I met Mr. Keating the one time, though. I didn't get any indication he was who some people thought he was. But he was in here with Sanscrit one evening, the two of them drinking, and I recall a conversation they were having. About Asher losing his job. I took from their words that he was fired."

"Fired from where?" William asked.

"The Ford plant. On the assembly line, I think."

"Why was he fired?" Barley asked.

The man took a slug of beer. "I gathered it had something to do with the boss's wife."

"Tanner Finn," said the white-haired man. "That's who runs the Ford plant. I think that's who we're talking about. Tanner's wife. Don't know her name."

"Sanscrit was talking sense to Asher. His boss wanted to rehire him. Sanscrit was talking Asher into returning. Asher Keating said he had better things to do than build cars."

William spotted a telephone behind the bar.

Skip allowed them use of it but gave them the hinky eye from across the way. Were the men in the bar catching on that Barley was no longer who they thought he was? It only took a moment for the operator to put William in touch with the residence of Tanner Finn. But it was the wife who answered, cautiously saying her name was Bethany. As soon as William mentioned Asher Keating, he heard a nervous gasp. And then a *click*.

"What'd she say?" Barley asked.

"She hung up."

After they'd left the American Legion, Barley decided he needed a drink. They drove to Twisted Tree's drugstore, called Melvin's. It was owned by a man everyone called Juice. He sold more booze than pills. During Prohibition, whiskey was his most widely scripted medicine.

William parked the car. "How about I go in. I wanna see if Juice will sell to me. Can I have your hat?"

"My hat? What for?"

"Makes me look older."

"Don't bend it. And don't pull it down too far. Your head's bigger than mine. You'll stretch the band out."

William placed it on his head and checked how he looked in the rearview. The brim partially concealed his black eye. Juice didn't even give him a second glance, counting out the change as if he'd sold William booze hundreds of times before. William left with a strut, the embarrassment from the coke ovens buried.

A blue Model T with a bullet hole in the driver's door had just pulled into the lot.

Bancroft straightened the lapels of his coat and smoothed the sides of his trimmed black mustache as he got out of his car. "You're the McFee boy. Didn't recognize you under the topper. Your journalistic efforts are juvenile, by the way." Bancroft started along. "Good day."

"Why haven't you got the door fixed?"

"Haven't had the time."

"But you'll do it." The hat gave William some Barley-power. "My mom gave you cabbage. Make sure you're not gonna be a wise guy."

Mr. Bancroft laughed pompously. "Look, sonny, I'll fix the door when I fix the door. I'm a busy man." He paused. "Expect a follow-up on all that potter's field nonsense in the *Post*. And then you'd best turn to the Lord before the Devil pulls you asunder."

"She thinks you're crazy," William said. "You know that,

don't you? She was only being kind and didn't know how to get rid of you."

"Your mother is a coquettish harlot." Mr. Bancroft entered the drugstore.

William went back to the car. He asked for Barley's gun.

"First my hat and now my gun?" Barley pulled the Colt .45 from the shoulder holster and handed it through the window.

William approached Mr. Bancroft's Model T. He pointed the gun at the back door on the driver's side and pulled the trigger, plugging the middle with a fresh hole. He walked around to the other side and put a bullet in both of those doors.

"Hey, you little scoundrel!" Mr. Bancroft yelled. He and Juice had run outside to see what was going on. William tipped his father's hat as he moved past them.

"You'll do time, McFee! You'll pay for this!"

William got in the car. Barley was wide eyed and slack jawed. William backed out of the lot. "Now his doors match."

FOURTEEN

The potter's field was inundated: blacks and whites, poor and well-to-do, and dozens in between, trampling the grass and leaning against the distillery houses. Men, women, and children walked to the grave and back to their cars, some crying, some chatting, others mute with emotion. A man rolled his wheelchair-bound wife over the bricked path to salvation.

"They started arriving after lunch." Samantha hurried from the front stoop to meet Barley and William as they exited the car. "They came in droves, Barley. I had control for a time, but now I don't know what to do."

Annie reached out for William to take her. She was excited about so many people. "Look, William, a party!" She whispered in his ear, "I think they know Henry is coming home!"

"Where's Johnny?"

"In the aging house with the Browders. Ronald said he'd die before he let anyone inside. He spent all day fixing it up."

"Hunt down Max then. I'm gonna need him."

Samantha wove her way through the throng while Barley hurried inside.

William perused the crowd, looking for Polly. He spotted dozens of women, even a few redheads, but none were lookers like Polly.

Annie hugged her hands around his neck and kissed his cheek. "I'm glad *you're* home."

"Me too, Sugar Cakes."

Barley returned to the porch with a rifle in one hand and the Chopper in the other. He looked through the crowd. Samantha and Max emerged, hustling toward the porch. Barley tossed Max the rifle. "You ready?"

"For what?" Max asked, his muscles bulging through a white cotton shirt.

"Don't know yet, but follow me." Barley looked back at Max. "Don't actually shoot anybody. Just stand there and look like you want to."

Barley entered the crowd. It parted as they noticed the automatic weapon. Barley let loose a barrage of shots into the air. A camera flashed. Across the circle, two rows deep, stood Bancroft. He must have followed them back to the distillery. Bancroft snapped another picture and stood on his toes for a better view.

Barley fired a few more bullets into the sky for good measure. Max popped a shot from his own with the rifle, which drew a respectful nod from Barley.

William stayed back with Annie, keeping her safe. A strange woman had already asked if she could touch Annie's legs.

When all was quiet, Barley spoke to the crowd. "I'd rather keep firing into the air, ladies and gentlemen, but if anyone gives me reason, I'm happy to introduce you to the Chopper."

Max spoke under his breath to Barley. "What's this one called?"

Barley, annoyed, hissed, "It's just a rifle."

Max raised the rifle high in the air and shouted, "And I'll introduce you to the Machete!"

Barley gave Max a look that said, "Close your big head," and then returned his focus to the crowd. "This is my home. Every last one of you is trespassing on my property. My business."

"You running the distillery again, Mr. McFee?" Mr. Bancroft yelled.

"It sure appears so," said a woman in the front.

Whispers spread through the crowd. "Is it true? Is the town's lifeblood returning?"

"I want everybody to go back to your cars and scram. I can't stop you from tenting in the woods, but I can and I will back you up out of my business."

Max pointed the rifle at the crowd and they instantly began to back up.

A woman cried, "But you have no right to keep this to yourself."

"I've got every right, ma'am. Back up."

"Give us time to assess the situation," William called out, still holding his sister in his arms. "We'll decide when and how to allow visitation."

Bancroft snapped a picture. "Is that the girl?"

The crowd surged in on them. William held Annie high, nearly on his shoulder. Barley fired into the air again and people froze. "As the boy said, we need time to assess."

William returned Annie to the porch, but not before a few more people swarmed to touch her legs. He pushed a bearded man away with his right arm and then elbowed another. Annie was crying for her mother.

Someone shouted, "Is this a ploy to draw attention to the distillery?"

A woman screamed, "No, it's real! I felt it the moment I touched that cross."

"I did as well," said another man. "The power of Christ is with us!"

"It's the Devil among you," yelled Bancroft. "Not Christ!"

Max fired into the air and shouted, "Disperse!" His voice was cavernous and deep, a rumble that sent fear into the crowd. He fired again. Barley followed with his Chopper. Slowly, the mob began to disperse, even Bancroft, who slunk away. Max herded them like sheep toward their cars, shouting, "Disperse!" every thirty seconds.

St. Michael's priest was in the crowd. Samantha had spotted him and beckoned him toward the porch. "Father Vincent! Over here."

The priest was wide eyed and bewildered, his face nearly as white as his hair. He made his way to the porch alongside Barley.

"Stay for dinner, Father," Barley said with benevolence. "I reckon we might need some saintly advice."

Father Vincent nodded, speechless, as he followed Samantha and Annie into the house.

Now that Annie was safe inside, William chased down Bancroft near the tree line.

Bancroft spoke first. "What happened to your eye?"

"Got into a fight with another reporter."

"You're not a good liar, William. And you have your father's temper." Bancroft watched the dispersing crowd. "A cheap way to bring attention to a broken distillery."

"We'll be boiling mash soon enough."

"So it's true?"

"No comment."

Bancroft patted William's shoulder. "Pick up a copy of the *Post* in the morning, you farce. You've had your moment. Distill your evil spirits and leave print to professionals."

"I want your camera. You took pictures on my property without permission."

"I had permission."

"From whom?"

"From the Lord our Savior. From my knees, I prayed to Him. He delivered me here. To cast all blasphemers back to the Devil. To wrestle free what was briefly stolen by the wicked. My advice, son? Repent now, if you want a chance of redemption."

"And if I don't?"

Bancroft got into his car; he shifted into gear. "Then you'd best get used to the heat." Bancroft peeled away, churning gravel, and disappeared into the cluster of departing cars.

<hr />

They ate fried chicken, green beans, and potatoes mashed with butter; the McFees, the Browders, Max, and their least likely guest, Father Vincent. After two glasses of red wine he'd regained his rosy cheeks, though he'd yet to offer an opinion on what was happening in the field.

William finished his green beans, wiped his mouth, and placed his napkin on his plate. Outside, dusk cast a red glow through the whiskey trees. Tents were set up for the night and campfires smelled of fall. "By the looks of it, they're here to stay," William said. "I say we let them in."

"But how do we patrol it?" said Mr. Browder. "They start rummaging through my corn, I'm coming with the Chopper *and* the Machete."

"I say we charge admission," said Johnny.

William said, "And bleed the already bleeding?"

"It's not some clip joint," Barley said. "And they may be eager, but they're not chumps."

"Bound to be a couple chumps." Johnny swallowed some milk. "I'll only fleece them."

A sudden pound on the table made the silverware jump. They all looked at Father Vincent, whose fist was shaking in midair. "This is not the time for playful banter! It's not a carnival act. This is . . ." He closed his eyes, let out a loud exhale through his nose. When he opened them again he had gained the fatherly, even-keeled control he displayed during sermons. "As much as I wished otherwise, I truly believe what is happening here is real. I don't know whether the Lord is acting through Asher Keating or he is, God save me, what people claim, but . . . but I walked to that grave and I felt something. I'll be cursed to my grave for sitting here, but I truly felt something! Look at Annie!"

Everyone did.

"Something spiritual is happening. We can't rightfully deny people. Belief in something . . . is a powerful thing. Especially now. Black clouds are raging across the plains." He looked at Barley. "Crime lords and mob bosses are filling each other with holes."

Barley looked away.

Samantha asked, "What do you propose we do, Father?"

"I don't know." Father Vincent rubbed his hair, sighed. "Something controlled."

"Not Father out there with his Chopper," said William. *Or his hidden men in the woods.* "What if the town spares a few coppers to help control the woods?"

"Four patrolmen, one standing guard each direction," said Carly decisively. "They can be armed, but people should not feel threatened. And to prevent chaos, let's take everyone's name and pull them from a hat. Allow them visits only during certain times of the day. They get five minutes at the grave to do what they need to do. Then they must go."

Max said to Johnny, "And you reckoned I married her on account of her prettiness."

Carly smiled bashfully. Mr. Browder put an arm around his daughter.

Samantha said, "Fitting that it took a woman to find an answer. Father, I think the police would be more agreeable if you were to approach them."

"I'll speak to them." Father Vincent pushed his chair from the table and stood. "I thank you for the hospitality, but I must return to the church and rest. It's been a day."

Everyone stood along with Father Vincent. The priest gently took William's arm as the rest of the room cleared. "Just a word." He kept his voice low. "The world is full of skeptics, and I admit I was one of them. Up until this morning." He scratched his forehead wearily. "I didn't believe your story in the *Times.* I was angered by it. And disappointed in you. That you would fall prey to such . . . such . . ."

"What happened this morning, Father?"

"I awoke with bruises and severe pain in both wrists and ankles. Throbbing pains, William. Stigmata—pain and bruises where Christ's wounds were. Believe me or not, but the pain was real. It subsided after I visited that grave."

"Why are you telling me this?"

"Call it a confession, if you will." He looked around to make sure no one was listening. "I want you to write about it. Lord knows I *don't* want the attention. But I'd feel more burdened should I conceal the truth. People need something to believe in, William. They will believe me because I am a priest." He put his hands on William's shoulders and looked into his eyes. "Something powerful is happening in Twisted Tree. As Saint Paul wrote in his letter to the Galatians: 'I bear on my body the marks of Jesus.'"

William couldn't sleep. The glass of Old Forester he'd had while writing about Father Vincent's transformation exhausted him, but after twenty minutes of tossing and turning he was again wide-awake. Bancroft would tell his version of the events, and William had every right to tell Father Vincent's version.

So why did he feel guilty?

He swung his feet to the floor and clicked on his lamp. The sound reminded him of Bethany Finn hanging up on him. He'd try her again, but pestering could clam her up for good.

William moved to his desk, sat in the chair, and stared at the page he'd typed out earlier. I bear on my body the marks of Jesus. He reread the article. The pacing was fast, and he'd done a thorough job detailing the facts while recreating the tension of the night. Would Barley paste him again? The damage had already been done—the people had already arrived.

William moved to his closet, and a minute later he had boxes of old newspaper articles spread around him. After ten minutes of rooting through stories—THE BRITISH OCEAN LINER QUEEN

MARY IS LAUNCHED; JOHN DILLINGER IS NAMED PUBLIC ENEMY NUMBER ONE; HITLER AND MUSSOLINI MEET IN VIENNA—he located the story detailing Tommy the Bat's escape from Eddyville prison. He knew he'd seen the picture of Borduchi before.

That face had somehow given Henry nightmares. William suffered from them too, then they'd stopped right about the time Henry's started.

He buried his face in his hands. The article on his desk would be published at the expense of his family's safety. Why had he written it? For selfish gain? Or because, as Father Vincent said, the people deserved to know?

He dug back into the boxes and scoured his collection for information on Tommy "The Bat" Borduchi. All he learned was that Borduchi had a twin sister. And she was a Carmelite nun at the Sisters for the Aged and Infirm.

William wrote down the pertinent information about Borduchi's twin, and then a sudden convulsion of memories left an acidic taste in his mouth: *A sharp blade cutting skin. Blood. A voice like a razor blade. "Left or the right, Boss?"* William blinked away Tommy Borduchi's face and the name Big Bang Tony came to him. Big Bang was Tommy's right-hand man, arrested the same day. He was prescribed the electric cure after Borduchi grabbed life without parole.

William pulled a story about the night Henry died, the night Barley collided with Preston Wildemere, and studied the picture he'd seen many times. Glass from smashed headlights and windshields littered the road. Two vehicles totaled. A torn fender coiled and resting like a python. Wildemere's Studebaker crunched like an accordion. He was in the car but not visible in the photo. And neither was Barley. He'd been loaded into the ambulance by then. Out of view, his little brother lay in the grass. Dying.

There was no evidence of any booze. William studied the wreckage, studied the road, studied the woods and the grainy black ink beneath the boughs, and there, in the darkness . . . *Is that a man?* William dropped the paper. *Holy Moses.*

He scrambled to his desk, pulled out the middle drawer, and rummaged for his magnifying glass. He positioned the glass an inch from the page. It was a man for sure, his contour half concealed by darkness, blurry and unfocused under the trees, but tall, broad shouldered, heavily bearded. William leaned in: two lumps dangled against his chest. *Henry's shoes.*

William dropped the magnifying glass. He felt like he'd seen a ghost. His mind felt clear, though, and he knew he'd deliver Father Vincent's story tomorrow before sunrise. He knew exactly why he'd written it.

For Henry.

It all came back to Henry.

Henry waved his arms above his head. "Over here, Will'm."

William kicked the ball across the dewy grass.

Henry trapped it with his right foot. Did a little shuffle before he kicked it back.

William had to run five paces to his left to retrieve it. He picked the ball up and punted it like Henry liked, except the wet ball thudded off the side of his foot and went sideways.

Henry couldn't stop laughing as he chased it down.

"See, Will'm. Told you."

William opened his eyes, whispered, "Told you we'd have fun."

His bedroom was dark, but his typewriter rested like a boulder on the desktop. Beyond it, on the seat of his chair, was the ball.

Henry's ball.

William supposed he remembered putting it there before going to bed.

FIFTEEN

Bancroft was true to his word; his article in the *Post* described Asher Keating as blasphemous and insinuated that he was possessed by the Devil. It also claimed that he had Negro blood, offering as proof an outrageous categorization of his physical features. "Christ is white!" Bancroft wrote. "Not a man blackened by the inferior race."

It was ludicrous. Luckily, the only picture they included was one of Max firing his weapon into the sky. Barley had his back to the camera. A caption beneath gave Barley's name, so Dooly McDowell was still in the clear.

Bancroft's article attracted protestors, and they gathered on the south side of the whiskey trees bordering Mr. Browder's cornfields early in the morning. William had seen them arriving when he returned from dropping off his article. Their numbers had grown to nearly four dozen by midday, all picketing against a palette of crisp fall leaves with signs of SACRILEGE and BLASPHEMY. Bancroft was the most boisterous, his face bright red and strained as he pumped his BLASPHEMER sign in cadence with his chant: "Christ was white! Christ was white! Christ was white!"

William had the remnants of Asher's bindle. He pulled out the picture of Asher, a black-and-white image. The scraggly beard dated it from after he'd returned from the war. He studied the skin around the beard and neckline and around the eyes. Asher's hair was long, covering his ears, but the hair of his beard was darker, coarser . . . *Was* he black, in part?

Asher's skin appeared more jaundiced to William than anything else, which made no sense given it was a black-and-white picture. Some called Asians yellow-skinned. Asher's cheekbones were wide, his face flat like his nose. His eyes could be described as lacking the typical crease of most Europeans. *What exactly was Asher Keating? Does it matter?*

Bancroft's chant carried across the distillery. "Christ was white!"

To many the bigotry would matter.

When William returned outside, Barley was on the porch. "Next time you write the truth, William, you have to reveal the bruises too. Or he will." Barley nodded toward Bancroft. "The drugs. You have to mention it."

William nodded, moved on. Barley was right. As Father Vincent said, the people deserved to know the truth, all of it.

The crowd in the whiskey trees, drawn by his stigmata article, numbered in the hundreds, closing in on a thousand. It appeared that a line of tension was developing between the believers in the whiskey trees and the protestors set up next to the cornfield. One of the police officers stood between the two groups, keeping them separate.

Still, Carly Charles's timed visits proved to be working, and believers were moving to and from Asher's grave in an orderly fashion.

William spotted Dr. Lewis with a sign of his own, a pro-evolution sign with a picture of a chimpanzee on it. And it appeared the doctor had brought a group of his own, a small cluster of passionate evolutionists. William felt a morsel of pity for him. Across the potter's field, a family of five deer watched the crowds.

Samantha called across the lawn, "William, there's a phone call for you. A woman named Bethany Finn? Says she's ready to talk."

Tanner and Bethany Finn lived in a one-story brick house on the north side of Iroquois Park. Although their garage was large enough to hold ten Ford cars and enough parts for three more, the plainness of their home lent William to believe they were living on the nut like the rest of the country. Under an obvious comb-over, Tanner was a handsome man. His eyes were marked with crow's feet and he wore a mask of worry. His smile was genuine, though, and he was eager to show William and Barley his collection of coupes and his 1934 Phaeton.

Bethany was petite and pretty in a white blouse and blue skirt. Her curly auburn hair was cut in a bob. She carried a tray with a pitcher of lemonade and four glasses with ice. The four of them sat at a square table and drank pulpy lemonade. "It was your article today that encouraged me to talk," she told William. "Thank you for coming."

Tanner gripped his wife's hand. "I think this will be good for her. For both of us."

Bethany exhaled deeply. "So you gentlemen would like to know about Asher Keating."

"Yes, ma'am." Barley reached into his jacket for his flask. He poured a splash of Old Forester into his lemonade and stirred with his finger.

William said, "We understand Asher once worked for you, Mr. Finn?"

"That is correct."

"It's taken years for us to come to grips with what happened," Bethany told them. "The man you mentioned on the phone. Mr. Oliver Sanscrit. We did meet him the once, after the incident. He claimed to represent Mr. Keating. He was under the presumption that Asher had been fired unjustly."

"We told him we'd made a mistake," Tanner said. "We tried to rehire Asher, but he refused to return."

Bethany said, "Mr. Sanscrit was an odd man, polite enough, but . . . his arrival caught us off-guard. We were having tea on our patio, and all of a sudden, there he was, standing beside us. Didn't phone as you gentlemen did."

"Dressed as if he'd just returned from the war. At the time we were not able to rationally talk about it with a stranger."

"But now?" William asked.

Bethany said, "Now we're eager to add to Asher's story. We never knew what became of him after he left the assembly line."

William removed his notepad and pen. "We appreciate your willingness to talk."

Tanner scratched his comb-over. "I believe now that it was the Lord, acting through my employees, who held me back from killing him."

Bethany interjected, "He had wild thoughts of an affair running through his mind."

"When my employee told me he'd seen my wife kissing

another man, I imagined the worst. Who could have known what was really happening?"

Bethany sipped her lemonade. "Luckily I was able to talk sense into him."

"What sense was there to discuss?" asked Barley. "Were you kissing Asher Keating?"

"I was," she said softly. "Indeed I was. But my words stopped Tanner cold."

"What did you say to him?" asked William.

Tanner looked down to the tabletop. "All she said was that it wasn't what it appeared. It was the fact that she spoke at all that got my attention."

"Before I met Asher Keating, I was deaf," said Bethany. "I couldn't speak at all. I was born deaf. I struggled to talk as a child. The look in my father's eyes . . . He'd try hard to understand me, but I knew he also wanted me to hush. It pained him to listen to the noises I made. I stopped trying to speak long before I met Tanner."

She gripped his hand and they shared a loving smile. "We learned to speak adequately with our hands. Well, there was an evil man who worked at the plant named Kirby Delpho. He often came to work under the influence. Around Tanner he pretended to be upright, which makes my blood boil. I occasionally visited the plant to have lunch with Tanner. One afternoon on my way out to the parking lot, Kirby Delpho grabbed me." She closed her eyes to strengthen her resolve. Tanner squeezed her hand.

"We can stop," William said.

She opened her eyes. "I'd never liked how he looked at me, like a predator. He'd been eyeing me for months. In hindsight, I hated myself for not taking precautions. Or for not telling Tanner my thoughts on the man. I didn't hear when he approached me, of course. I kicked and fought to no avail. He raped me."

Tanner's jaw was quivering. Barley looked angry enough to hurl the lemonade pitcher into the wall. Bethany regained her composure. "I am thankful I couldn't hear him. I thought I would never be able to escape the smells—of him, of the deed itself. My senses of smell and sight were ones I cherished, and he stole them from me that day. Kirby said he'd kill me if I tried to tell Tanner. Turned my face to his so I could read his lips. So I didn't. And Tanner suffered the brunt of my moods. I was sharp with him, ill-tempered, and I even stopped loving him. No, that's not right."

She gave Tanner a glance before looking back to her guests. "I always loved him. It's just that there was a part of me that blamed him because he'd failed to protect me. But I also knew that was unfair. I stopped sleeping with him. I just couldn't bring myself to . . ."

She took a sip of her lemonade and nodded toward Barley. He handed her his flask. She poured a finger into her lemonade, swirled the glass, and took a deep drink. "Thank you. For months there was a great sadness in our home. But then Asher Keating was hired at the plant. He'd been there a month when I showed up to give Tanner the lunch pail he'd forgotten. I was drawn to Asher with an urgency I could not explain. He smiled at me, and I smiled for the first time in months. Kirby was there, putting back bumpers on a run of coupes. I felt ashamed smiling in his presence. I gave Tanner his lunch pail and I went on my way. Before leaving I looked for the new man, Asher, but he was nowhere to be seen."

William scribbled into his notepad. "Mrs. Finn, could you describe Asher for me? What do you think he looked like?"

"What do I think? He was handsome and tall, but that's not why I smiled at him. I smiled because for some reason I felt things would get better for me."

"I mean . . . ," William said.

She shared a glance with Tanner that made William think they'd discussed it before. "You want my opinion on . . . his physical traits?"

William nodded. "The more I've studied his picture, the more mysterious he seems. I'm looking for clarity when there seems to be none."

"What are we talking about here?" Barley asked.

"Your son wants to know if I think Asher was colored."

Barley froze his glass in midair and then slowly lowered it back to the table. "Christ was white."

Tanner said, "Excuse me?"

William said, "The protestors at our distillery are chanting it. 'Christ was white.'"

It was Tanner's turn to dump a splash of Barley's bourbon into his lemonade. "When I first met him and shook his hand, I did a double look. We didn't have any Negroes on our line. I thought he was colored, but then a minute later, I convinced myself that I was being foolish. I asked one of my employees what he thought, and he said he looked plenty white. I asked another and *he* said Asher must have Asian blood in him. Or Middle Eastern." Tanner shook his head. "I don't know. Another guy asked me if I thought Asher might be Red Indian. Or Mexican or Spanish. I didn't much care. He was a good, loyal worker."

Silence spread across the table. "I'm sorry, Mrs. Finn. I didn't mean to interrupt you." William looked to his notes. "You were saying that when he smiled at you, you felt like things were going to get better?"

She took a drink of her lemonade. "There was a break room on the way out to the parking lot. On a typical day it was thick with cigarette smoke, but the morning was young and the room was smoke-free and Asher was sitting on the couch, reverently, with his elbows on his knees and his hands folded under his chin. 'Please, sit,' he said. He knew me and I knew him, although I can't say as to how. I'd been afraid to look at any man for months, but I stared deeply into this man's eyes, this stranger who was really not a stranger at all. He knew what Kirby had done to me.

"Asher lifted my chin and said, 'I can take away the pain, Bethany. And the hurt.' I'd never told him my name. 'I can remove the guilt,' he said. 'The sadness.' He asked me to close my eyes and I did. He kissed my ears and told me to hear the words, and I did. The first words I'd ever heard in my life were Asher's. Every noise of the car plant rang true. He kissed the tip of my nose and whispered for me to smell again. His soft breaths had sound. He kissed my forehead and told me my thoughts would be born anew. He kissed my head and said the bad memories would be wiped clean, and they were. I grabbed his hand and moved it down my body. I pressed his palm into the folds of my skirt for no longer than a few seconds. He told me to love again.

"He leaned me back on the couch, put his hands to my throat, casting his warmth, and then he gently ran his fingers to my mouth, which he kissed. That's when one of the employees walked in and saw us. Neither of us jumped as if we'd been discovered doing anything unseemly; on the contrary, nothing had ever felt more right. Asher's lips left mine in his own time. After he'd completed his miracle. Even then I knew that's what I was a part of. He pulled away from me and told me to speak." She paused for another sip of her drink. "And I did."

Tanner took over. "Asher told me he was quitting the next day. I tried to keep him, but he said while he appreciated the chance to make cars, the poor needed him more."

Bethany said, "And Kirby Delpho died that afternoon working on a red Ford Phaeton."

"Collapsed right into the open driver's seat," said Tanner. "The men thought he'd eaten some bad food at Duke's Diner the night before. Others believed he'd had a stroke. Doctor said it was a massive heart attack."

"I know what you're thinking," said Bethany. "As much as I'd wanted that man to pay, after Asher's miracle, I no longer had hate in my heart for Kirby Delpho. So don't think I wished for it and it came true."

"And Asher?" Barley asked. "Could he have had anything to do with it?"

"Couldn't hurt a fly."

"How do you know?"

She finished her drink. "Because I know."

William closed his notepad respectfully. "Thank you for your time and honesty, Mrs. Finn. And I have your permission to publish this?"

"You do. Tanner and I, we truly believe Asher Keating was a conduit to the Lord. It's important that people know what happened."

Tanner said, "We didn't feel comfortable talking to the man who stopped by last night."

William immediately thought of Bancroft. "Was he from the *Post*?"

"No," said Bethany. "I don't think he was a reporter at all. We told him nothing of significance. He left disappointed, I'm afraid."

Tanner said, "Had a bunch of scars across his cheeks. And he had a woman with him."

Bethany playfully slapped Tanner's arm. "Go ahead and say it, Tanner."

Tanner grinned. "Okay, then. She was a doll. A real looker."

William took a sharp turn too quickly and the wheels felt as if they'd lifted. The tires squealed. Barley braced himself, digging his shoes into the footwell and his fingers into the dashboard. The exhaust pipe had a loose-bolt rattle by the time they'd finished their trek through the wooded back road. Lantern lights flickered under the whiskey trees as they approached the house; it looked like hundreds had set up camp. William parked the car, and the two of them bounded up the porch steps to the front door as if racing. When they saw their family safe in the living room, they exhaled, but then their attention focused on the couch.

"William, there you are." Samantha sat next to Polly, who was lying beneath a blanket on the couch. Johnny and Annie watched silently from across the room. "She got here an hour ago. She was delirious, dehydrated. And what's with the two of you? Coming in here like your britches are on fire."

William approached the couch. Polly's face was pale, freckled across the nose and cheekbones. Her lashes were long with hints of blonde. There was a pockmark just above her right eyebrow. "Did she say anything?"

Samantha sighed, looking from Polly to William, then giving him the hinky eye. "No. I got very little out of her. Why?"

Barley lit a Lucky Strike, played off the fact that he'd been panicked seconds before. "All the girls in the world and he's stuck on a jingle-brained hobo."

"What?" asked Samantha.

"Boy drove home like the street was on fire. Turns out it *was* his britches."

"Polly," William said. "Can you hear me? It's William. William McFee."

Her eyes opened. William moved a glass of water to her lips and lifted her head from the pillow. "You need to drink."

She took enough to wet her lips and on the second try managed to swallow. "They tried to burn us..."

"Who? Polly, did someone try to hurt you and your friends?" *Persecuted.* That was the word that came to mind. *Religious persecution.* "Pauline? Pauline?"

"Polly. Friends call me Polly." She whispered, "I returned the book."

And then she went back to sleep.

The woods were quiet. Campfires smoldered under the trees and tents rustled as their occupants sought comfort. William found Barley and Johnny at Asher's grave, their bodies lit by the glow of an oil lamp one of them had hung on the arm of Asher's cross.

"Would you hang a lantern from Christ's cross?" William joined them.

"If I recall," Barley said, "that cross was up pretty high. This one isn't."

"We were praying," said Johnny. "Among other things. Heard you filled Mr. Bancroft's doors with holes."

Barley lit a Lucky Strike. "If you really want to know, William, I prayed for that man we met by the river. The fisherman and his son. Their bucket was empty." He exhaled a smoke cloud and waited for it to disperse in the lantern glow. "Hopefully they'll catch a fish tomorrow."

William shared a look with Johnny, one that showed that his younger brother had also noticed some changes in their father, a transformation of sorts that was ongoing. But they'd best not bring it attention and risk spooking him.

Barley shared the cigarette with his oldest.

William took a drag on the Lucky and blew smoke from the corner of his mouth. Johnny reached toward William for the next drag, but William wouldn't give him one. "Too young."

Johnny didn't like it. "I suppose you're still too young for your first kiss."

"Close your head, Johnny."

Barley said, "Your mother said your bum can stay in the Glousters' old cottage after tonight. If she's gonna hang around."

"She's not my—mine," William said defensively, unconvincingly, and handed the cigarette back to Barley. "The Glousters' cottage? That's the one farthest away from the house."

Johnny laughed.

"Your mother was born during the day, William, but not yesterday." Barley started to take another drag but froze with it a few inches from his mouth. "Shhhhhh." He passed the cigarette back to William and slid his Colt .45 from his shoulder harness. Black-Tail had joined them. The squirrel stood on his hind legs no more than ten feet away, watching them over the smooth surface of a nut.

"You little runt." Barley slowly cocked the pistol.

"Do it," Johnny whispered. "Do it."

"Bang," Barley said, reeling the gun back into his holster. Black-Tail gnawed on the nut for another couple of seconds and then took off running.

Johnny watched, openmouthed and disappointed.

Barley took the cigarette back from William and finished it off with one long, cheek-sucking drag. "I had my first kiss when I was ten. Your grandfather took me to the races at Churchill. Little sandy-haired girl was there with her parents. Pink dress. Cute white hat with a pink ribbon. While your grandfather was studying the horses, she and I, we snuck behind the barn. We took turns skipping rocks across a rain puddle. Then we started tossing them atop the barn's pitched roof. Drove the horses crazy. The last thing betters want to see is a skittish horse just before the starting gun. I'd like to think we changed a few odds that day.

"Well, her parents called for her, and we hid behind a bush. I put my hand over her mouth because she'd started giggling. And she bit it. Bit the middle finger and I nearly screamed. But to quiet me, she put her lips right up against mine until she felt sure I wasn't going to make a noise. When the coast was clear, you know what she said? 'The next one will cost you.' 'Cost me what?' I said. 'One of them root beers. With the ice cream in it.'"

"And did you get it for her?" William asked.

"Of course."

"So . . . what happened to the girl?"

Barley looked toward their house. "She's in there putting your sister to bed."

SIXTEEN

William finished his article at three in the morning with achy eyes. Part of him had hoped his key-clacking would wake Polly, but it didn't. Barley's chair was available across the room, but he couldn't hear Polly breathing from over there. So he scooted the throw rug closer and slept fitfully on the floor next to her.

He awoke the next morning with a stiff back and a crick in his neck. The couch was empty and Polly's blankets were folded on the far cushion. The dining room was vacant, although the table still held dishes from a breakfast that hadn't included him. The kitchen smelled of baked apples. At the sink he splashed cold water on his face, dried it with a hand towel, and glanced out the window toward the woods.

The crowd had grown; he recognized both Catholics and Baptists and some of the town's Jewish population. A black man slept in a hammock. A few yards away, a white family raked leaves into a pile with their hands so their kids could jump in them. There was no sign of Polly.

"She's outside with Mommy."

William spun away from the sink and placed his hands on Annie's shoulders. Then he hurried out of the kitchen and up the stairs. He came down fifteen minutes later, shaved, washed, and decked out in a suit and tie. He'd sprayed some of Barley's cologne, smoothed his hair back with a glob of pomade.

"William?"

"Yeah, Sugar Cakes?"

"You going to church? There's white stuff on your chin."

William rubbed off a smear of shaving cream. He touched it on Annie's nose and opened the door. Four armed men in suits and hats guarded the front porch.

"They're friends of Daddy's," Annie said. "They came this morning."

William jerked a nod and looked over at Barley, who tiptoed on the middle rung of a ladder, painting the top of a porch column.

"She's around here somewhere." Barley said nothing about the men standing guard. "You off to church?"

William shook his head, turned away.

Inside the grain mill Mr. Browder was making adjustments on the hammer mill. Carly was cleaning one of the vats in the cooking house. Next door at distillation, Max was hammering and Johnny was with him.

William eyed the woods. No sign of Bancroft. The protestors were only now arriving and they'd yet to begin their chanting.

He found Polly inside the aging house with Samantha. "Your mother was showing me around." Her color was better. She inhaled the lingering angels' share and took in the expanse of naked ricks. "It'll be beautiful."

Samantha looked unusually happy. "Are you going to church, William?"

"No." He scoffed, straightening a button on his pin-striped jacket.

She stepped toward him, sniffed. "You smell like your father."

William glanced toward Polly. "Mom . . . quit gumshoeing, eh? And what's with the suits guarding the house? Where'd they come from?"

"I don't know, but Barley said they'll be here for as long as this circus lasts. I'll leave you be." His mother winked. "She's been waiting for you all morning," Samantha whispered, touching his arm fleetingly. "We've had a nice talk."

"Mom, you're glowing. What is it?"

"It's your father. Out of the blue this morning, he surprised me with a root-beer float."

William and Polly sat side by side on empty bourbon barrels as the sun cast windowpane shadows across the floorboards. He explained the aging process, how the barrels age differently depending on the floor upon which they've been stored. They inhaled the angels' share with their eyes closed, announcing the different flavors as their senses discovered them—vanilla, caramel, toasted sugars, sweet and smoky aromas, and Polly shouted out, "Butterscotch!"

They took a walk together and ended up behind the house, on a wooden bench facing the woods where the deer gathered. William learned that Polly and the other eleven—she was not shy in calling them apostles—had crossed the river into southern Indiana, to New Albany and Jeffersonville, to speak to anyone who would listen about Asher Keating's miracles. They preached that God had sent another son to earth. Most assumed they were lunatics, but their following was growing.

When they ventured north to the Knobs, their sheer numbers helped sway more to listen. They were hugged, kissed, spat upon and cajoled, heckled and hated, but still they walked on, heading north toward Salem, where they found an abandoned church thirty miles south of the town, an adequate wood structure where they could camp for the night.

"We . . . all twelve of us, slept inside, along with fifty others. Dozens more slept outside, and the mood was of cheer and promise." Polly shook her head. "Near midnight I had to relieve myself. I ventured fifty paces into the woods for privacy, and no sooner had I dropped my drawers I heard the horses. Klansmen."

"Why would the Klan get involved?" Indiana once had the most powerfully active Klan in the nation, with roots that ran all the way to the governor. They spread hateful propaganda in the *Fiery Cross*, their newspaper. But the Klan had mostly disbanded by the end of the twenties. He thought it had dissolved even further with the onset of the Depression.

"The Klan's heavily Protestant, William. They hate anything Catholic. Anything to do with the pope and his influence."

"Asher had no claims to Catholicism, did he? Did he have any specific denomination?"

"Your priest made them think so. Your article on his stigmata—"

"You read it?"

"I read it."

"And?"

"I believe every word, if that's what you're asking." She picked at dirt under one of her fingernails. "But it equated Asher with

Catholicism. The Klansmen circled the church, condemning your priest's sacrilegious claims. They called your distillery the true mark of the Devil."

"What does our distillery have to do with any of this?"

"Prohibition was the cornerstone of their reform agenda: 'Demon Rum.' They attacked bootleggers. Broke up speakeasies. It united Klansmen across the country. And now this man buried on the grounds of a famous bourbon distillery where a priest claims stigmata wounds—"

"You sound like you're rationalizing for them!"

"I'm only explaining where they're coming from, William."

She shuddered. He put his arm around her shoulders and she leaned into him.

"I watched as the cowards circled the church. They set it on fire and called for the apostles to watch it burn. Followers rushed out the door, others out the windows. But the apostles didn't. The roof caught fire, and the Klansmen got nervous. It was not their intention to murder, and they shouted for the apostles to come out. I was so afraid they were going to die as martyrs! They finally did come out, praying. The Klansmen hurried off as the church crumbled."

Polly didn't cry. She'd cried too much on her walk back home, across the river to the coke ovens, before she decided to return to Twisted Tree. She'd collapsed atop Asher's grave and wept, and that was where Samantha and Johnny had found her.

"Where did the rest of them go? The other eleven?"

"They moved on. To continue our mission. The attack fueled their cause."

"But not yours?"

"The truth is, William, I was scared. I believe in our mission, but I was tired of being scared. And I feel safe here."

Polly rested her head on his shoulder. He'd wanted to ask about Asher's connection to Henry, but with talk of the Klan, he asked another question instead. "Was Asher a Negro?"

Polly jerked her head up at his bluntness. "Why do you ask?"

"A man named Bancroft. He's a reporter at the *Post*. He's spreading rumors that Keating had Negro blood. He's written about it in the paper."

"I don't know what blood Asher had, William. And I don't much care. To be honest, I thought he was of Mediterranean descent. His skin had an olive-colored tone. The question was posed to him often."

"What would he say when asked?"

"His answer was always the same. 'I am every man.' That's what he would tell them. 'I am every man.'" She looked in his eyes. "This worries you?"

"I'm thinking of how bad things come in threes."

"Such as?"

"The Klan burned that church because of their views on Catholicism. And the link to the distillery. If they hear that Asher Keating had Negro blood—all three could bring fire to our doorstep."

"Then let them come, William. We'll be safe."

"How do you know that?"

"Your mother. She told me about the angels' share. They'll keep the distillery safe."

⸺⸺⸺

After dropping Johnny and Annie at the schoolhouse, William drove to the *Courier-Journal* building in Louisville to deliver his article to Mr. Crone. Along with Bethany Finn's revelation, he also wrote about Asher's darker side. He softened the news of his drug use by proposing it stemmed from war horrors. Asher had an addiction, but he'd fought for his country and should be remembered as a hero.

Mr. Crone asked for more, more, more, but now that the distillery had life, William found himself wanting to give him less.

The main roads leading to Twisted Tree were clogged for miles. William knew the back roads well enough to venture off into the woods, but this extended his return trip by twenty minutes. A mile from the distillery, he slowed to a stop on a narrow path, which was partially blocked by Frank and his corpse wagon. He'd had the same idea as William, but with the cart's rickety wheels, Frank had bitten off more than he could chew. He was stranded and the horse looked beat.

"The wheels stuck?"

"No." Frank eyed his horse. "Betsy refuses to go another step." He gazed at the colorful fall foliage. "At least it's peaceful here. Can't say I was looking forward to this delivery."

William sized up the bundle on the cart. "Suppose I take it the rest of the way for you?"

"I wouldn't burden you with a job like that."

"I can fit it in the trunk. Wait until nightfall. Get Barley to help me bury it. We've watched you enough to know the routine."

"What say you, Betsy? Should we turn back around?"

Betsy whinnied and snorted, and Frank took it as a yes.

William unlocked the trunk. "Does this body have a name?"

"Afraid not." Frank helped William lift the bulky bag. "Found in a back alley in Bricktown is all I know."

The body was heavy. *Probably a man.* William slammed the

trunk closed with an urge to scrub his hands pink. "Do you need help turning the wagon around?"

"I'll be fine, thank you. Might even sit here for a bit."

Before getting into the car, William called over, "When you delivered Asher Keating's body, did you notice anything different?"

"He was heavier than most. But can't say I felt anything different at all."

As soon as he stepped out of the car, he saw Polly. She wore clean clothes—a beige ankle-length skirt and purple sweater William guessed belonged to his mother decades ago—and her hair shimmered in the sunlight, pulled back and braided in an ornate plait against her ivory neckline.

She waved at William, a quick wiggle of the fingers before resuming her conversation with Carly. With all her clunky layers gone, William could see her true figure, which was petite but curvy.

She is stunning.

William suddenly felt small. Not good enough for her.

Barley was still painting the porch, and policemen were stationed north, south, east, and west around the house. A young black couple walked hand in hand from the whiskey trees toward Asher's grave. They passed a white family that was returning. A few words were exchanged, then a compassionate handshake between the two men followed. Bancroft's article had failed to produce any violence. *Good.* Samantha rushed an empty barrel across the run and into the door of the distillation house.

"Hurry up and wait," Barley said from his ladder. White paint stained the tip of his nose and fingers. He spoke to himself more than to William. "Old Sam ages four to six years." He pointed to the hanging swing. A brown fedora rested on the seat. "That's for you. It's one of my old ones, but it'll do."

William stepped up to the porch to try the hat on. It fit like a glove.

Barley jerked him an approving nod. "We need to look for Asher's friend from the war today. Oliver Sanscrit."

"We'll have to go out the way I came," William said, proudly fingering the brim of his new hat. "Roads are clogged for miles."

Barley tiptoed to reach the top of a column. "I'll finish this, then we'll go."

William cut his eyes to Polly. Then he asked Barley, "Why should we wait for all the bourbon to age? Can't we sell at least some before it's aged? Isn't it still whiskey? We could market it as something new, something everyone should want."

"White lightning is nothing new, William."

"But ours will be from *this* distillery." William breathed the corn-scented air. "We'll call it White Barley. Or Johnny White . . . or . . . or William—"

"We can call it nonsense." Barley stepped down from the ladder, taking a good whiff of the air himself as he wiped his hands on a towel. He glanced over at Polly as well. "Cleans up good, doesn't she?"

"What? Yeah, I suppose so."

"Too bad she's probably off her tracks." Barley straightened William's new hat.

"Did Mother have to put her in the most unflattering clothes possible?"

"What's wrong with them?"

"Not exactly the cat's meow."

"You expect her to give up her glad rags?"

William shrugged, watched Polly in the distance. "Suppose it doesn't matter what she wears. She's still a doll."

Barley grinned, watched his son. "Make sure after they distill, they use some of the sour mash as backset on the next batch. Your mother will know the amount. The rest they can sell to cow farms. Haven't been drunk cows around here in years. And the first batch will probably be unsuitable. So don't be too— Oh, what am I talking about." Barley tossed his towel down. "Our coopers left us over a decade ago."

"Excuse me, Mr. McFee. The officer let us pass."

It was the fisherman from the river, and his son, Peter. He held two buckets overflowing with fish and his son carried a third.

"I'm John Swell. We met yesterday under the bridge?"

Barley stared down at the fish. "Dear God."

William's legs wobbled. He braced himself on the porch rail.

"Last night the fish were practically jumping at us from the river. And when I slept, I had a dream. A voice said to come visit the grave. Said to come here and earn my keep."

Barley's voice was unsteady. "What'd you do for a living, Mr. Swell?"

"I was a cooper, Mr. McFee."

The cooperage behind the distillation house was in fine shape, Swell said. Most of the bilge hoops were free of rust. After some easy cleanup he could have barrels rolling in a matter of days.

Although many of the leftover staves were unusable, there were enough to make at least ten initial barrels.

John Swell made hogshead barrels during his years at the Burnsley & Klingsmith cooperage on Main Street. He also had experience with wine casks, buckets, butter churns, and puncheons. As he and his son ate fried fish at the McFees' dinner table, he spoke confidently about his ability to make the barrels needed for the distillery.

Polly had joined them for dinner. A couple of times she'd smiled at William, but now that she'd turned gorgeous and smelled of lavender, he'd reverted to his bashful self.

Barley, William, and Johnny grew silent when John told the story of how he'd caught the first fish of the morning—none of them was willing to admit to the table that Barley had prayed for it to happen.

"Peter screamed, 'I got one, Daddy.'" John took a healthy bite of fried fish and continued talking as he chewed. "He'd taken the bucket to the shoreline to gather water and an eight-inch bass leapt right into it! We sat for the next two hours and snatched a fish every sixty seconds. I knew then that I had to follow that voice in my dream. The one that brought me to that twisted tree the town was named for. Never seen such a thing. But it was a miracle, those fish."

Polly reached down the table and touched John Swell's hands. She held them long enough to utter a silent prayer and make William envious.

When dinner was over and everyone stood from the table, Polly brushed William on the way to the living room. She was pretty enough to paint and he'd planned to tell her as much, but his sweats began and his neckline flushed.

"Are you okay, William?"

He nodded, looked away, acting all high hat.

She grinned. "Well, would you be so kind as to escort this lady to the new cottage your mother just offered me?"

"No." He wiped his brow, then stammered an even more confounding, "I can't. Not right now. I'm busy."

"Busy? I see." She folded her arms. Her shoulders sagged, but she faked a smile on her way to the door.

He watched her out the window as John Swell and his son served as her escort. For a few heartbeats they looked like a family, and the thought made William sweat more. His hands shook. His breath quickened. Tiny bee stings embraced his heart, and a tingling sensation crawled up and down his spine and neckline. Then his skin went cold and clammy, and the attack ended as Polly and the Swell family disappeared behind the fermentation house.

William balled his hand into a fist and punched the meat of it against the window frame. He stewed for a minute, then gathered his wits and then his memory.

John Swell's arrival had forced them to postpone their search for Oliver Sanscrit.

It also made William forget that he had a dead body in the car trunk.

So later, when Barley asked him if everything was jake, William said, "No. But I do have an idea about how to kill Dooly McDowell."

Samantha was up reading until well after eleven, so it was close to midnight by the time William and Johnny met Barley in the driveway with a wooden cart and a Louisville Slugger. At the potter's field, a lone man sprinted away from Asher's grave. Access was closed after ten, but they'd begun to see "prayer robbers" stealing time after hours. Except for a few distant lanterns, the rest of the tents had turned down for the night.

Barley rested an oil lamp on the gravel behind the car and opened the trunk. The stench made them gag, but Barley quickly got down to business and they lifted the bulky sack out and onto the cart.

Johnny asked, "So are you gonna tell me who Dooly McDowell is?"

"Man I once knew," Barley said. "Now grab that corner and hush."

Together, they pulled the cart toward the hammer mill.

Once inside the mill, Johnny unzipped the sack to reveal the deceased's head. He was a dark-haired man, wide eyed, with a face that looked like it had been in the boxing ring.

Johnny fell back on his butt. "He's looking at me!"

"Johnny," Barley hissed. "Quit being a wise guy." He drew his hand across his face. "It'll be best if you turned your heads." He shucked down to his shirt and suspenders. Johnny turned away as soon as Barley raised the bat; William did too, but the sound—not the sight of it—nearly forced his dinner up. On the second, third, fourth strike, he covered his ears.

"That should do it." Barley wiped the bat with a towel and handed the Slugger to Johnny, who took it with reluctance. Then he pulled a pigskin wallet, with Dooly's identification, from his pants and slid it into the pocket of the old suit he'd put on the dead man before he'd ruined his face.

"Father's gone off the track," Johnny whispered as they

watched Barley slide a switchblade into one of the dead guy's pockets.

"He knows what he's doing, Johnny."

But the lantern glow did give Barley's deep-set eyes a catatonic look. And when he removed a piece of wire from his shirt pocket and staged a stranglehold, William unwillingly composed a sentence in his head: *The look on his face could have been construed as insane.*

"He said this would be duck soup." Johnny cringed. "It ain't easy at all."

William already regretted suggesting this plan. Barley clapped his hands together—job well done—and told them to get the feet while he got the arms, and together they shuffled "Dooly McDowell" back in the trunk.

Barley wiped his face, took two long pulls from a flask, and slipped his jacket and hat on. "Ready, boys?" He closed the trunk and patted it like a dog. "Next stop, Rose Island."

By the time they parked in the trees flanking Fourteen Mile Creek, William's hands were cramped from clutching the steering wheel and his shoulders had grown stiff from stress. Barley smoked in the front while Johnny leaned forward with his elbows propped on the seat backs. Then Barley peered through the trees at the mouth of the creek where it entered the Ohio River. "The Devil's Backbone."

William looked at the ridge of exposed rocks jutting above the water. Most of Rose Island's visitors arrived by ferryboat or steamers, like the *Idlewild* and *City of Memphis*. Some of the wealthier businessmen from the city hired private speedboats for quick lunch trips. Boats weren't an option this time of night, and crossing the Devil's Backbone was out of the question. Barley looked upward to the swaying footbridge for passage.

The suspension bridge stretched fifty feet across the mouth toward the peninsula. Across the black water a craggy hill rose up the Indiana bank to the seven-acre bluff upon which the popular Rose Island Amusement Park had been built a decade before. William had gone there three times, and the park, every time, teemed with people swimming, riding rides, and taking pictures of the caged animals. But at night it was eerily quiet.

As the three of them inched across the footbridge with Dooly McDowell in their arms and the wind swaying the rickety boards side to side, William brooded on the island's legends, dating back before the time of Christopher Columbus. Indians told stories of yellow-haired Welsh giants roaming the dark and forbidden land. The natives buried their dead on the bluff overlooking the river. Children were told not to scale the walls because they were cursed by the Devil. *Don't look down*, he told himself as they closed in on the middle of the bridge. He could feel it sag from the weight of four men. *Don't look down. Don't look down. Don't look—*

"Look at that owl down there." Barley pointed with a nod.

Johnny made a hooting sound and the owl flew off toward the tall ferns.

William glanced down, long enough to see the water rushing underfoot. He quickened his pace, which nearly made Barley trip.

"Easy now." Barley backed his way to the end of the bridge. Over his shoulder in the distance, lit by what moonlight the clouds let through, was the entrance to the park. Two stone pillars twenty feet apart held a rainbow-shaped sign above the bluff that read ROSE ISLAND in large white letters. Barley directed them away from the entrance. "To the tennis courts."

It took another ten minutes of grunting and slogging through the ferns, but eventually they made it to Barley's precise destination, which was down the hillside from the tennis and horseshoe courts. The net on the closest court was barely visible.

Johnny asked, "Why are we dropping it here, where nobody will see it?"

"Used to bury cases of whiskey here. In this spot." Barley placed a shovel he'd brought along inside Dooly's limp hand. "Deals were made here. Hands were shook." He pointed to the river below, slivers of it visible through the trees. "Close enough to hear the water and tennis balls thwacking at the same time. When Tommy the Bat reads of this body in the paper, this location will make sense to him."

"That's it, then? We just leave it here?" Johnny asked.

Barley, hands on his hips, looked up the hillside, where a large hotel towered behind a merry-go-round and Ferris wheel. Twenty summer cottages slept vacant for the season. He looked eager to get back to the Kentucky side of the river. "Let's go home."

He started to retrace their steps, moving at a clip that William didn't like, bracing himself on various tree trunks. The river rocks could make corpses out of them if they fell.

"But who will *find* the body?"

Barley threw a thumb toward William. "Your brother the *Courier* reporter, first thing in the morning."

SEVENTEEN

William stayed up all night writing about Dooly McDowell's murder. He had the peculiar advantage of being able to check details with the victim himself, and Barley was particular about what he wanted in print. Dooly was a known bootlegger who attempted to legitimize after repeal. Dooly's network was crushed by the deaths of his three partners—the collective foursome known during the twenties as the "Micks." Barley wanted nothing mentioned about family or relatives but did allow mention of the recent burning down of Dooly McDowell's house.

William left right after sunrise, as the believers began to emerge from their tents. He drove to Rose Island and parked twenty yards from the suspension bridge. He was the first one there, but soon others began to arrive. He slid the Kodak Brownie in his jacket pocket and merged with the early birds heading toward the footbridge.

With his new fedora and two-toned wing tips, he felt like an experienced reporter. The cool river breeze shook the bridge as he crossed. The sun was bright, the sky a brilliant blue—perfect

weather for the last weekend of the fall season. A full ferryboat—
the *Idlewild*—cut through a patch of low fog, whistle blowing
its arrival, the calliope playing "I'm Looking over a Four Leaf
Clover." The *City of Memphis* approached from the west. The
captain sounded the landing whistle with gusto, as if in friendly
competition with the *Idlewild*.

The plan was to take pictures of the zoo animals, roam for a
bit, and then "stumble" across the body. Rose Island was a place
to take the family for a day of fun, but daily attendance had been
on a steady decline due to the Depression. Yet by the looks of the
crowds approaching on steamboats, parents were taking a pleasure day without their children. Today looked to be a throwback
to the years when men and women had jobs and families had food
on their tables. Which was all for the better; "finding" the body
would cause that much more fervor.

William's pace increased when he stepped off the bridge and
joined the men and women who funneled from three directions
with picnic baskets. White and cream were the most popular
colors—dresses, blouses, skirts, and suits, all with accompany-
ing shoes: wing tips and spats, heels and flats. Men wore fedoras
and top hats, walked with canes and bottles of wine and whiskey.
Genteel women moved about in dresses that showed waistline
curves, toting umbrellas for those wanting to avoid the sun. He
saw old cloche hats, small plate-shaped hats, lamb chop hats, cut-
let hats—some tilted at jaunty, flirtatious angles—and even a
few that resembled fake fruit baskets. Chic and charming, Coco
Chanel and Greta Garbo, faces made up and lips painted bright
enough to kiss. The smell of fried chicken and biscuits mingled
with cologne and perfume, and William was giddy by the time he
squeezed through the gate. Signs said it was BUSINESS DAY, and

general admission was only fifty cents. William told the ticket taker he was a reporter and showed his camera.

Once inside, he moved along with the crowd. It was too cold to swim—the pool was closed—but he took pictures of the shimmering water. He imagined Polly swimming in it, wearing a skimpy suit. He sidestepped through the crowd and took pictures of the Ferris wheel and roller coaster. He took pictures of the new golf course, the baseball diamond, shooting gallery, and dance hall. The zoo was soon packed. Men and women petted the goats and took pictures of wolves, monkeys, and a black bear named Teddy Roosevelt.

William snapped a picture of the popular bear and moved along toward the sound of clanking horseshoes and cleanly struck tennis balls. "Forty-love," a man shouted.

His opponent, an athletically built woman in a knee-length white dress and shoes, swung much too quickly and the ball thudded off the wooden racquet frame and sailed toward the woods.

"That's off the court, dear."

He went to retrieve it, but his wife beat him to the fence.

"I hit it, Harvey. I'll get it."

Let her, William thought. *She'll yell much louder than you.*

A few seconds later a dirty tennis ball sailed over Harvey's head and onto the court. Then a terror-filled scream scattered birds from trees and everyone on Rose Island froze.

By the time William made it across the tennis court to the hillside, the husband had already wrapped his arms around his distraught wife and led her away.

William approached the body with trepidation, aware of the quickly forming ring of onlookers. In the sunlight, it looked more gruesome. The hands had taken on a greenish tint, as had the back of the neck. William snapped pictures of the body. He removed the wallet and identification and took a quick picture of the Dooly McDowell ID.

"He's robbing the poor man!" shouted someone from the crowd.

"I'm a reporter," William said from his squat next to the body, as if he'd covered dozens of murder scenes, and then added quickly, "For the *Courier-Journal*."

"Vulture," shouted another man.

"It's the job of the police," said another.

The crowd, aside from some crying, was mostly quiet as William went about taking pictures, trying to get all he needed before someone ordered him to stop. He flipped the dead man over. The face was unrecognizable, smashed in and disfigured. William lowered his head. He didn't have to fake disgust. The tumble in his stomach was real. He took the picture.

A baby-faced security guard arrived, huffing. Mr. Rose, the park's owner, arrived with him. William told them who he was, and suddenly his palms grew wet. His forehead dripped sweat. The camera shook in his hands.

"Do you have credentials?" asked Mr. Rose.

"I've only just begun working there. I was here enjoying the—"

"He's the one wrote the articles about that man," someone said, stepping forward. "The stories about the Potter's Field Christ."

Whispers spread across the crowd. All eyes settled on William. *The Potter's Field Christ.* He liked the name and would use it. In any event, it registered credibility with both Mr. Rose and the security guard. Mr. Rose hurried to phone the police while the security guard, all three hundred some-odd pounds of him, navigated the downslope toward the body. A patch on his uniform read SMITH.

Smith said, "We should probably cover the body until the police show."

William had gotten what he needed. All that remained was to borrow a phone and call Mr. Crone at the *Courier*.

But then the crowd parted, and a tall, broad-shouldered man in a cream-colored fedora and matching suit entered the circle. In his jacket pocket was a red rose that matched his buttoned vest. In his hand was a Louisville Slugger. His face was tanned and hard lined; his cheeks were hatched with scars and his chin looked chiseled from stone. A busty brunette in a tight red dress had her hand wrapped around his arm. She looked both sophisticated and devilish, her lips painted as starkly red as her eyelashes were black.

William remembered the picture from the newspaper and had no doubt who the man was. Tommy Borduchi. The Hash Man.

Borduchi nudged Dooly's leg with the bat barrel.

"He's been coming round here a lot," Smith said to William. "Like he's casing the—"

"Shut your head, Fat Pants," Tommy said to Smith. "Who is this man at my feet?"

William feared his bowels would turn to liquid. At least now they wouldn't have to hope Tommy read about the body in the newspapers. "According to his identification, sir . . ."

"Sir?" Tommy said to the woman at his side, who laughed as she lit a Lucky Strike. "Have I said anything yet to make these people fear me?"

"No, Daddy," she said, blowing smoke.

William shook his head. "I'm sorry . . . sir."

"Drop the sir or I'll make you a bed next to his."

"His name, according to his identification, is Dooly McDowell."

Tommy touched William's chin with the bat. "I smell something foul. Did you just lose your bladder?"

William shook his head, but warm urine trickled down his right leg. *He doesn't know who you are. Stay calm. He doesn't know what you've done.*

Tommy handed him a handkerchief from his jacket. "Wipe that forehead off before you drown in it." He returned his focus to the body, squatted next to the corpse, removed the wallet, and studied the identification. He closed the wallet, slid it back inside Dooly's pants, and stood. "I heard them say you're the reporter what wrote about that Potter's Field Christ?"

William nodded. "Yes, I'm William. William McFee."

Tommy casually swung the bat, a slow practice swing before stepping into the box. "Do you believe Babe Ruth really called his shot, William McFee?"

Tommy's woman finished her cigarette and tossed the butt to the ground, not too far from where Dooly's hand decayed in mud. Flies had started to buzz. "Come on, Daddy. Let's drift."

"In a minute, babe. I'm chinning here with my new friend." Tommy swung the bat again in a slow arc. "Well? Did the Babe call his shot?"

William didn't know. His wet pants clung to his leg.

"He called his shot, sure as the night, mister!" Someone in the crowd didn't know when to shut his head. "Wrigley Field, 1932 World Series. Game three against the Cubs. The Chicago bench jockeys were ribbing Ruth hard, and he did it to toy with them."

JAMES MARKERT

Tommy pointed the bat. "Now there is a baseball fan, ladies and gentlemen."

"Let's drift, baby," said the woman, antsy.

Tommy looked back at William. "Of course he called his shot. And do you know why? Because he's Babe Ruth. The best baseball player to ever live."

"Darn tootin'," said the man in the crowd.

Tommy kept his eyes on William but pointed the bat at the fool who kept talking. "See, even that little guttersnipe agrees with me." Tommy beat the bat barrel against his palm. "Do you believe in miracles, William McFee?"

"Yes . . . I do."

Tommy pointed the bat at the corpse. "Here lies proof of a miracle." He turned to the crowd and spoke like a God-fearing preacher. "One of Christ's own has perished before us today, ladies and gentlemen, in a most gruesome and heinous manner. Clear work of the Devil, no doubt. I was once burdened by such evil, but Christ has a way of righting all wrongs and saving the good man from further sin, the righteous man from falling off that track to redemption. Can I get an amen?"

The baseball fan gave him one, but no one else did.

Tommy waved the bat lazily as he talked. "Perhaps, in the eyes of lesser men, this man before me now, this man we now know as Dooly McDowell, deserved to be beaten, bludgeoned, strangled, and left for dead. But even the vilest of men shall be called back to the flock and rest peacefully under the warm embrace of Christ. Let us not judge this sinner, this lost child of God. Instead, let us commend him to the mercy of God. Earth to earth, ashes to ashes, dust to dust. Let us pray that he will be resurrected to eternal life with Christ."

192

Tommy motioned the sign of the cross over Dooly's body. He bowed his head. Many in the crowd did likewise. The tension faded. Smith had multiple chins, and they were all squeezed together at his neckline, his head bobbing in prayer, although his eyes never left Tommy the Bat.

William prayed as well, prayed like he'd never strayed from God, not even for a thought. He prayed as hard as he could for the police to come. And then Tommy the Bat backed away from the corpse and turned toward his woman. He grabbed her outstretched hand, started up the hill with her toward the tennis courts.

"You're the man who crushed out of the Eddyville prison!" By Smith's expression, it was a thought he didn't mean to verbalize. But once he'd said it, he stood tall with forced confidence. "Your picture was in the paper. Sir."

"Close your head," William whispered out of the side of his mouth.

"Keep walking, Daddy," said Eva Carcolli in a sultry voice.

Tommy pulled his hand free. "I can tell you like to eat, pal. Is it true, Fat Pants? Do you like to eat?" Tommy stepped closer. "Open your mouth. Wider."

Quick as a snakebite he plunged the end of the bat into Smith's mouth, forcing the security guard back. Tommy removed the bat and brought it down, ax-like. Smith groaned and whimpered.

"Fat Pants squeals like a pig, ladies and gentlemen!"

No one dared move to help. Everyone stood frozen.

William felt paralyzed.

Tommy swung the bat again, and again, sending Smith into avoidance rolls until Tommy choked up on the bat for easier leverage. "Like hitting a pillow," Tommy said, finally backing away, his face red. He straightened his fedora and wiped the bloody bat on William's jacket. "Go pray to your Potter's Field Christ that he lives."

Tommy walked toward his woman, using his bat as a cane. "Let's dangle."

William sat in the lobby of the Rose Island Hotel, wrapped in a white bathrobe, waiting for his shirt and pants to dry. He'd gone mute after the episode. Then he had told the police everything he wanted them to know: *"Tommy Borduchi killed that man. Borduchi was here to witness Dooly being found. How did I end up in the pool? I walked in. Took my hat off first. And shoes. His blood was on my jacket. I walked into the pool fully clothed."*

The glass door opened across the lobby and Sylvester Crone stepped in, adjusting his glasses as he approached. "Are you okay, McFee?"

"Getting there, sir. Have you seen the body?"

"I did. Excitement seems to follow you like a shadow. Of course, the untimely always makes for a good story."

"I suppose it does."

"Our building was defaced with eggs and tomatoes this morning. People took offense to your mention of Asher Keating's drug use."

"I called him a hero too."

"If it makes you feel better, the *Post* was vandalized also." Mr. Crone waved it away. "Don't worry yourself with that. You're not doing a good job unless you're stirring controversy. I assume you got pictures? Of this Dooly McDowell?"

William pulled the camera from his satchel. "How's the security guard?"

"On a speedboat to City Hospital. He's alive. For now."

"I couldn't help him."

"Best you didn't. Are you okay to write the story?"

"The story's already finished." William pulled out the pages he'd written the night before. "At least up until that beating. And today's daily." He handed over the story about John Swell's miracle with the fish.

Mr. Crone scanned the Dooly McDowell article. "When did you write this?"

William couldn't wait to get off the island, where the air didn't smell like blood. And he wouldn't lose sleep if he never had to write another article about it all. "I wrote it before you got here." William may not have been as good at lying as Johnny, but he was improving. "Mr. Rose let me use his typewriter and phone."

"Well done, Mr. McFee."

William closed his eyes and saw the face of Tommy Borduchi. He opened them and saw the baseball bat forced into Smith's mouth. He'd never escape what he'd seen.

EIGHTEEN

The sun had set. William had spent the rest of the day in his bedroom, heartsick and dizzy from the bottle of Old Forester he'd bought after leaving Rose Island. Everyone in the house was asleep. He unlocked the door and stumbled to the bathroom to throw up in the toilet. He stole a bottle of Old Forester from Barley's stash in the kitchen and slunk back to his bedroom, arms and legs achy, his brain sloshy like an ocean wave inside his skull. A skull that had a heartbeat, a slow thud that made him want to throw up again. So he did.

The window was open. Outside he heard the protesters alternating chants of "Christ was white!" and something about Asher being a fraud. Johnny knocked on his door and told him ten people had been arrested. And that the Klan had arrived.

Annie knocked on his door at lunchtime. He mumbled, "See you later, Sugar Cakes."

He drank bourbon until nightfall. Samantha threatened to

knock down his door but ultimately left his dinner in the hallway. The bourbon helped him forget Rose Island. It took the edge off his sweats. It helped settle surfacing memories of Tommy Borduchi.

"Left or the right, Boss?"

He buried that voice with the bottle.

Barley talked through the door like the rest of his family, though in more of a whisper. Even sounded drunk himself. Like father like son. "I know what happened put a scare into you, boy, but I have a feeling what we did worked." A soft *thud* sounded on the door. Probably his father's head leaning on the other side of it. "You know it?"

William didn't know it. Barley hadn't seen the fanatical spark in Borduchi's eyes as he'd prayed over Dooly McDowell's body. Maybe Tommy the Bat was a cat, and they were the ball of yarn. He hadn't seen the way Borduchi's face lit up at the mention of the Potter's Field Christ.

Barley cleared his throat outside the door. "Polly asked about you."

Maybe Samantha was right and he should go into the priesthood. That way he could sweat and panic and not give two hoots about who saw his red, embarrassed face.

Barley eventually left. William didn't feel relieved. It was quiet, too quiet, and his bottle was nearly dry. He went ahead and finished it off.

The soil at the grave was disturbed, overturned and left in clumps of root, dirt, and sod. At first he thought someone had been at it with a shovel, but then it made sense that Asher had climbed out. Laughter drew him toward the aging house, laughter and footsteps and shuffling.

He looked through the window and there they were. Asher half covered in earth and Henry in his dancing shoes, the two of them sidestepping and clapping in tempo. Henry did the Black Bottom and the Jitterbug Jive and Asher did the fox-trot. The aging house glowed with so much energy that the window glass was hot to the touch. Henry looked at the window and waved. His mouth didn't move, but William heard Henry's thoughts. I'm a prodigy, Will'm. Sometimes God puts a little extra in the recipe.

Fingers splayed, William put his hand against the glass. Henry did the same, mirroring the motion from ten yards away. William couldn't bear for the magical connection to be lost. I'm sorry, *he thought.* I know, Will'm.

William awoke with tears in his eyes. He accidentally kicked an empty bottle across the floor and it clinked against the baseboard under the window. He wiped his eyes and felt warmth around his sockets, as if his hands truly radiated from touching the hot glass in his dream. He turned on his desk lamp and searched through the drawers. *Child prodigies.* He'd done a day of research on the subject after Henry won the dance marathon. William had never transformed the research into an article as intended, but in the right bottom drawer he found the page of notes he'd taken.

Child prodigies are usually under the age of ten with talents performed at the levels of an adult. They are so rare as to immediately garner attention and awe. More definitions of prodigy: *Person with exceptional talent or powers ... an act or event so extraordinary and rare as to inspire awe and wonder ... a portentous event or sign ... an omen ...*

William loaded a clean sheet of paper into his typewriter and began to peck out his thoughts. Sometime in the middle of the night, his eyes grew heavy and he fell asleep, comfortable this time, on his bed.

NINETEEN

William came downstairs, having splashed his face with cold water, brushed his teeth, and slicked his hair down with a scoop of pomade, to rejoin the world of the living.

Polly was at the kitchen table. "Next time I ask you to walk me back to my cottage, are you going to be too busy?"

He smiled, relieved. "I'll have to check my schedule."

"You do that." She stood, straightened her dress—another one from his mother's closet.

"While you were hibernating, the distillery continued on. We are about to fill the first barrel." Without another word, she went out the door.

After eating two boiled eggs and rushing through a cup of joe, he followed her out into the cool morning. Barley was on the porch, one column away from completing his painting project.

William surveyed the porch. "Looks good."

Barley carefully edged the top of the column, then looked down at William. "I went into Louisville. No one seems to know this Sanscrit. The bums aren't as willing to talk about Asher anymore, and the ones willing told me nothing we hadn't already heard."

"You went to the city by yourself? Who drove you?"

"I did."

"When did you start driving again?"

"Since you turned turtle."

William watched Barley paint. "They're filling the first barrel. You coming?"

Barley acted uninterested.

The whiskey-tree crowd and the protestors were all currently subdued. Even Bancroft and the Klan stood silent. Most of the folks knew the distillery's history, and many had prayed for its revival, and so they watched, knowing something important was about to happen.

William entered the cooking house first. His footfalls echoed off the wooden walls. The cooking tub was three-quarters full with milled corn grist and limestone-filtered water. It would be the first batch to include 25 percent of the sour mash backset from what was currently being distilled two houses down the run. Which was why, even though they would age the initial barrels, they wouldn't sell them as Old Sam. Tradition would have them age those barrels until the whiskey completely evaporated and the angels were good and drunk.

Old Sam's mash bill included 80 percent corn, 14 percent rye, and 6 percent barley—the latter two added after the corn mash had boiled and cooled slightly, to 140 degrees, because they cooked at a lower temperature than the corn. William braced his hands on the lip of the cooker, imagining he was Old Sam's master distiller.

He moved from the cooking house and followed the barrel

run outside to the fermentation house a few paces away. It was empty as well, but not void of sound, and certainly not of aroma. The next batch to be distilled was nearing the end of the fermentation process. Inside the massive cyprus vat the yeast feasted on the mash's sugars and starches, eating and multiplying, the golden liquid popping and bubbling as the sugars converted to alcohol and the room became thick with corn and carbon dioxide.

It was important to keep it under 80 degrees, hot enough for the yeast to work but not so hot to kill the yeast too early. The McFee Distillery used the same yeast strain since its first days. According to legend, Samuel took the strain home with him daily, locking it in a safe between his bed and the shotgun propped against the wall. Apparently Mr. Browder had kept the yeast strain alive through Prohibition.

William walked from the fermentation house and entered distillation, where he found everyone gathered around the three stills: Samantha, Johnny, Annie, Polly, Mr. Browder, Carly, and Max, and then John Swell and his boy, Peter. The first still was fifteen feet tall and shaped like a column. By the time the fermented mash entered the distillation house, it was known as distiller's beer, because it looked, smelled, and tasted like a rich beer. It was heated to just over 200 degrees inside the still, and the alcohol was vaporized, cooled, and condensed into a clear liquid called "low wines," testing at about 125 proof. From there it entered the onion-shaped thumper still, where it was distilled a second time, resulting in a water-clear whiskey known as "high wines," and it was this "white dog" unaged whiskey William was hoping they'd sell right away.

The group had gathered around the McFees' third still,

another copper thumper, where Mr. Browder had just cut the first batch of white dog with water to get the proof down to about 110 and was now pumping it into the first barrel.

"There he is," said Samantha. "He's finally risen."

William joined the group just as Mr. Browder pulled the hose from the barrel. "And we've got company." William pointed to the window. The top of Barley's hat was visible.

Samantha rolled her eyes.

Mr. Browder held out a tray of shot glasses full of the white dog. It smelled heavily of corn and made William's nostrils flare. They toasted the first batch of the new era. William winced, wiped his eyes. It was sharp and potent, but the aftertaste was a precursor to the bourbon it would one day become. Johnny choked and his eyes popped, which made little Peter Swell laugh. William patted his little brother on the back.

"Save some back for the well," Samantha told Mr. Browder.

The well? Just as William was about to ask what they were talking about, Mr. Browder handed him the bung mallet. "You want me to hammer it in?"

"I'll do it if he doesn't," said Polly.

William grabbed the hammer and winked at Polly.

Mr. Browder positioned the bung in the barrel's hole. "Hit it flush."

William eyeballed the target and hit it dead center, and then again to make sure it was flush. Mr. Browder kissed the barrel and removed the wedges holding it on the track. The five-hundred-pound barrel turned down the sloped run and thundered across the wooden floor. Boards popped and creaked under the weight—a giant awakening from a decade-long slumber. The barrel made the curved turn and rolled toward the opening in the far wall, where the run would carry it across the walkway, through the sunlit potter's field, and into the aging house.

William was the first out the door, with Johnny and their mother right on his heels, but they were not the first to follow the barrel across the field. Barley had kindly taken that position, walking alongside as it rumbled along the run. Every ten feet or so Barley put his hand on the barrel to coax it along. The tent folk applauded as Barley accompanied the barrel toward the aging house.

William could tell by the strut in his father's walk and the sway of his arms that he was giddy, and quite possibly crying by the way his head bobbed. William urged Samantha forward. She hesitated at first, then took off running to catch up. She and Barley shared a glance that warmed William's heart. Together they escorted the barrel around the next turn and down the slope toward the aging house.

William gripped Polly's hand and took off running. He wanted to see the barrel enter the house himself. The rest of the crew wasn't far behind, even Annie, who was racing Peter Swell in a slant across the potter's field.

The crowd cheered, and in every man's face William's paranoia saw Tommy Borduchi.

Bancroft arrived snapping pictures of the rolling barrel. He waved sarcastically to William. Polly said, "I'd like to smash that man's camera into a hundred pieces."

William liked her grit, but what he liked more was the sound of that heavy barrel rumbling toward the opening of the aging house. Once inside, the angels' share hit him like freshly baked bread—hard, in all his senses at once, an overload that made him hungry, tingly, thirsty, alive, and, dare he even think it, dizzy for Polly, whose palm had begun to sweat in his.

The barrel slowed inside the aging house and settled against a block at the end of the run. From there, Barley and Mr. Browder positioned it on the mechanical lift and watched as the barrel inched upward. At the lowest row of ricks, Mr. Browder transferred it to the platform. William let go of Polly's hand. He started to roll the barrel on down, but Mr. Browder stopped him. Max held his arm out to stop the barrel's progress.

"Bring it back," said Mr. Browder, a surgeon eyeing a prepped patient.

He waited for Barley to get on the opposite side of the barrel. Together, the two rotated the barrel clockwise two precise ticks, and then one more, before they both backed away, studying the angle. "Good?"

Barley nodded, looked at his son. "Bung hole needs to stop at high noon. Don't want to give the whiskey a chance to leak. Go ahead. Now you can push it."

William did as directed. He invited Johnny and Annie, and together the three McFee children got the barrel rolling. William followed it inside the rick, watching the bung hole pass underneath only to show itself a few seconds later on top. After ten more revolutions, just as Mr. Browder and Barley had calculated, it stopped against the end of the rick, two feet from the stone wall, and the bung hole was exactly at high noon.

Barley shook Mr. Browder's hand and patted him on the back.

Bancroft entered with his camera; Barley looked up. "Scram. You have no right to be in here." Bancroft snapped a picture of the initial barrel resting in the rick like a handheld egg.

Barley looked away from the flash so as to hide his face and then moved toward the reporter. "Take another and you'll be figuring how to digest it."

William jumped in front of his father. "Get out, Bancroft."

He held up his hands. "I'm going. No need for violence, Mr. McFee."

William slammed the door behind him. When he turned back toward his family and the crew, they stood silent. Barley clapped his hands and smiled. "Come on, boys. Quit bumping gums. We've got barrels to fill."

William took a break around midday, because Barley forced him to. Once he'd gotten his hands dirty with sour mash, he didn't want to stop. Distillery labor was invigorating; it was in his blood. He felt connected to the lineage and history of what they were doing. And it filled his mind with better images than those that had occupied it since Rose Island. But that didn't mean he was going to let Bancroft steal his story.

Barley said, "Do what you need to do so you can get back to work."

William wiped mash from his hands, put on his topper, and ventured into the woods in pursuit of Lulu Bancroft. It wasn't the first time William had mingled with the crowd, but it *was* the first time he didn't feel safe. The euphoria from earlier in the day was gone, and the overall mood had changed from excitement to annoyance. Tempers were growing short; not everyone's prayers were coming true. William could hear whispers as he passed. "There he is, the McFee boy." He felt exposed and vulnerable maneuvering around the tents, nodding to some while shaking the hands of others, blessed and cursed for his articles in equal measure.

The Roman Catholics, led by Father Vincent, had huddled into a group and were holding a small service while a cluster of Protestants did the same twenty paces away. Their voices rose in competition until both sides seemed more aware of the other instead of the service itself. And there Bancroft stood, in the foreground of Mr. Browder's cornfields, taking notes, a line of KKK standing centurion-like around him.

"You make me sick," William said, closing in. "You spread drivel like right or wrong, black or white. It's not that simple."

"It is if you read the Bible."

"Well, maybe the Bible needs to be rewritten."

"Blasphemer," Bancroft said. "Your day of judgment will be swift. Those who don't accept Christ into their lives will burn in the eternal fires of hell." Bancroft pointed toward the tents dotting the land. "As will all who give credence to this Potter's Field Christ."

"You're too much of a lunatic to recognize your own sins. Where's your camera?"

Bancroft pointed to the trunk of a nearby tree, where his camera lay shattered in the grass. "Your lady apostle saw fit to destroy it an hour ago. She said the distillery story is yours." He stood toe-to-toe with William, who didn't back down. "I don't want it."

One of the protestors snapped a picture of the two of them.

"I have other cameras. Readers need to know that their Potter's Field Christ is being championed by a temperamental boy who will turn toward the Devil just like his father. Your little brother is dead because of his sins. What exactly were the McFees up to the other night?"

"What are you meaning?"

"Middle of the night. Lights on in the mill house. The three of you loaded something bulky in the trunk of the car and drove off. And then the next morning you conveniently happen to be on Rose Island and report the discovery of a body firsthand? I don't believe in coincidences, Mr. McFee."

"What do you believe in?"

"Choices and repercussions."

William turned away. Bancroft called after him, "Advice, Mr. McFee? Don't cross me again. Tomorrow's story is a grain of sand. I can unleash the entire beach."

⁂

By the time the sun set over Twisted Tree, ten more barrels of white dog had been rolled into the aging house, and the day's sour mash had been added to both the cooking and fermentation vats. Barley was in full throttle as master distiller, and William was his understudy.

As the final arc of sunlight bled orange over the whiskey trees, Barley stood by the stone water well with his sons and Mr. Browder. He hung an oil lamp from the pitched roof, casting a hazy nimbus of light off the mossy stones.

"So why are we standing out here?" Johnny asked.

Mr. Browder held out a pitcher of liquid, samples of white dog from every barrel they'd filled during the day.

"I'd like to take a moment to thank a former employee." Barley looked across the well toward Mr. Browder. "The most loyal of loyal, who stayed when all the others so rightfully moved on. I'd like to thank him for believing this would happen, no matter how many times I insisted it wouldn't. To Ronald Browder, you stubborn son of a gun."

Mr. Browder nodded. Barley said, "The minute we start rolling barrels onto those ricks, the tax bills will come in. I've enough saved to float us for a while, but we need our initial work to bear fruit. Because of this I'd like to announce a new flavor to sell while our barrels age." He looked to Mr. Browder. "Named after our famous grower of grain, our corn connoisseur. Ronald's Ghost."

Mr. Browder smiled, truly honored.

"But ghost makes it sound like he's dead," Johnny said.

"It's because of his white hair," said Barley. "And the whiskey is clear."

"I like it," Mr. Browder said. "Ronald's Ghost. Unaged corn whiskey. I like it, Mr. Barley. I'm honored."

Barley held up his hand, urging Mr. Browder to keep the pitcher. "Boys, my father—your grandfather—had a tradition. He set aside a cup from every batch of high wines. Said if the angels got their share from the aging house, then the Devil needed his share off the still. So he'd walk to this well and pour it down. Give the Devil his share. In doing that, he believed it would keep anything evil from the distillery. Pour it down, Ronald."

Mr. Browder tipped the pitcher and slowly poured the white dog into the well.

"Give'm his share," Barley said, lowering his voice. "Every last drop."

William stayed by the well after Mr. Browder had given the Devil his share; he'd hoped to see Polly. Instead, he watched a finely dressed man walk side by side with his finely dressed woman. Watched them emerge, arm in arm, from the whiskey trees, approaching Keating's grave. The closer they got, the more William wished he'd gone inside with the rest of them.

They didn't pray long before the man genuflected, making the sign of the cross on his head, chest, and shoulders, and they headed back toward the trees. It couldn't be him. He'd seen Tommy the Bat's face in every man tenting in the woods, and he'd been able to blink those faces back into the real thing. He blinked and this man still had Borduchi's face.

Keep walking. Keep on walking and never come back. We gave the Devil his share already, so you keep on walking. He convinced himself that that was exactly what Tommy the Bat was going to do, but then Borduchi looked over his left shoulder and tipped his hat to William.

His heart stuttered, but he played it cool. He nodded back and watched as Tommy Borduchi and his moll disappeared into the whiskey trees. After they'd gone, William braced himself on the curved stone wall of the well and gagged into the abyss.

"Keep on walking," he said softly. He didn't like how it echoed back to him, so he talked in his head to keep from soiling his pants. *He didn't recognize me. He tipped his hat because that's what men do when they want to say thanks for allowing them time at Asher's grave. He didn't recognize me. Dad never needs to know he was here.*

The longer he stood out by the well, the more William convinced himself that the man hadn't been Tommy the Bat at all. Just had a striking resemblance, he and the woman. And now they were gone. Gone for good and no harm done. They'd given the Devil his share just in time. William hoped they'd given him enough.

TWENTY

The porch looked new. William found Barley sitting on the stoop with a bottle of Old Forester. Henry's shoes dangled around his neck like weights; his shoulders drooped.

"Porch looks nice." He wouldn't share what he might have seen by Asher's grave.

Barley took a swig from his bottle, scooted over. "Where you been?"

"Heard you made Mother a root-beer float the other day."

Barley's suited men stood guard in the shadows all around the house. William would have felt more comfortable if they were watching the woods instead of the police.

Barley shrugged and wiped his mouth and scruffy jawline. "Thank you, William."

"For what?"

"Didn't realize how much I needed the distillery until I saw that first barrel roll." Barley smelled the air. "Sometimes I feel like my heart's been torn by buckshot. This smell fills a few of the holes."

He gazed toward the family cemetery. Henry's headstone was visible from where they sat. "I used to joke that Henry was growing up to be too much like you. I suppose that wouldn't have been such a bad thing." Barley patted William's knee. "That boy could be so stubborn, though. I'd tell him to do something until I eventually did it myself."

"You never did that with us."

"No." Barley took a drink. "The youngest gets away with certain things."

"I was guilty too," William said. "Those dimples, and that smile. Blue eyes, big as saucers. He was impossible to say no to. But then . . ."

Barley appeared to be crying, but when he moved his hands from his face, his eyes were dry. "I want you to become the next master distiller." Barley glanced at William. "I don't question your passion for journalism. But Old Sam runs in your blood. Mr. Browder is an old man. And Johnny is too jingle-brained."

"I'll have time to learn from you—"

"Time is never guaranteed. Learn now. I could die tomorrow or in fifty years, but—"

"Dad, stop."

"I want you to be prepared when I'm gone, William." With the bottle, Barley motioned out toward the distillery. "It was your grandfather's dream for this distillery to thrive for generations. Do you know what he said the first time he saw you, the first time he held you? 'Feels like a master distiller to me.' And then you cooed some gibberish, and everyone laughed when Sam said that you already talked like a master distiller." Barley smiled at the memory. "And then you loaded your diaper and he handed you back to your mother and said, 'But he smells like Barley.'"

"You smelled like dirty britches back then?"

"I don't know what I smelled like, William. Grandpa Sam liked to needle me."

"Is that what you do when you call me a daisy?"

Barley took another swig of bourbon. "I suppose."

He offered William the bottle but he declined. He had a clear head and didn't want it altered. "The other night. You were telling me about Old Sam being stored in the concentration house. How'd you get involved with Tommy Borduchi?"

"I'd heard rumors Old Sam was being leaked. McVain's contacts put us in touch with Borduchi. He was a runner for George Remus early on, then split with the know-how to copy what Remus had done in his hidden distillery at Death Valley Farm." Barley caught William grinning. William wiped it away; he shouldn't find this amusing.

Barley said, "Like Remus, he bought up distilleries and pharmacies to get his hands on good whiskey and bourbon. A lot of the whiskey stored with ours came from distilleries bought by Tommy."

"So he had access to all of it?"

Barley nodded, flicked a leaf fleck off his pant leg. "He found the holes in the Volstead Act just like Remus did. Sold bonded liquor to himself. Under government licenses for medicinal purposes. He'd hijack his own trucks and then sell it illegally."

"And this is where you come in?"

"We had a meeting with Tommy at the Seelbach Hotel. Hidden room off the Oak Room, where Capone played cards. That's where Tommy liked to do his business before Rose Island."

"What about now? Where do you think he's hiding out?"

"I've heard whispers of Shippingport."

"The police have been unable to find him—"

"*Unable* isn't the word. Connections don't end when you're in the big house."

"You mean the coppers are protecting him?"

"He's in some of their pockets, yes." Barley finished off the bottle and placed the empty between his feet.

"Wouldn't those same coppers help him find you then?"

Barley patted William's leg, as if proud. "Trousers got two pockets, William."

"You're paying them too?"

Barley eyed the empty bottle, probably wishing he had more. "Been paying the coppers big cabbage for months to throw him off my scent. And they've been fleecing me for more ever since Tommy burned the house down. Bulls ain't dumb, and they know I've got it."

"Seems like a dangerous game for them, you know, straddling the line."

"Coppers gotta make a living too."

William took it in, in awe of his father. "Tell me more. What happened next?"

Barley puffed his cheeks and exhaled. "We came to terms with Tommy. His trucks would leave the concentration house with full loads. Taken to his pharmacies all over the state. Sometimes we drove those trucks. Other times we were hijack men and we'd steal from them. He was moving Old Sam inventory, and it became my goal to rescue every bottle. I wanted to hide it until Prohibition was repealed. But McVain . . . If he was going to risk his life—because Tommy would have killed us for sure—he was going to profit from it. So we hijacked our own trucks, made off with anything Old Sam, and kept the rest for Tommy."

"And you sold it? The Old Sam? Behind Tommy's back?"

"Yes. We formed our own distribution lines." Barley stood from the porch step. "If anyone was going to make money off what *my* father distilled, it was going to be me."

William stretched out on his bed with a yawn, feeling the window-reflected morning sunlight on his eyelids before he opened them.

"This is very poignant, William."

His eyes flashed open. Polly. In his bedroom. He leaned up on his elbows, remembered he didn't have a shirt on. Polly sat at his desk with a cup of coffee steaming, the article he'd written about the distillery in her hand. His bedroom door was wide open.

"Thank you."

"William, get dressed and meet me outside."

"A guardian angel?" William asked.

He was trying to digest what Polly had just told him of Asher and Henry's connection.

Clouds had moved in. The sky was full of circling blackbirds. More deer had gathered in the woods behind the aging house, staying put under the boughs but watching, waiting.

"Asher claimed he could feel it every time one was born," said Polly. "Children with inexplicable gifts that leave people in awe. In wonder. That make people smile. Laugh. Cry. He felt a hug of warmth around his heart. The same surge he'd get from an opium high."

"He felt this for prodigies?"

"Henry wasn't the only one Asher kept track of." She moved a strand of red hair from her brow and folded her arms as they walked. "There was a boy in Salem who played violin at three. A girl in Bardstown doing complex mathematics at age four. A little black boy in Frankfort born blind, who could paint a sunset perfectly without ever seeing one."

William scratched his head.

"Pascal, young David of the Old Testament, Joan of Arc," Polly continued. "Lovecraft reciting poetry at two, writing poems at five. Mozart playing at four. Picasso painting *The Picador* at eight. Beethoven and Chopin performing at seven. Capablanca beat his father at chess at four—"

"Henry won a dance marathon at four." William stared at the aging house. "My little brother could *dance*, the Charleston and the Black Bottom. The Lindy Hop and the Jitterbug Jive, the Shimmy and the fox-trot—his hands clapping and feet stomping, sweat dripping. Said he could outdance all the folks in Twisted Tree, and that's what he did. Nothing, not even the share, brought angels to the ricks faster than his shuffling feet."

"Asher was there, William. At the dance marathon. He watched."

William had wondered as much. "The day Henry was born, a tornado swept through Twisted Tree. It was coming toward the distillery. It jumped our house. There were deer just like there are now . . . Why are they here?"

"I don't know." Polly moved toward the trampled grass path surrounding the aging house. "Asher wasn't always forthcoming. I didn't know him when Henry was born. But Asher told me he felt heat on that day. He set out to follow it, saw the destruction here. Saw the untouched distillery and the evidence of uprooted trees where the tornado touched back down. He stood in the woods and wept for Henry, he said, because—"

"Henry didn't cry when he was born," William finished for her as they walked side by side toward the barrel run.

"Asher said we can be molded and shaped, but some can't escape their nature."

"Some things just already are," William said. "That's how Henry described his dancing. 'Not everything is learned. Some things just already are.'"

"'Sometimes God puts a little extra into the recipe,'" Polly said, suddenly stopping in the shade of a yellow-leaf tree. "That's what Asher would say. 'And sometimes God doesn't put enough.'"

William's eyes grew as he recalled the similar way Henry described things. "And sometimes, even though God must try to keep the Devil away, the bad stuff still gets in."

"Asher felt that too. Like little bee stings. When one of the other kind was born."

"But babies?"

"The bad stuff can get in." Polly started strolling again, and William followed her into the sunlight. They sat together on the barrel run. "Asher felt his first 'bee sting' as a boy. Felt the warmth and the sting simultaneously and it made him sick. He was six houses away from his own when he saw teenagers arguing. A boy and a girl." Polly gave William a preparatory glance. "At four, Mary Borduchi was known on her street for having seen a vision of Mary and Jesus. Tommy and Mary Borduchi."

She paused to let it sink in. "Mary was the first prodigy for Asher. He didn't understand why he needed to do it, but he watched over her all the same, despite her being older. He felt the need to protect her. There was something reverent about her just as there was something evil about her twin brother. Something not right."

William rubbed his face with shaky hands. "Mary Borduchi, she's a Carmelite nun. Cloistered at the Sisters for the Aged and Infirm."

"Asher never stopped looking after her. Their order is believed to be under the special protection of the Blessed Virgin Mary."

William gazed toward Asher Keating's grave, just as the deer were doing. "Is that why Asher Keating was born? To protect prodigies like himself?"

"I believe it's bigger."

"When did he start believing he was Christ?"

"Not sure he ever believed he was. He never knew exactly what he was. Claimed he was confused with his degree of . . . giftedness. Until the war."

"So he came back knowing he was more than a prodigy?"

"You're looking at it wrong. He came back understanding there are different degrees."

"Of what?"

"Of giftedness. And that he was closer to it than any prodigy since Jesus."

"You're implying Christ was a prodigy?"

"Why not? You've read the Bible, William. Was Christ not the greatest prodigy of all?"

William gave Mr. Crone his story about the revival of the distillery, and in turn he was handed a copy of Bancroft's latest in the *Post*. It included a picture of William standing nose to nose with Bancroft. He scanned the scathing article, then tossed it into the garbage on his way out.

At City Hall he told two officers he'd heard rumors in the newsroom that Tommy Borduchi was hiding out at Shippingport or the Seelbach Hotel. He said that Borduchi recently harassed Tanner and Bethany Finn about the Potter's Field Christ. They nodded, promised to look into it. "Why's this so important to you anyway?"

"I told you, he came to the distillery. He visited Asher Keating's grave."

"And he left?"

"But that doesn't mean he won't come back."

"Then the men we have on-site will take care of it."

"Take care of it? They let him waltz right in and out," said William. "Thank God we . . ." He trailed off before revealing Barley's old boys were guarding their house.

"Look, kid, you work for the paper. Leave investigating to those in the know-how. The Feds are sweeping the city. Borduchi's cornered and he's running out of hidey-holes."

The trees in the gardened courtyard at the Sisters for the Aged and Infirm bloomed gold and red above trimmed shrubbery and a gurgling central pond. Four nuns sat on benches, praying on rosaries. William leaned back on his simple concrete perch, closed his eyes, and allowed the daylight to warm his face.

"Mr. McFee?"

William sat up straight and blinked. He'd nearly dozed off. "Yes, Miss Borduchi. I mean, Sister Borduchi. Sister Mary?"

"Sister Mary is fine."

She sat beside him. She was more striking than he'd imagined; she had a youthful yet sculpted face. Because of her white, brown, and black head and neck garments, he couldn't see her hair color, but her eyes were bright blue. The sister shared physical characteristics with her twin, but while Tommy made William's heart race, Sister Mary's presence calmed him.

"Thank you for taking time to see me, Sister."

"We get two hours of recreation each day. Some sew and knit. Some make rosaries. I prefer on nice days like this to sit in the courtyard and listen to the pond." Her smile was kind, though her lip tilted similarly to her brother's. "Incorporate conversation into the fold, Mr. McFee, and it makes for a lovely day. So what can I do for you? You're a reporter?"

He fought back the sweats. "I wrote the article on the Potter's Field Christ. But I'd be content with never writing about it again."

"We're cloistered here to prevent distraction from prayer, but some news can't be shielded by these walls. I know about Asher Keating."

"If I tell you some things, can it be just between you and me?"

"Well, of course. What's on your mind?"

"My little brother, Henry, he was killed in a car wreck." William looked around. No one was close enough to overhear them, but he lowered his voice anyway. "Asher Keating was buried in the field next to our house on the one-year anniversary of his death. To the day. When my brother died, his shoes were missing. Well, they showed up in Asher's bindle. Turns out Asher and Henry had a connection."

William paused to study her reaction; it wasn't one of surprise.

"Henry had a talent." William looked over his shoulder again. "He could dance like an adult. Better, in fact. Had the talent before he learned to walk. Like it was God given. Do you see what I'm saying?"

She folded her hands. "Should I?"

"I don't know. I'm afraid you'll think me crazy."

"No crazier than choosing a life of prayer and solitude."

They shared a laugh. He liked the ease he felt with her. "Okay, well, I'd figured Henry was a prodigy. I've learned that Asher Keating watched over my brother, like a guardian angel. That he was a prodigy himself. But more so. Henry wasn't the only one he watched over."

She adjusted the brown scapular around her neck, then faced him with a serious look in her eyes. "When I sat down, you were wondering what color my hair is? It's brown. As a kid, during the summer, it would turn the color of sand. Not now, of course. I also know you're here about my twin brother."

"Sister . . . can you read my mind?"

"And your heart," she said warmly. "And it's in a good place, William."

It was the first time she'd called him by his first name.

"And yes, I was one Asher watched over. I was three when I first surprised my mother by saying what she was just about to do. But a gift can also be a curse. Not everyone's thoughts are kind. I was a gangly and long-nosed child. The other girls teased me without saying a word. Passing them on the sidewalk, I knew what they thought."

"A friend of Asher's told me that you had visions of Mary and Jesus."

"You're in love with this friend. You've yet to kiss her and this drives you batty." She patted his hand. "You're worried that you won't know how to do it and she'll laugh."

"I'm more worried now that a nun knows this about me." William blushed.

"Don't be. Your wait will soon be over, I predict." She watched water trickle across the pond stones. "I did see visions of Mary and Jesus. Five times."

"How well did you know Asher Keating?"

"He was younger than me by several years. We spoke a handful of times, mostly kind greetings in passing. He took up for me on the street on the sly, although I knew. One afternoon I fell running after a ball. I skinned my knees bloody. There was a car coming. Asher hustled me from the pavement to the grass, although I was twice his size. I thanked him and he nodded 'you're welcome.' And that was it. Until, around the age of ten, he got the courage to talk to me in more depth." She chuckled as she reminisced. "He told me he loved me. Loved me like the days are long. And then he just stood there."

"What did you tell him?"

"I told him I was flattered, but that was not the path chosen for us."

"And?"

"And he agreed. He wished me a good afternoon. Two days later he was in an orphanage. We never spoke again, but I knew he watched over me, all the way up until he died."

"What do you think of him now? I mean, with everything that's being said?"

"I think Asher Keating was a very special man. A kind man. A flawed man. An especially gifted man." She shrugged, pursed her lips. "Could he have been the second coming of Jesus Christ? That I can't answer with certainty. But the fact that a woman of the cloth gives pause is one kind of answer."

"You mentioned the paths chosen for you. You knew that you'd become a nun?"

"I knew I wanted to serve the Lord. I knew I wanted to be in a place where people didn't have mean thoughts." She motioned toward the courtyard. "And I've found that here. I came as soon as I could. Joined at sixteen. You don't know what it was like living with Tommy, being able to read his mind. Tommy once spotted a cat snooping for scraps around our porch. He ran into the house. I just knew it was to get his bat. I shooed the poor thing away before Tommy could get to it. He would have beaten it to death, he was in such an ornery mood. He glared at me, knowing what I'd done. Wanted to take the bat to me, and probably would have tried had I not walked away."

William felt sick to his stomach. "They say he's found Christ. In prison."

"I pray that he has. I've prayed for him all of my life, but I'm hard-pressed to believe he's changed." She shook her head. "Or that he'll ever change."

"He came to visit Asher's grave. He wants my father dead, but he thinks my father is somebody else. I'm not making sense—"

"I understand you perfectly, William." She sighed, touched the scapular around her neck again. "I will add you to my afternoon prayers."

"But do you think . . . ?" He trailed off, started over. "Asher felt your presence on the street. You *and* Tommy, he felt it. I know it has to do about how we're brought up, but is it possible . . . ?"

"To be born evil?"

"Yes, that's what I'm asking. My little brother, he said sometimes the bad stuff gets in."

Sister Mary exhaled. "My mother told me she once woke to the smell of smoke and singed fabric. She sat up, and there was Tommy hunkered like a troll, sitting on the foot of the bed with a lit candle. She asked him what in the world he was doing. He said he was thinking about when he was born. He wanted to know if there were any more babies in there. 'Why?' my mother asked. 'Better not be,' he said." Sister Mary kissed her rosary and then motioned the sign of the cross. "He was two years old."

An aroma of boiled corn and rye escaped the cooking mill, and the air of the fermentation house was thick with yeasty mash. Mr. Browder was the center of attention amid the whiskey-tree crowd, handing small samples of Ronald's Ghost to anyone willing to try it.

"He's on his second barrel," Polly told William as they faced the crowd. "The Klansmen barked their disapproval of the Demon Rum. And they don't like the fact that a Negro is handing it out to white folks."

Polly had spent the morning collecting stories.

Kenneth Smart, after visiting the grave, found a dollar alongside the road. He took it as a sign to reopen his hardware store. He started removing the plywood from the windows at lunchtime.

Mario Benvito, a widower of five years, found his wife's wedding ring. He'd lost it months ago. At the grave he'd prayed on whether or not to close his restaurant. Moments after he found the ring—in the restaurant, near the cash register—a woman entered and he served her spaghetti and a glass of wine. He even sat with her while she dined. She was a widow herself and looking for work. She could wait tables, she'd told him, to which he responded that he didn't have the business. Two minutes later two families from the crowded main road arrived with empty bellies and pocket change. The woman stood and grabbed a dusty apron from a hook on the wall.

Taking advantage of the cars continuously coming in and out of Twisted Tree, Charlie Pipes's Gas & Taff corner store was seeing more business than it had in the past two years. He dropped his gas to eight cents a gallon and gave his taffy away free on fill-ups.

Brooks Madden found his old hot-dog stand in the garage and set up shop alongside the main road. He'd visited Asher's grave the day before. His hot dogs with chili and cheese were a hit—especially with Margie Fitzgerald, because he'd gotten all his ingredients from her Twisted Tree food store, which itself had seen a resurgence of customers of late—and those who couldn't afford to pay for the hot dog were asked to do something kind for a stranger.

George and Hope Sparrow, who'd for the most part lived a loveless marriage, had prayed at the grave for God to rekindle their flame. That night, according to George, he'd kept Hope awake all night long.

Dr. Lewis knocked on the McFees' front door shortly before lunchtime, fidgeting with his hat when Samantha opened the door. She'd asked him inside for coffee, but Dr. Lewis declined. Couldn't stay long. He'd visited his wife at the Waverly Sanatorium, and she'd made a remarkable turn for the better.

The doctors said her breathing was stronger and even mentioned her "making the walk" soon. The sanatorium sat upon a tall hill. If the patients could make the walk up and down, they were healthy enough to go home. Dr. Lewis thanked Samantha for praying for his wife and apologized for some of the things he'd said about Annie.

They shook hands and Dr. Lewis went on his way.

"I believe," William admitted. "I trust in it all like I trust the sun to rise every morning."

Polly slid her arm around his. "Did you find Sister Mary?"

"I did. And now I'm confused. When I was little, my mother explained why we're baptized as infants. To cleanse ourselves from original sin. The repercussions of Adam and Eve eating the fruit off the tree. Our entire family was baptized. But I'm wondering now. Does it really matter at all?"

"William, what are you saying?"

"That I think it's all a sting, Polly. Tommy and Mary Borduchi were baptized. One became a nun and the other a monster. Maybe God put a little extra into the recipe with Henry and Sister Mary. But sometimes the bad stuff gets in and there's nothin' to be done about it."

"Which is exactly why I pray."

A letter from Nashville arrived in the afternoon mail, dated two days prior. The Fancannons were sad to report that their son had passed, overwhelmed with a fever the doctors were still trying to explain. It was their son's wish that the letter be written in thanks. The short time he spent at the grave, the boy said, had given him "confidence to walk the long road." And he was "no longer afraid." Mr. Fancannon added a postscript, stating that the boy, after he'd returned home to their estate in Nashville, seemed to understand more than they ever would about life and the hereafter.

"Negroes should have their own line," a man shouted along the front line of whiskey trees, waving his right arm in the air. He was yelling at a black man and his family who'd just returned from the grave. He was a mean drunk, and a racist to boot.

Bancroft was there with his camera; probably said something to instigate it all. Around him stood hooded Klansmen.

Mr. Browder and his son-in-law, Max, came hurrying from the fermentation house as scuffles broke out. Barley fired his Colt into the air. Blackbirds scattered and leaves filtered down in golden drops. Everyone stopped. The Negro family who had been accosted packed their tent quickly.

"Take your time," Barley told them calmly. "No one's gonna hurt you."

"Negroes should have their own line," the drunk said again, now that he'd gotten the attention he craved. "Don't you reckon, Mr. McFee?"

Barley didn't answer, but William said, "What I reckon is you should get on out of Twisted Tree. There's no room for your kind here."

"My kind?" the man asked, offended. "Look at'chu, boy. Our kind, you mean. Huh?" The Klansmen behind him nodded. "And I ain't yet got my turn to pray, boy."

"You're drunk."

"Negroes in their own line!" the bigot chanted, trying to get others to join in.

"Christ is white!" one of the Klansmen shouted. "The Devil has taken root here!"

William didn't like the icy feeling sweeping through the woods. It was obvious how segregated the crowd had become. Barley spoke as if a revelation had hit him. "Anyone opposed to having two lines? Speak up."

More people toed up to the imaginary line between them as if to face off. Like they'd all been waiting for a reason.

"Then it's agreed," shouted Barley. "Two lines it will be."

William's heart sank.

Barley punched the drunk loudmouth, knocking the man out cold like a felled tree. The crowd was stunned. Whispers spread through the trees, then became louder as Barley grabbed him by the collar. "Here you go, ladies and gentlemen. A most-needed second line. For palookas."

The crowd cheered.

Bancroft raised his camera and got a perfect shot of Barley's face.

TWENTY-ONE

S on, we're going out on the town."
       At first, Barley's words had come as a shock. But he had
been strutting around like a peacock since he'd pasted the drunk
and created that second line. And now Barley, dressed to the nines
in freshly shined shoes, slapped Samantha gently on the rump.
She smoothed her knee-length dress and did a bad job concealing
her pleasure.

"We're going out," Barley repeated. "Me and your mother."

"Now?" William grinned.

"There's potato soup on the stove," said Samantha. "Make
sure Annie's in bed by nine. And I invited Polly to the house
for soup."

Barley nudged William's shoulder and winked.

After the dishes were done, the sun looked like half an orange sliding into the woods. The temperature was dropping, so William

offered Polly one of Samantha's sweaters. They walked in a clear arc around the whiskey trees. Would she allow him a kiss before the night was over? She was so beautiful, her fiery hair pulled back in a braided plait. He held her hand as they walked. Leaves crunched underfoot and bats fluttered through the naked trees overhead. Campfires burned in the distance and a few tents had broken out into foreign song.

"It's Polish, that tune," Polly remarked. "Your parents were cute tonight, weren't they?"

"You never knew my father before Asher. *Cute* wasn't the word to describe him."

"Your mother told me Henry kicked so much inside her belly she should have guessed he was a dancer." She'd begun to swing their arms a little.

"When did he start wearing Henry's shoes?"

Polly grew silent for a few steps. "The night he died. He . . . we all noticed the new shoes. The next morning . . . we read the paper, about the car accident. Asher said, 'I tried to stop him.'"

"Tried to stop who?"

"Don't know." She kicked a twig across the footpath. "That's all he said."

They walked over deadfall and navigated a half-cleared path that curved around a narrow creek bed. Polly let go of his hand and reached inside her sweater for the flask. She unscrewed the top and took a drink. She offered William a nip but he declined.

She took another and pointed at him with the flask. "I'm not a boozehound. But I came back because the distillery was running again. I thought I could get a job as a taster so I'd never have to beg or steal for booze again."

"Really?"

"No, William. *Not* really." She took another sip, wiped her mouth. "But there's that word again. *Really*. Now, would you like a nip or not? Are you afraid I have cooties?"

William reached for the flask and took a quick swig.

"It calms my nerves. Helps me forget."

"My father told me about the cooties," said William as they continued through the woods. "During the war he and his dough-boys were walking a road in France. Muddy from their heads to the hobnails of their boots. Grouchy and scratching themselves. They came to a wooded shack with steam pouring out the chimney. It was a disinfecting plant set up by the American Red Cross. My father told the guard he'd caught all the cooties France had to offer. The guard called him a liar. My father said, 'I thought this was a graveyard for cooties, not a session of Congress.'"

Polly's laugh was delicate, like birdsong.

"They showered and got clean and sang 'Suwannee River' and 'What the hell do we care?' He stole a glance. "I heard you singing that morning. You've got a beautiful voice."

"I was a singer in another life. So what happened to your father and his doughboys?"

"Their clothes went into steam chests to kill the vermin. They wrapped themselves in big Turkish towels while they waited. Then it was back to the trenches to get cooties again."

They'd reached a clearing in the trees where an abandoned stone house stood pocked with age marks, the roof weather-damaged and dented where a tree had fallen on it.

"The Crawley mansion," said William. "Hasn't been lived in since before the war." The chimney soared toward the darkening sky. "Johnny says it's haunted. The couple who built it founded this town."

Nearby were the two trees that had given Twisted Tree its name. Polly touched the entwined trunks. "I've never seen such a thing."

"My grandfather hung himself from it."

Polly removed her hand as if burned. "I'm so sorry, William."

"Don't be." He rubbed his hand up the smooth bark. Two trunks, each round enough to hug, had grown side by side until about the four-foot mark, at which point they'd begun to twist into one another, coiling upward for another hundred feet into one massive tree with boughs wide enough to shade half an acre.

"I told him to go away."

"Told who, William?"

"Henry." He bit his lip but tears came anyway. "That's the last thing I ever said to my baby brother. I told him to go away." Polly squeezed him tight, and the embrace gave him strength. "He kept pestering me to go outside and play. Usually I couldn't say no, but that day I did, several times in a row. I yelled at him. Told him to go away. He did. And never came back."

"He knows you loved him." She rubbed his back affectionately.

"But you didn't see his face. I found him in the aging house later, dancing. I watched him through the window. Decided to let him be. To wait until the morning to apologize; take him into town for an ice cream or something."

"He knows, William." She held him. They stared at the twisted tree.

"Asher didn't die." Polly broke the silence. "He was murdered. I witnessed it."

William pulled away, far enough to look into her eyes. "Tell me about it."

She nodded. "I will. But not here." She squeezed him, hard. "Promise me."

"Promise you what?"

"That your feelings for me won't change after what I have to tell you."

He leaned down and kissed Polly on the lips, kissed her with confidence. It felt like a first kiss should feel—sweet, soft, and naively everlasting.

"My father once had a farm," Polly said as they sat side by side on the cottage stoop. Night had fallen like a baize curtain. "He grew corn and wheat, and for a while raised pigs. Overproduction sent prices plummeting; our bushels of corn were worth barely a dime and wheat even less. There were seven of us children. I was the oldest. We were about to lose the farm, and then my little brother Timmy's appendix burst. We bartered our last pig to pay the doctor."

"Did he live?"

She nodded, sipped from her flask, and offered it to William. "He lived, and we put him right back into the eating rotation. Timmy, John, and Joseph ate on Mondays; Deli, Francine, and Clare got to eat on Tuesdays, and then I would eat with my parents on the third day, although my father gave half of his to the young ones, feeding them around a dinner table that we'd eventually use for firewood. By then we stopped burning coal to keep warm. We switched to corn. It was cheaper. Our neighbors did the same."

"Did the town smell like popcorn?"

"It did." She put her soft lips against his for the tenth time since they'd sat down. Each time they held the kiss longer, until William's hair stood on end. This time her tongue brushed his teeth. He shifted on the step. She giggled and touched the tip of his nose with her index finger. "Quit interrupting me."

"You kissed me."

She folded her arms against the cool air. "The popcorn smell only made us hungrier. But it was either that or freeze to death. At eighteen I started to substitute spirits for food. I'd encourage my younger siblings to split my share when our parents weren't looking. There was an old distiller down the road, illegal moonshine. It's where I got my first taste. I thought it was free, until he tried to take what he thought was owed. I slapped him, and luckily he was too drunk to chase me down.

"If I left, there would be that much more food for my younger siblings. So I left. A cousin in Louisville had invited me to sing at his theater—he had vaudeville shows and talent acts. I was naive in thinking that the theater would still be open. People didn't have money for food, let alone entertainment. I found it boarded up and partially burned down. And my cousin was nowhere to be found. I slept in the doorway that night, freezing. The next morning I was blanketed by the shadow of Santa Claus."

"Santa Claus?"

"He was pudgy, with a white beard and hair. 'Do you need a place to stay, lovely lady?' I didn't like that he'd referred to me as lovely, but he had a voice I thought I could trust. And a hand as soft as a pillow. He covered me in a blanket and walked with me until we'd reached a brick building on Liberty Street. It had a sign that read Book Store, and a bell that tinkled when we entered. The walls were stocked with leather-bound books. The man introduced himself as Devlin. I was in awe of the books. I liked to read. He asked if I knew how to do laundry. Yes, I told him, and so he showed me up to the second floor where there was a hallway splitting four rooms down the middle. Knew right then that he'd brought me to a house of ill repute."

She paused for another drink, the last. She'd drained it dry. They'd drained it dry.

William was starting to feel it in his head.

"He put me in charge of washing the sheets. My pay was room and board and access to his library. The books had a smell to them that made me feel safe. And how bad could it be to do laundry? Well, it kept me plenty busy, and at night my hands were raw. But it wasn't long before men took me for one of the doves. One in particular was obsessed with redheads."

William wanted to paste someone.

"It's okay, William. He never got me in that way. It was a butter-and-egg man who wasn't used to hearing no, and so my Santa Claus told him yes. Yes, he could come to my room and watch me sleep; yes, he could watch me dress and undress; yes, he could sketch me; and ultimately yes, because this was how he courted his doves—he could have me if he wanted. His pockets were deep and he paid up front for a full night. He didn't count on me having a pocketknife. He leaned in toward my ear, asking me to undress slowly, and got a knife in his jugular."

William stood and breathed into his hands, pacing the grass.

"Please sit back down. I warned you. Don't do this to me."

"The man," William said. "What happened to him?"

"I pulled my knife from him, took his wallet, and ran from

the room. But Evil Santa was waiting with a knife of his own. And then the door opened and a man, bearded and broad shouldered, bundled in layers of dirty clothes, made Claus freeze in his boots.

"I fell into Asher's arms. I'd been slashed across my right calf by Devlin and could barely stand."

Polly turned her right leg to reveal a cruel white smile etched across smooth skin. William ran his fingers over the wound; it had barely a raise to it.

"Asher rested me gently on the ground. He spoke to Devlin. 'Give me the knife, my son.' Devlin jabbed at him, but still Asher approached, his arms raised in a gesture of peace. 'Drop the knife, my son.' Devlin drove the knife into his right shoulder. But Asher showed no sign that he'd felt the blade at all. He placed his palm against Devlin's forehead and prayed as Devlin cowered, first kneeling and then flat and unmoving on the floorboards. Asher stepped over Devlin and walked up the creaky stairs. He came back down with the four doves behind him, their satchels packed. They never returned to that place."

"But you . . . you'd never seen Asher before that night?"

"No."

"How did he know you were in danger?" William looked directly into her eyes. "Polly?"

She sighed. "I gave my first concert when I was five."

"First concert?"

"Something small for the town folk. I was terrified. The newspapers were there. My father invited them. Come see the girl with the angelic voice. I couldn't tie my shoes, but they say people wept when I'd sing. Left people in awe, the newspapers said. A child touched by God. I didn't want it. I was frightened by so many people. So I stopped singing. Until I decided to jump that train and start a life of my own."

"And Asher began watching over you then?"

"He'd been watching over me for months. It's the first thing he said to me. He pulled the blade without a wince of discomfort and dropped it to the floor. Said he felt the warmth of my arrival. He picked me up, opened the door, and walked out into the night. I wrote a letter to my family and told them I'd found a life in Louisville. I never heard back from them. I followed Asher for the next year and a half. Watched his followers grow. Watched him perform miracles. Watched him heal the sick and comfort the dying. Watched him feed the hungry and clothe the naked."

"Do you think there could be more?"

"More what, William?"

"People like him? Like Asher? If he is some kind of guardian angel?"

"I've never thought about it, but I suppose it's possible." An owl hooted and the wind blew a pinecone across the path. Polly said, "I also witnessed him suffer. Asher, he was taking pain and suffering from the inflicted and storing it in his own body. It was subtle. But it was not our greatest fear." Polly shifted on the stoop. "Evil Santa lost his doves the night Asher rescued me, and his bordello. So he recruited followers of his own, sinners and sneak-thieves, pickpockets and swindlers, murderers and rapists. 'Blasphemy,' they cried. 'Asher Keating is an opium fiend bound by illusions,' they claimed."

"John Swell once referred to him as a magician."

"Many believed he was," Polly concurred. "Devlin dubbed his followers the New Sanhedrin. The original Sanhedrin had its own police force that could make arrests—as they did with

Jesus. But they never had the power to execute. That was in the hands of the Romans. That is why He was crucified instead of stoned. Devlin's New Sanhedrin was a gang of thugs. We avoided alleyways and confined spaces, preferring to keep Asher out in the open, in large crowds."

Polly chewed on a fingernail. "A man came begging us to help his little boy—claimed he was suffering convulsions. Asher followed him up Floyd Street, and he stopped at an alleyway between Market and Jefferson. A boy was there. Asher followed the man into the alleyway, and the boy took off running. As the man lowered the knife into his back, Asher bowed his head in prayer, as if he'd known it was coming and he was asking forgiveness, even before the rest of his attackers emerged, ten of them. They attacked with brutal force, slashing and stabbing until they were sure he was dead. Never once did Asher resist. Never once did he cry out in pain or give them the pleasure of struggle. They shouted insults and cried 'blasphemer' as they ripped and tore garments from his body—"

William put his arm around her and pulled her close. "I'm so sorry, Polly."

"Devlin yelled out, 'Let him save himself if he is truly chosen.' I knelt beside Asher's body. Blood bubbles escaped from his lips as he spoke. 'Father, forgive them; for they know not what they do.' He smiled at me. At that moment I had no regrets about leaving my family. Asher was my family. They were all my family. He refused to drink from a container of water, but he did grip my hand and urge me not to hold anger. 'Do not plot revenge,' he said. I watched him die. He did so in anonymity. Few watched and many jeered. I will never forget his final words, his grip loosening around my fingers. 'Father, into Your hands I commit my spirit.' I closed his eyes."

For a minute they watched the wind move shadows through the woods.

"Devlin was found along the riverfront the next morning with his throat cut."

"Who did it?"

"I don't know. Asher said not to seek revenge. I didn't. But I won't deny the relief I felt." Polly stood, pulled him with her. "I'm tired." She kissed him on the lips. "I need to lie down."

William waited until she was safely inside and heard the bolt lock. He turned back into the woods and walked forty yards until the rear of the distillation house was visible.

"So do *you* think Babe Ruth really called his shot?"

He felt the end of a baseball bat poking against his spine.

"That idiot had an answer, but I don't recall one from you."

William put his hands up as if the bat could shoot bullets. Given a choice he'd rather take a bullet than get bludgeoned to death. "Everyone knows Babe Ruth called his shot."

Eva Carcolli stepped out of the trees with a Louisville Slugger of her own. She swung, connected with his rib cage, doubling him over, and then the burlap sack turned everything dark.

TWENTY-TWO

William's rib cage throbbed. He was sitting in a hard-backed chair. They pulled the sack from his head. All of the abandoned distillery cottages had the same simple floor plan, and he was in the living room of one of them. Two oil lamps glowed along with the tips of several cigarettes. Eva sat ten feet away with her long legs crossed, her eyes hawkish. Behind her stood three suited trouble men, all armed. Tommy paced, tapping the bat against his palm.

"Got a smoke?" William was determined to be tough.

Eva pulled a small tin container from the bust of her tight blue dress and handed it to Tommy. He opened it for William to grab a butt, snapped the container shut, and handed it back to Eva. She slid it in the front of her dress.

"Give him some fire," Tommy said.

One of the men behind Eva tossed a lighter across the room and William caught it. He lit up and then tossed the lighter back to the brute who'd thrown it. He exhaled, fought the tremor in his voice. "I'd ask for dope if I didn't know where she kept it."

Eva laughed, and then so did Tommy.

"I don't smell urine this time." Tommy sniffed the air. "I smell fear. You smell it, Eva?"

"I can smell it, Daddy."

Tommy tapped William's kneecap with the bat. "You asking about me around town?"

William didn't deny it.

"You carry a torch for a skirt from the streets. Isn't that right, William McFee?"

How much do they know? "What do you want with me?"

"Do you believe in this Potter's Field Christ?" Tommy's hash marks glistened in the macabre light.

"Left or the right, Boss?" William understood now. *One scar for every kill.*

"I believe in God," continued Tommy. "So deeply it makes me weep. I believe in this Potter's Field Christ. I believe your sister's legs are healed because of Asher Keating. Do you know how I know? Because I believe in signs. That man you found dead on Rose Island. The body you discovered facedown in the mud. Dooly McDowell."

Here we go. His ribs throbbed.

"That day dredged up negative press about me. It had died down, but that day rekindled it. And now the Feds are breathing down my neck. Would you believe it if I told you I once wanted that man dead? Dooly McDowell. He put me behind bars and then walked free. And you found him dead." Tommy smiled. "I don't believe in coincidences, William. I never met your grandfather, but I heard he took it pretty hard when they locked up his houses. And then he did the dance from the Twisted Tree." Tommy tapped William's chest with the bat. "Your father. Is he not the master distiller now?"

William nodded.

"Barley McFee. Is that his name?"

William nodded again. Sharp pains shot across his chest.

"I never met him either, I'm afraid. Perhaps I should go up to the main house now and introduce myself. Congratulate him on restarting Old Sam. Thank him for allowing me to visit this Potter's Field Christ. Huh?"

Eva lit a cigarette. The three men behind her stood still as statues.

Tommy tapped William's right shoulder. "I noticed the suited men with guns on your porch."

"The protestors—"

"Yes, I know, they can be most brutal." Tommy slammed the bat down against the floor and William jumped. "But we digress. Back to the signs and this dead man found on Rose Island. I once prayed for his death, William. I told Christ, on my knees, 'Just this one more. I'll give this man what's owed to him and wash my hands of crime.' And there he was, dead. I'd only recently found Christ, and He was already keeping me on the straight and narrow. I had to see the grave of this Potter's Field Christ. We prayed over that cross. And tell him, Eva, what we felt."

"The power of Jesus."

"Yes, the power of Jesus Christ," Tommy said. "Felt it coursing through my veins like Edison's current. I knew it was real. The hairs on my arms and legs stood on end. I baptized myself in the river that evening, from the rocks of the Devil's Backbone, and cried as the water trickled down my face."

Tommy snapped, and Eva immediately stood from her chair so he could sit. He rested both palms on the bottom end of the bat, propping the barrel tip against the floor. Eva slithered behind him and draped her arms around his shoulders. She kissed his neck. "You're so warm, Daddy. I can feel the power moving through you even now."

William watched her slender fingers move up and down Tommy's thigh.

Tommy said, "I read about that woman Bethany. I wept for that poor woman. Then she wouldn't give me two words. But she talked to you. You are the conduit, William. Do you see?"

"I'm only a journalist—"

"At the grave I heard a voice. It told me to repent. And I did. I cleansed myself in the waters of my sins. It told me to go forth and spread the word. And that's what I plan to do."

"Your sister doesn't believe you can change."

"My sister is a witch."

"Have you ever wondered?" William took a chance. "Why you two are so different?"

Tommy's face softened. "You know she came out first. Her face was blue. The umbilical cord was wrapped around her neck." Tommy laughed. "Maybe I tried to kill her—tried to wrap that cord around her neck even as we lived together in the uterus. And so we come to the main purpose of our conversation this evening."

Is that what this is? A conversation?

"You will write about how I've changed since I allowed Christ in my life. God has forgiven all of my past transgressions. I wish to be left alone to spread the word."

"You think it will stop the authorities from looking for you?"

"Don't be a fool. Of course it won't. But you'll say I made a journey to Jerusalem. A pilgrimage of sorts. I can divert the bulls from my scent and begin anew."

"Is that where you're going?"

"Don't test me." He pointed to his thugs. "Not all of us have been baptized. I expect our interview in tomorrow's paper."

"The scars?" William looked into Tommy's eyes. "How many have you killed?"

Tommy pointed to his left cheek. "The first was an accident when I was fifteen. Not an accident that I pierced his heart with a knife but an accident that my face got clipped by his. Right here on the cheek. So it became a ritual." Tommy removed his jacket. "Count them yourself."

There were at least a dozen on each side of his face. "Which is for Dooly McDowell?"

"Seeing as I didn't kill him, there isn't one. But I would have cut off an ear to put him in his grave." Tommy was unbuttoning his shirt. "Look upon me."

Tommy's chest was slashed with so many inch-long scars they'd be nearly impossible to count. Running parallel and perpendicular, north to south, east to west, diagonally and at tangents across his pectorals and abdominals, up around his powerful shoulders; and then he turned to reveal the same across his entire back. Some looked fresh.

William averted his eyes, fought back the urge to vomit.

Tommy slipped his shirt back on and tucked it into his pants, making room for Eva to approach William's chair. She sat on William's lap, straddling his waist, and gripped his face, forcing him to stare into her baby blue eyes. "You will do exactly as he says." She kissed his forehead. Her breath smelled of smoke. Her lips were soft.

"You've recently found first love," she said, pinning him

harder against the seat back, holding his face straight in her hands. "What a shame it would be for her to find these pictures."

One of Tommy's men had a camera and William flinched when it flashed.

She kissed his mouth, then moved to his right ear and licked the lobe. She caught the lobe between her teeth and bit down hard.

William screamed and Eva stood, wiping blood from her mouth. She spat. He dry heaved and wheezed. Tommy had left the room, and now his men were sliding out into the darkness like rats, one after the next. And then finally Eva, after she'd whispered for him "not to tell," straightened her tight skirt and disappeared into the night.

William touched his ear and his fingers came back bloody. He hobbled to the open door and leaned against the frame. Then he labored down from the porch and made his way through the woods toward the main house. With each step taken, the throb in his ribs increased and his ear had taken on a beat of its own.

But his wounded ear, he now realized as screams filled the woods and Klansmen thundered by on horseback brandishing torches, was the least of his worries.

The distillery was on fire.

TWENTY-THREE

Through thick, billowing smoke William made out Max and Mr. Browder. Their faces were masks of rage. Max gripped a shovel and looked eager to use it. The near corner of the distillation house was blackened and smoldering. Twelve Klansmen circled on horseback; three held torches that flickered and hissed through the breeze-blown smoke.

"Get on back to the cornfield," one of the officers said. "Go on."

"We'll burn the distillery down first," said one Klansman, his voice muffled by fabric.

"Don't do it," said one of the policemen, aiming his rifle.

"Christ ain't no Negro," said another. "Ain't I right?"

The surrounding crowd watched, transfixed.

Then a bullet knocked him off his horse.

"Get the hell off my property," Barley snarled, firing his rifle again into the air. He was flanked on both sides by his four armed men. Behind him William saw his mother, keeping a close grip on Johnny.

The Klansman closest to Asher's grave tossed his torch. Asher's cross was immediately engulfed in flames. The horses whinnied, and one got so spooked he flipped his rider.

William sprinted across the potter's field, screaming, his ribs and his ear forgotten. He removed his shirt and started thwacking Asher's cross with it until the flames died.

Behind him was an all-out brawl. Three of the officers were on the ground; one was getting trampled by a panicked horse. Barley used the butt of his rifle, and Max was in there with the shovel, swinging and connecting but also taking hits. Mr. Browder was easily knocked down by a blow to the back of his head. Then Barley was on his knees, and William was leveled by a blind punch on his left. Two hands clasped his neck, and he recognized the eyes. The knowing gave him strength. He head-butted the man, gripped the hood, and revealed Lulu Bancroft.

And then the crowd parted as Tommy Borduchi emerged from the trees.

Tommy was followed by his three goons. He immediately began swinging his bat with complete control, connecting knock-out blows. He doubled a Klansman with a shot to the gut and then broke his face with a swift upward swing.

Barley grabbed a pipe and used it to knock another Klansman to the ground. Klansmen fell; several attempted to crawl away; the horses had fled.

Bancroft was one of the crawlers. William allowed him the brief freedom of ten feet before stepping on his back. Bancroft looked up at William, pleaded for his life. William leaned down. "Advice? Don't needle Barley McFee."

Bancroft made it to his feet and ran back toward the woods.

In the middle of the potter's field, Barley stood with a pipe in his hands next to Tommy and his Louisville Slugger. Around them were clusters of wounded men. Smoke from the smoldering fire floated like a fallen cloud. Barley looked at Tommy Borduchi and offered his hand. Tommy stared at Barley's hand, then Barley's face.

TWENTY-FOUR

D o you think he recognized you?"

After he washed Eva's scent and the night's blood away in a warm bath, William had wrapped his chest tightly and bandaged the lower portion of his right ear. He found Barley in the kitchen, drinking straight from the bottle. They had spoken to the police, the wounded had been removed, and the rest of the house was finally sleeping.

"I know he did." Barley was cut and bruised but he wore it well, and only winced when he took a drink. They both stared out the window. New policemen had been posted on all four corners, and Barley's men were back at their posts.

"Do you believe he's found the Lord?"

"I don't know." Barley took another drink. "Where's Polly? I assume you don't want her alone tonight."

"She's safe. Staying with John Swell and his boy. But she's not one to scare easily."

"You did good tonight." He handed the bottle to William.

William nodded, sloshed the bourbon. It was half full. He

followed Barley into the living room, toward the stairwell. "Where you going?"

Barley stopped with his hand on the rail. "To bed."

William looked at the recliner chair and the couch.

"With your mother." Barley winked.

William wrote all night.

He left for the city before his parents came downstairs for breakfast, and twenty minutes later he stood in the *Courier-Journal* building. Mr. Crone was stunned. He questioned him for an hour and then urged him to have his ear checked by a doctor and to try to get some sleep.

William promised to do both and drove directly home.

Barley and Samantha were working together inside the distillation house, where Max was replacing the scorched boards. William waited on the porch for Polly, remembering what she'd told him Asher had said the morning after Henry's death. *"I tried to stop him."*

When she didn't appear, William grew worried. He questioned each of Barley's guards and none of them had seen Polly all morning. "Keep an eye out," he told them, "and make sure my brother and sister don't go into the woods today." Just as William started down the porch steps, Samantha approached.

"Honey, you doing okay?"

William nodded, then jerked away as she reached for his bandaged ear. "It's fine, Mother. Stings." Despite the horror of the previous night, she glowed. "You?"

"Yesterday I was doing the dishes," she said. "The dog was

curled at my feet. Your father, he walked into the kitchen. He said, 'Do you want to go out?' I knew he was talking to the dog, but I said, 'Sure, Barley, I'd love to go out tonight.' He stood there, shocked, I think. He said, in perfect Barley McFee fashion, 'Well, okay then.'"

"And so you went out."

"And so we went out," said Samantha. "We had a wonderful dinner. And ice cream. We went to the picture show and watched *Stand Up and Cheer!* With that lovely little Shirley Temple, who completely stole the show, and your father actually sat through it all without complaining. He even took me dancing afterward. He was a fine dancer when we were first courting. Hasn't lost too much. But then he said we needed to leave. Felt like something wasn't right at the distillery."

"Good thing he showed when he did."

"I suppose so."

"Does he know? That *you* know he was talking to the dog?"

"I don't know, William. Does it matter?"

He looked out over the distillation and fermentation houses, looking for Polly but remembering the sounds from his parents' bedroom last night. "No, I guess it doesn't."

A minute later Polly emerged through the trees, walking fast.

William waited with Polly inside a sterile room with no windows, and fifteen minutes later Preston Wildemere took his seat and rested his cuffed hands on the tabletop. He didn't look any better than the last time.

William said, "You saw Asher carry my brother off the road. Was my brother still alive?"

"He was still alive."

"How could you tell?"

"He knelt over the boy." Wildemere scratched his chin and his cuffs rattled. "Said something to him. I saw your brother nod, then reach his arms up to be held. Asher held him. Then he put your brother down and rested his arms on his chest. He was crying."

William tightened his jaw.

"Took the shoes off his feet. Real respectful. One and then the other. Hung them around his neck. Then he looked at me." Wildemere buried his forehead in his hands. "Your dad. When he came to . . . I'll never forget his wailing when he saw the boy. That's the sound that keeps me up at night."

"Mr. Wildemere," Polly said. "I saw Asher the morning after the accident. He said something. 'I tried to stop him.' He said it twice. 'I tried to stop him.'"

William asked, "Who did he try to stop?"

"Me," Wildemere said softly, looking up. "He tried to stop me." He looked at William. "About a quarter mile before the accident, I came up fast on a man standing in the middle of the road. It was so dark. I had to slam the brakes. I rolled down the window and yelled he was going to get himself run over. He looked at me like he'd seen me before. Asked if I knew who he was. I said I didn't. He said he was Asher Keating, like it should somehow matter to me. It didn't, so I gave him the hinky eye and started to coast along. But then he tried to talk me out of the car. Walked right along with it. Said I wasn't fit to be behind the wheel. But I didn't listen. He grabbed my side mirror, like he was going to stop me, but I was too drunk for reasoning. I thought he was a lunatic. Just another lunatic walking near Lakeland. They escape all the time. It's a lunatic asylum."

"I know what it is," said William. "It's four miles from Twisted Tree."

"That's where Asher said he was going. He was on his way to visit his mother."

TWENTY-FIVE

⁘

Central Kentucky Asylum for the Insane, formerly known as Lakeland Asylum, rested in seclusion, nestled between acres of water maples and evergreens. Dr. Givens, a white-haired gentleman with thick eyebrows and outdated muttonchops, looked overwhelmed but relieved, for the moment, to be outside, where the air was crisp, and the sun was warm. "We're carrying twenty-four hundred patients but only have room for sixteen."

Patients working on the grounds gathered leaves onto carts. He showed William and Polly to a wooden picnic table that bordered the egg-shaped lake that had once given the asylum its name. Ducks skimmed the surface, picking at the reeds, immune—as were the lunatics—to whistles from the nearby train depot.

"Maryanne Keating rarely has visitors; in fact, her son was the only person to see her. About once a month. But when he came," said Dr. Givens, "she liked to visit at this table, which was where I preferred they talk as well. The few times he went inside caused too much of a disturbance for the other patients."

"How so?" asked William.

"They grew overly excited. I don't know how to explain it really."

Polly asked, "Have you read the newspapers lately?"

"What I've read is quite consistent with my thoughts on the man."

"Which are?" Polly asked, taking offense.

"That he was delusional. And that he inherited his mother's unfortunate illness. She's what we call schizophrenic. She's suffered a splitting of the mind—"

"Asher was not mentally ill," Polly interrupted. "I knew him well."

William asked, "How do you explain his miracles, then?"

"Timely coincidences?"

"You're wrong." William shook his head. "Every person we meet has a story."

Dr. Givens said, "Was Asher hearing voices? Abusing drugs and alcohol? Having grand delusions? Did he exhibit disorganized thinking and speech? Social withdrawal, poor hygiene, sloppiness of dress? All symptoms of schizophrenia."

"You're wrong, Doctor."

Dr. Givens was professional enough not to argue with Polly, especially when patients roamed freely and liked to eavesdrop. Several had come closer to rake grass that had clearly been raked.

"Forgive me. I've upset you," said Dr. Givens. "That was not my intention. I only mean to prepare you for Miss Keating. You may ask about the weather and she'll answer with her views on abortion or insist scaly brown creatures are trying to kill her with kitchen appliances. I'll be back out with her in a few moments. Please enjoy the surroundings until I return. Our work-out patients take great pride in the grounds here."

"You said Miss Keating. Was she not married?" asked William.

"To our knowledge, Miss Keating never married."

As soon as the doctor was out of earshot, Polly said, "He's wrong. I mean, what he says is true. But he's wrong too. Why does he think Asher excited the patients? Because they *knew*. They could *tell*."

"Asylums have been steering lunatics away from religion for decades."

Tall maples partially concealed the Tudor revival façade, but the checkered brick-and-stone edifice was visible, as were the twin turrets and white-painted porch. Flowering trellises and colorful perennial beds flanked adjacent sidewalks. The American flag rippled from a pole.

Dr. Givens escorted a petite elderly woman with long silvery hair wearing a sky-blue uniform across the grounds. She couldn't have weighed more than a hundred pounds.

William squinted. "Are those hand muffs? Why would they need to muff such a tiny woman?" As she sat across the table from them, his first thought was: *Asher Keating's father must have been a giant.*

William and Polly introduced themselves and waited for Dr. Givens to give them privacy. The doctor leaned against a nearby tree to review charts and spy over his clipboard.

"Miss Keating, I was close to your son." Polly reached across the table. "I believed in him. Do you understand what I'm telling you? That I believed in him?"

"The bearded man came up from the core and plucked his eyes out." Her voice was thin but clear, still molded by an Irish accent.

"Do you understand what's happened to him?"

"He's dead, if that's what you mean." She nodded. "I was told that much by Mr. Boy over there." She glanced at Dr. Givens. "Asher has moved on, but not away. The bearded man killed him, didn't he? Asher told me the bearded man had been following him. Watching him. Was it him?" She looked at Dr. Givens and raised her restrained hands, hidden by what looked like oven mitts. "I need to scratch my nose. Do you know how hard it is to scratch my nose with these on?"

"What did you do?" William asked. "To have those put on you."

Dr. Givens spoke from the tree. "She tried to scratch an attendant's eye out."

Polly and William looked at each other.

"I no longer need medication," said Miss Keating. "I am no longer mentally ill."

Dr. Givens said, "She has moments of clarity. Don't let it fool you."

"Only fools get fooled by fools. How long have I been in this place, Mr. Boy?"

Dr. Givens stepped away from the tree. "Twenty years, Maryanne."

"Yes, around the time my Asher turned fourteen. Or was it ten? He was alive, I know that much. The poor boy was in and out of orphanages until he enlisted. Beaten at one. Kept in a closet in another. For a month with only bread and water, mind you. He healed a young girl's leg and they accused him of being perverted, so they put him in a closet. And, Mr. Boy, have you ever known me to be this chatty and understandable?"

"This is very positive, Maryanne, which is why you should be taking—"

"Can we have our privacy back, please?"

Dr. Givens stopped. "Why, yes, of course, Maryanne." He retreated to the tree.

"Thank you." She looked at William. "Where was I? Oh yes. You believe and so do I, and I no longer have schizophrenia. Asher visited me two days ago, you know. Or maybe it was three. But he put his hands on my head and told it to be at peace. He commanded it. I was sure he was a delusion, as Mr. Boy over there would have me believe, but I felt the weight of the Holy Spirit on my hair, so it had to be true. And I would have touched him back had I not been bound by these dang oven mitts. But they didn't rake the leaves, and so act one was a disaster," she whispered. "And then the brown men with scales tried to rip that man's nipples off with a soup spoon."

"You see?" said Dr. Givens.

William ignored him. "You believe your son came to you after his death?"

She leaned forward, pounded her bound hands on the table. "He visits me every night. And what is it you want from me, Junior? Why can't he heal himself? Did Jesus Christ heal Himself on the cross? No, He most certainly did not. Although He could have had He wanted to."

William asked, "Miss Keating, do you know why your son wore shoes around his neck?"

"To keep warm." She banged the table again, unraveling before their eyes.

"Miss Keating." William hated seeing the illness take over. "Your son had my brother's—"

"Keep your hands off of me, you monster," she hissed at William. "I'll run this knife from throat to belly. You will not treat me like cattle. Only he has ever touched me there, and no one shall ever touch me again. I'm with child and you force me into steerage with the wolves? With a bastard in my belly! How dare you!" Miss Keating was screaming now, startling the other patients. "Stay away from me. All of you. *Stay away from my baby!*"

Three attendants corralled her, one for each arm and the third grabbed her feet. But they were delicate in how they lifted her. They'd done it many times before, William could tell. She was crying when they carried her away.

"He wore them to make sure," Maryanne Keating shouted back to them. Her voice faded into the wind that circled the lake.

"I'm sorry you had to witness that," said Dr. Givens. "Perhaps it was a mistake to allow visitors this close to her son's passing."

Miss Keating's last words, *"He wore them to make sure,"* replayed in William's mind. "Please give Miss Keating our apologies," William said.

Polly touched the doctor's arm. "Dr. Givens. Her words were not senseless. She feared for her life when she was pregnant. She said only he has touched her there, and no one shall ever touch her again. She referred to the baby as a bastard."

"What do you know of Asher's father?" William asked.

"Very little, I'm afraid." Dr. Givens paused. "She came over on a steamer from Ireland, with no male companion. Full term and alone. From what I've gathered she was running away from something. Someone perhaps. But I've learned not to venture too deep into Miss Keating's past. It's not a pleasant place to go."

"Was Asher born on the steamer?" Polly asked.

"No. But soon thereafter. It was a White Star Line ship from Liverpool. Twelve days at sea. Docked at East River pier. From there the steerage and third-class passengers were transported by ferry to Ellis Island for legal and medical inspection. That's where she gave birth to Asher. On the floor of the Registry Room at Ellis Island, the Great Hall, they called it, right there in New York Harbor."

"Immigrants without a home," William said, thinking aloud.

"Yes," Dr. Givens said, as the likeness to Christ's birth dawned on William. "Yes indeed."

"Doctor, when was Asher born?"

"In October, I believe, 1901. Why?"

William's knees buckled as sweat broke out across his brow. "Same age."

"Same age?"

"Asher," said William. "He and Jesus. They were both thirty-three when they died."

<hr />

Barley was smoking on the porch steps when they returned from the asylum. William approached, having prepared how to tell him what they'd learned from Wildemere and Maryanne Keating.

"He finally dug deep enough." Barley stood and forced a newspaper into William's chest.

William unfolded the *Post* to the latest Bancroft article. Hidden Identity Revealed. Barley McFee Is Dooly McDowell.

Barley showed a cool lack of concern. "Three Klansmen invaded one of our hidden warehouses back in '26. Tried to set fire to our inventory. Me and the Micks were there. It got bloody; mostly theirs. Bottom line is the Klansmen died and they were friends of Bancroft. He's been looking for dirt ever since."

"That's why he started snooping around our church?"

"And your mother."

"You knew about that?"

Barley nodded. "I like to keep my enemies close."

"Wait . . . Are you saying Mother knew too?"

"She knew what Bancroft was doing. She knew what not to say."

William skimmed the article. Bancroft revealed that Barley McFee had lived an alternate life during Prohibition, the life of the recently found dead man on Rose Island, Dooly McDowell. Two pictures were displayed next to the text: one of Dooly's identification and the other a more recent photo of Barley punching the racist drunk man in the woods.

William lowered the paper, handed it to Polly, who began reading. "You think this could bring him back? Borduchi?"

Barley exhaled cigarette smoke. "He looked me clear in the eyes, William. He knows."

"And claims a fresh start."

Barley dropped the cigarette to the gravel and squashed it with his shoe. "Can't trust a man with that many scars." Barley turned toward the front steps. William and Polly followed him into the house, nodding to the guard on the porch just as Barley had done.

William closed the door.

Barley removed his hat, placed it on the table next to his recliner, and reached for his bottle of Old Forester.

Polly looked into the dining room and let out a quick scream. William and Barley turned to find a curly-haired man dressed in full military uniform sitting at the dining room table with his arms folded and a pistol on his lap, waiting.

"I came in through the back door. House was empty."

The man lit a cigarette and exhaled toward the ceiling. His brown hair was a corkscrew bushel, his eyes dark marbles.

"You don't find him; he finds you." William asked, "Oliver Sanscrit?"

The man nodded. "William McFee."

Barley said, "We've been looking for you."

"I know. I've been following you."

<hr />

The four of them sat at the dining room table to talk.

Oliver Sanscrit was a private detective, budding, he said after thinking on it. His true profession was lawyer. He "only dabbled in the clandestine." (*"How did I get past the guards? I told them who I was."*) He admitted that on many levels he didn't exist, and that he'd done his due diligence and knew more about William and Barley than he probably should.

"How close were you and Asher?" William asked.

Sanscrit gulped his steaming coffee like water after a hot day in the fields. "Friends, I'd say, although we were not without our squabbles. About whether or not he should be in the asylum."

"And you decided not?"

"I decided it wasn't my decision."

"As his legal counsel?" Barley said.

"I only give advice. He had enough believers down to the very core, gentlemen, who would have run me out of town on a pike had I continued to pursue it. But I was acting out of love. I feared for his life. There was a growing number who wished him dead."

William asked, "When was the last time you saw him?"

"Four weeks ago, perhaps five." Sadness crept into Sanscrit's face. "He was never afraid to die, but he did fear dying alone."

Polly said, "I was with him, Mr. Sanscrit. He didn't die alone."

Sanscrit finished his cigarette, smashed the butt against the tabletop. "I've seen you."

Polly said, "And I've seen you."

William waited for the quick give-and-take to expand, but it didn't. Sanscrit wasn't one to embellish. "Why did he not have protection?"

"He didn't believe he needed it. He believed he was some-thing, but he didn't believe he was *that*. Others put that on him, the stuff about him being Jesus. The last argument I had with him was about just that—protection. He gave me a lecture on loving thine enemies. His apostles . . ." Sanscrit rubbed his temples, gave Polly another glance. "He didn't call them that, but they did. They created a ring that made him a little less vulnerable." Sanscrit fin-ished his coffee, stared out the window, watching the potter's field and Asher's charred cross. "Is that it?"

"It is," William said. "The visitors are allowed five minutes."

Sanscrit slid the empty coffee cup between his hands. "I miss him."

Barley removed a bourbon flask from his vest. He offered it to Sanscrit, who declined. "Asher ended up with my dead son's shoes. Why did he wear shoes around his neck?"

Sanscrit smiled, scoffed at the same time. "We met as Marines, in training. Became friends overseas. When we returned home, we made a pact not to let what we'd lived through change who we were. Made a pact to get real jobs and become successful mem-bers of society. I thought Asher was on a good path at Ford. Cars were booming. But then . . . he started talking."

"About?"

"About God. About Jesus, the Bible. He'd always been reverent, holier than whoever was around. It wasn't in a condescending way. It's just the way he was. Very soft-spoken for a man his size. He wore a cross around his neck, on the outside of his uniform. Kissed it before he went into battle. Kissed it when he closed his eyes at night. Some of the men called him Father Keating, jokingly, you know, but he was honored. He was comfortable with who he was."

"And who was he?" William asked.

"Just a man. A man who did some things that defied logic or explanation, but just a man. He did his business in the trenches like the rest of us. He took to the streets after he left Ford. I tried for years to get him other jobs, but he refused. He lost the apartment he'd been living in. I offered for him to stay with me until he could get back on his feet. 'Am I not already standing, Oliver?' He kissed me on both cheeks and went back to the hovels and coke ovens, back alleys and street corners, sleeping under bridges. I offered him money. 'Give it to those in need, Oliver.' That's what he'd tell me as he stood there in rags, clothes that smelled of filth. 'Give it to those in need.' I stood as his lawyer on three separate occasions when he was arrested for being stoned. There were other times he was arrested for stealing food in order to feed the poor. The food didn't appear out of a hat, gentlemen."

"You're not a believer?"

"Do you truly believe Jesus caused the blind to see? Turned water into wine? You lived the horror of the war, Barley. Any hope of God that I had was left overseas."

"Yet you survived," Barley said. "And my little girl went from crippled to walking."

"Believe in something wholeheartedly and your mind can make it so."

"My mind had nothing to do with it." Barley pointed at Sanscrit. "He declined your every offer of help. Yet you remained steadfast. Why the obligation to him?"

"Because I owed him my life. We all did. I would do anything for Asher Keating."

"Quit running around the barn then," Barley said. "And start helping us."

Sanscrit slid his empty coffee mug toward Barley, who added a shot. "We were a fresh unit. Full strength at ten thousand men. In late May of 1918, Germany's Spring Offensive penetrated the Western Front. They'd reached to within forty-five miles of Paris, dangerously close to the Reims. General Black Jack Pershing ordered a counteroffensive on June 6 to drive the Krauts out of the Belleau Wood, a former hunting preserve northwest of the Paris-to-Metz. By the time we arrived it was a jungle of cut-up fields and half-blown trees, and the French had begun to retreat. There was a suggestion that the Marines join them. One of our captains shouted retreat. Retreat? Hell, we just got there!

"Black Jack Pershing was known for costly frontal assaults, but he won battles. Under Pershing's order, General Harbord led the Second Division Marine Corps against four German divisions. We first captured the ridge overlooking Torcy and Belleau Wood. But our men missed a regiment of Kraut infantry, a dug-in network of artillery and machine-gun nests. Taking Hill 142, the First Battalion lost nine officers, and of three hundred–plus men, most got cut to pieces. We continued across an open wheat field stained with blood, every inch covered by Kraut machine-gun fire. Men dropped left and right. Those who made it through were immediately engaged in hand-to-hand combat.

"We'd never lost so many men in one day. I was grazed on my left shoulder. Hit again in my right thigh. Asher made it through unscathed. He never shot to kill. He'd blow off arms if he needed to, but I never saw him go for the kill shot. On his run through that field, he didn't fire a bullet. Didn't even lift his gun. Just ran. Ran through the field like it was some Olympic race and he came out clean."

Sanscrit drank the bourbon fast. Barley refilled without being asked. "Once the shock of being shot wore off, I realized a hot shell casing had landed inside my right boot, and my ankle was on fire. I unlaced that boot as bullets zipped overhead. And when I got that one off, I unlaced the left as well. I was delirious by that point and couldn't tell which foot was burning. Asher spotted me. I shook my head no, but he ran *back* through that wheat field! Lifted me on his shoulders. He saw my boots. He squatted down with my weight across his back, tied the boots together, and draped them over his neck. He ran with me toward the woods. Men were dropping all around us, cut up with machine-gun fire, but we didn't get touched.

"He placed me on the ground, surveyed the carnage, and then took off running. Came back a minute later with another soldier and placed him beside me. Kid had his arm blown off and was half out of his wits. His eyes weren't focused, looked like he was seeing something magical that nobody else could see.

"'Walked on the shoulders of angels,' the boy said to me. 'Walked on the shoulders of angels . . .' Then he closed his eyes and died. Asher crossed that field all day long, my boots bouncing against his chest. He carried at least a hundred wounded men to the tree line. Most lived to see the next day."

Sanscrit shook his head. "That night I thanked him. He just smiled. The most peaceful smile I'd ever seen. Jerry Jones, another man from our unit, was one Asher carried. Had his left knee blown. Came over on crutches. Asher still had my boots around his neck. Jerry handed over his, already tied at the laces.

"After that, it became a thing. The wounded gave Asher their boots while they convalesced. For good luck, you see. They wanted to walk on the shoulders of angels. If Asher wore their boots, even for a night, it would protect them. That's what they believed. And dang if most of those boys didn't make it back home. We expelled the Germans from Belleau Wood after twenty days of fighting, and we captured the villages of Vaux and Bouresche. Belleau Wood and the Battle of Château-Thierry ended the last major German offensive. The French renamed the wood *Bois de la Brigade de Marine*."

Barley said, "Wood of the Marine Brigade."

"In honor of how fiercely we fought over those three weeks."

"You earned the name Devil Dogs."

Sanscrit nodded. "After Belleau Wood and Château-Thierry, we ended up in the battle of Saint-Mihiel. Asher entered no-man's-land like you'd go to the kitchen for a cup of water. Recovered bodies from the barbed wire and the scorched battlefield. Risked his life claiming the wounded. Did the same thing at Meuse-Argonne, Blanc Mont Ridge—every battle. If he got hit, it never clipped his skin; or if it did we never saw him bleed, although his uniform was seared with the blood of others. He received every medal of honor bestowed on a Marine."

William said, "We didn't find any medals in his bindle."

"He sold them. Used the money to buy food for the poor. He still wore shoes around his neck. But by then he only wore

those of the recently deceased. 'As an escort into heaven,' he said."
Sanscrit paused to let this sink in, like he knew exactly where it
was hitting them. "So they could walk on the shoulders of angels
for a few days. To get acquainted with things."

Polly said, "He wore Henry's shoes for months."

"That boy's death hit him hard. Rattled some things loose in
his brain."

"Why did he keep some?" William asked. "There were two
other pairs in his bindle when he died."

Sanscrit spoke like he didn't believe what he was about to say.
"He kept those that belonged to the ones who were extra touched
by God. Whatever that meant."

"Then who did the other shoes in the bindle belong to?" Polly
asked.

Sanscrit shrugged. "Mind if I use your bathroom?"

William knocked after twenty minutes but didn't get an
answer. He opened the door to find the window was open. He
returned to the living room, and Barley pointed out the window
toward Asher's grave.

Sanscrit's boots dangled over the horizontal arm of the
charred cross.

TWENTY-SIX

The heavy barrel shot out of the distillation house like a bullet. Barley walked along one side, his son's shoes dangling around his neck, and William accompanied it on the other. They'd learned all they could about Henry's shoes, and the finality of it made him melancholy. He'd been shadowing Barley most of the day. They hadn't spoken about Sanscrit's visit, but they had shared a brief look at Henry's grave that said they were ready to move on.

The crowd in the whiskey trees hadn't diminished since the fighting, though the protestors had stopped chanting and the KKK had evacuated.

William wanted them all gone. They'd outstayed their welcome.

He looked at Asher's grave, where Sanscrit's boots dangled. Then he watched his father, the intimidating way he swung his arms as he walked. William still had questions about the night of the accident. *Why was Henry in the car?*

William gave the barrel a coaxing nudge and Barley did the same. His father's hands were thick fingered and big knuckled. How many men had those hands killed?

"Look." Barley pointed to Black-Tail, standing on hind legs.

They watched the barrel disappear into the opening on the side of the aging house. They headed for the door to reconnect with it inside, and Black-Tail darted in with them, skittering toward the back wall and hiding in the ricks.

William made sure the barrel stopped at the appointed spot at the lift. Barley moved toward where the squirrel was hiding. "William, grab that broom over there."

He grabbed it and followed Barley down the center row. They stopped at the far wall. There was a six-foot space between the last rick and a sunlit window.

"Come on out, Black-Tail. Done past makin' plans for your funeral."

Black-Tail appeared at Barley's summons, stared for a moment, and then darted between his legs. The squirrel clawed against a loose board and then backed into a corner. Barley approached with slow steps, stomped on the loose board, and Black-Tail sprinted out the open door.

"That was easier than I thought." Barley knelt down, wiggled the loose board. "William, reach me that hammer."

He grabbed the bung hammer and handed it to Barley, who had his hands inside the floor prying the board up, nails and all. A wave of angels' share emerged from the subfloor.

"There's something down there . . ."

They pried up the next board. Together they cast it aside. Light from the window shone toward the opening they had created. "It's a barrel. Holy smoke!"

They hastily ripped up the next board. It was definitely a barrel, resting on a rick inside the subfloor. They took another board up, and then another, until the opening was large enough for William to slide under the main floor. He looked up at his father. "Do you think?"

Barley took off running. He returned a minute later with a small, dented tin cup. "Bust it open. Use the hammer. But be careful!"

William was so careful his hands shook. He tapped it lightly at first, then put more muscle into it. The top board splintered. The smell of bourbon was strong. Barley was practically salivating as William pulled the stave back. The inside was blackened to near tar and rich with aroma. He pulled another stave free and peered inside. "There's bourbon in here, Father!"

"How full?"

"Looks like about a third is left."

"Do you believe this? Your grandfather hid a barrel before Prohibition."

William thought on it. "It's been aging for . . ."

"About fifteen years." Barley smiled large. "What are you waiting for? Dip the cup!"

William gave his father the first sip.

Barley nosed it, then nosed it again. He closed his eyes and took in enough to coat his tongue. "It's Old Sam, alright." He opened his eyes and they were wet with emotion. "But better. Smoother. Richer."

He handed William the cup. William nosed the bourbon. The note was strong, the vanilla and caramel tones distinct but not overpowering. He also smelled hints of spice and fruit. The oaky scent was more noticeable than anything he'd tried before.

The first taste burned but went down smooth with an abundance of flavor, and he instantly wanted more. The next he took in a gulp and didn't regret how it lit his eyes on fire.

"He always wanted to age a batch for ten years. I never had the patience." Barley shook his head. "He went and did it anyway. That's why the angels' share never left—"

"Dad. There's more barrels."

Barley gripped the next board in line and pulled until the nails bent. He yanked again and ripped it free. Together they did the next board in two pulls. There was another barrel nest-egged in a rick beside the first. From there they used their hands and feet, the broom and hammer, kicking and pulling and nudging and prying board after board.

Samantha arrived first, thinking all the noise meant they were in danger, that the ricks had collapsed. Polly arrived with Annie and Peter. Johnny hurried in with the entire Browder family, and John Swell showed with a bilge hoop still in his hand.

By that time William and Barley had ripped up every board alongside the wall, from corner to corner like an excavation site. Father and son stood side by side wearing goofy smiles and sweating profusely.

Barley looked up at Samantha. Then they all stared at the barrels, exposed like a row of dead soldiers. Fifteen barrels in all, and the bung holes all pointed to high noon.

"Old Sam. He hid them. He left a note."

Samantha's eyes glistened. "What does it say?"

"Read it, son. Go on. Read it out loud."

"It says . . ." William paused for a chuckle. "'The Prohibition agents can go dangle.'"

They all either smiled or started laughing, but then Samantha said, "That's it?"

"Signed Old Sam McFee."

<hr />

While the adults shared the fifteen-year-old bourbon, Johnny was sneaking a shot of Old Forester into each new Coke he poured. He'd begun an hour before dinner, so by the time the chicken and mashed potatoes had settled in his stomach and the plate of blueberry cobbler was placed before him on the table, he could hardly keep his head up.

William helped Johnny from the table before anyone noticed his condition. Or maybe they had noticed but were too intoxicated to care. Even Father Vincent, who had joined them, was slurring words, laughing as he retold the story of Barley firing a gun in church.

"And you know what he says to me," said Father Vincent, ruddy faced. "He says thanks!" John Swell laughed so hard he started coughing. Max, who wasn't Catholic, didn't see what was so funny. Father Vincent explained, "He was supposed to say amen! When I say, 'The Body of the Christ . . .' when I say, 'Corpus Christi,' you say . . . ?"

Max said hesitantly, "Amen?"

"Yes, my son. Not thanks." Father Vincent slapped his leg and almost fell over.

Polly was drinking Old Sam but taking her time with it, and so, along with William, was the most sober of the group, excluding Annie and John Swell's boy, who were on the floor playing cards. Mr. Browder was passed out on the couch with an empty bottle of Ghost wedged between his thighs. Carly leaned her head on Max's shoulder and hummed out of tune.

Barley stuck his hands out toward Father Vincent, as if waiting for Holy Communion. "How do you say 'Kiss my big chunky butt' in Latin?"

Without hesitation Father Vincent punched Barley's nose. Then the men drunkenly hugged, which made it okay for everyone to guffaw. Barley had been paid back for interrupting mass and putting a hole in St. Michael's stained glass window.

William got a smile from Polly as he half dragged Johnny to the stairs. He motioned for her help, and together they walked his brother upstairs to his bedroom. They plopped him on the mattress and Polly tucked him in. She walked around the foot of the bed and held her hands out to William, who leaned down and kissed her lips, enticed by the taste of bourbon on her breath. She kissed him harder.

"William, have you seen Johnny?" Samantha called from the bottom of the stairs.

They both froze. Polly bit William's lip to stymie his laughter.

He pulled his lip free with a pop, which made him laugh. "He's in bed, Mom." Polly licked his left ear; the right one was still bandaged.

"What are you doing up there?" Samantha asked.

"Johnny isn't feeling well, Mrs. McFee," Polly said, her neckline flushed. "We helped him up into bed."

"Thank you, dear. William, come on down. Your father wants to make a toast to your grandfather."

"On our way," William said.

Polly tiptoed to kiss his lips. "Later?"

He nodded, kissed her back. "Yes, later."

<hr />

Barley grew paranoid as the night drew on. By nine o'clock he began rushing people out the door, and for the most part the guests were too intoxicated to be offended. Father Vincent was only halfway finished with his third piece of cobbler when Barley took his plate.

"You can stay in one of the cottages tonight, Father." Barley walked him to the porch. "You're in no condition to drive back to the church."

Father didn't object; he was still looking at his empty hand where the cobbler plate had been. Carly aided Father Vincent out the door.

Barley patted Max on the shoulder. "Time to go." He found Mr. Browder snoring with his head on the dining room table. He nudged him. Ronald snorted awake, asked if it was morning. Polly offered to walk him back to his cottage and said she was ready for bed. She smiled at William and said good night. He couldn't tell if that was code for seeing him later.

After everyone had departed, Barley locked the front door.

"Barley, what is it?" Samantha asked.

He turned, kissed her on the lips. "Nothing. Early to rise. We need to start bottling what we found under the floorboards. First thing in the morning."

Samantha kissed him back, rubbing the palm of her right hand against his chest, which reminded William of how Polly had touched him hours ago. He knew that work wasn't the reason Barley ended the party—the bourbon had worn off enough for him to remember his face in the *Post*. William checked all the doors in the house. When he returned, Samantha had already taken Annie up to bed, and Barley stood with the Machete next to the window.

"Go on up, William."

William stretched out on his bed and stared at the whorls in the ceiling as the wall clock ticked toward the next hour. Every thought returned him to Polly's lips, the feel of her fingers inside his belt line, and the look in her eyes when she'd said, *"Later."*

His bedroom door opened around midnight. Disappointingly, Barley entered. He wasn't drunk, but he didn't look altogether sober. William sat up, worried about the foreboding tilt of Barley's shoulders and the urgency with which he closed the door.

Barley sat at William's desk, placed his rifle next to the typewriter. "Eventually Old Sam ran out, William, but we were in too deep to get out. The Micks were in charge of a distribution system that couldn't be shut down, not without some blood spilled. Our initial problem was with Tommy; he caught wind of what we'd been doing. And this is where Rose Island comes into play. Tommy loved the place. He had four kids with his first wife, who he divorced and had killed, and Rose Island was where he liked to take them for fun. He had the run of the place, even after closing hours. So any liquor that needed to be hidden, it was stored at Rose Island, in the hotel, the summer cottages, buried.

"Tommy scheduled a meeting one night for all the thugs and crime bosses we sold to. Capone came down from Chicago. Like I said, Tommy suspected us; we weren't distributors for him, remember. We were hijack men and runners. But the men in the room that night knew us as distributors because that's what we were doing behind Tommy's back. The buyers were surprised to see us all in the same room. Tommy wanted to see their reactions. He wanted it to turn into a bloodbath. He had his men ready to bury all four of us.

"What I didn't know was that Fop McDougal had been contacted by Prohibition agents. They'd been following him for months, and to save his own hide he said he could get them Tommy Borduchi. Fop asked for immunity for all the Micks. It was granted—as long as we got them Tommy the Bat and his right-hand man, Big Bang Tony."

"Left or the right, Boss?" Sweat spread across William's brow and he felt clammy. "Why did you just watch him?" He blurted the words as if from a long-dormant volcano.

"Watch who?"

"At our old house. In the garage. Tommy beat that man to death and you watched! And then Big Bang Tony, he said, 'Left or the right, Boss?' And then he cut Tommy's cheek."

"What are you talking about?"

"I was there." William swung his feet from the bed. "I was seven." He walked to the window. "You were home early. I followed you to the garage. I looked inside the window and I saw it all. Why didn't you help him?"

Barley looked stunned. "Because he'd done Tommy wrong. He lied."

"What was his name?"

"Cranston? Creighton? I don't know."

"You don't know?"

Barley shook his head. "And I don't know what he lied about. We were fresh fish, and Tommy wanted to show us what would happen if we ever crossed him. His way of feeling me out. Checking my loyalty. Letting me know he could end me and my family. I can't believe you saw it." He startled. "Tommy said he saw a face up in the window. I didn't believe him."

"It was me. I pushed it way down deep. But it came out in flashes over the years. Came out in gushes of sweat and me flinching every time you gutted a deer. It's why I don't like to see things bleed. Saw too much of it on the garage floor."

Barley stood from the desk. "William . . ."

"And when he got me inside our own cottages? His shirt was off, and he's got hundreds of scars. 'Left or the right, Boss?' Left or the right? You should have seen the way he looked at me. Like he knew it was me up in that window. I was seven." William stared into the night. "She *bit* part of my *ear* off."

"I'm sorry." Barley's breath moved William's hair, and then William felt his father's arms around him. He resisted at first but then turned into the bourbon-scented warmth of his embrace. William pulled Barley against his chest, not worried about what he looked like or what others would think, because none of it mattered. He cried on his father's shoulder, cried until he'd had his share. Then he sucked in a deep breath. "You were saying?"

"I don't remember."

"Rose Island. The meeting."

Barley wiped his hands across his face. "Doesn't even sound important anymore."

"I want to know."

Barley nodded. "There were two undercover agents posing as buyers with deep pockets, new distribution lines from Newport. They offered up their guns before our Bruno patted them down—they had backup waiting north of the Devil's

Backbone. Whiskey was flowing directly from the barrels and everyone in the room had had too much of it. Tommy exposed us. His men moved in with bean-shooters. The doors crashed open and the Prohib agents moved in. It got bloody fast; two agents died. I escaped with two Micks. Tommy got out with Big Bang, and they took Fop McDougal with them. We heard later that Tommy beat him to within an inch of his life, fit him with concrete shoes, and sunk him into the Ohio, still breathing. The agents caught up to Tommy and Big Bang the next day, arrested them. Big Bang got a fast track to the chair. Tommy got life without parole."

"Did the agents come after you?"

"We stayed away from the crosshairs for months to make it appear that we'd gone clean. But Gio and Tad weren't finished making money, and they weren't going to let me out so easily. Truth is, I also saw the money that could be made. And we wanted to stick it to the government. Gio took over Tommy's pharmacies and the bootlegging went on. I made three million dollars during the twenties, William."

William's jaw dropped.

"If anything should happen to me, your mom knows where it's kept. Make sure the distillery survives. And you run it."

"Dad, don't talk like that—"

Barley patted William on the shoulder and headed for the door, but he stopped just before clutching the knob. When he turned, his eyes were wet. "I *was* drinking that night, William. The night of the accident. The other Micks were dead. I was closing out my last line. My last delivery. I intended to wash my hands of it all. It was supposed to be easy. It would have been easy. A hundred bottles packed in four fruit crates that fit in the trunk.

Except one crate I put in the passenger's seat. Easy drop on the back porch of a fruit market. In and out. Wouldn't even have to turn the car off."

Barley tightened his jaw. "Henry thought it was funny the way I couldn't stay in the lane. I was laughing too, because *he* was laughing. Then we saw Wildemere's lights coming around the bend. I think I got mostly back in my lane, but I can't be certain. We blinded each other. Henry stopped laughing, but not until we made impact. Up until then he still thought it was funny."

Barley stood in the doorway, nodding, silently coming to terms with what had happened.

William had cried out his emotions on Barley's shoulder. Now he was a dried-out husk, a hollow shell. He looked at his father. "He was laughing?"

"Yes. He was." Barley smiled, reminiscing. "We were having us a good time."

"Did he say anything? About me?"

Barley thought on it, nodded. "Said you were mad at him earlier. And it made him sad."

The lump in William's throat was instant.

"But then he danced it all out in the aging house."

"I watched him."

"I know. Henry said he saw you out the window."

"And?"

"And that's how he knew it was okay."

William wasn't completely dried up after all. Moisture came to his eyes and puddled there. "Father, why did you take Henry with you? Why was he even in the car?"

"Because he asked me if he could come, William. He asked

me if he could come. And you know I never could tell that boy no."

Sometime in the middle of the night, William's bedroom door opened for the second time. The floor creaked and William felt his father's breath on his forehead, smelled Old Sam bourbon. Barley kissed the skin above William's eyes and whispered that he loved him.

The floor creaked and the door closed, and William was alone again, heart pounding so hard he feared it was audible. Next, he heard Johnny's bedroom door open down the hallway, and a minute later it closed. Then Barley entered Annie's room. Barley closed her door and walked down the stairs. William waited to hear the front door open, but it never did.

The rock hit the window at three minutes after four. Polly was bundled in a coat that may have been Carly's. It was cold enough for steam to escape her mouth. She waved him down. He contemplated the wisdom of sneaking out. Barley was on high alert and armed men stalked the porch. But then he looked at her pretty face, imagined her lips against his, and motioned that he'd be right down.

He tossed on some clothes and lifted the bedroom window. It wasn't the first time he'd exited this way. Samantha, soon after Henry died, had a sudden fear of the house burning down. She'd made them practice climbing out the second-story windows in case a fire ever blocked their passage down the stairs.

"Like a cat out of a tree," Polly said after he jumped the last three feet down.

"How'd you get past my father's men?"

"I told them I was dizzy for a young man."

"Really?"

"That word again, William." She slapped his arm. "Yes, I said it. And I also meant it."

"Well then, so do I."

"So do you what?"

"You know . . . I guess I'm dizzy for a dame. *Really* dizzy."

She grinned bashfully. William looked back to the house, specifically to his open bedroom window. The wind would rattle the door and make noises that could alert his parents of his absence. Before he had time to dwell on the repercussions, Polly grabbed his hand.

She ran and William followed, tethered at the fingers, feet pounding across dewy grass and moist leaves. A man and woman knelt praying, illegally taking a nocturnal turn with the Potter's Field Christ. Apparently the police were easily bribed. The couple looked up at the sound of footsteps, so Polly pulled William behind a thick-trunked tree. Would their steaming breath give away their position? Polly kissed him, a deep kiss. Her lips were so cold, but her breath was warm. Then she giggled. "Steam comes out our noses!"

"Should I kiss your nose and see if it comes out our ears?"

The couple finished praying. As soon as the coast was clear, Polly and William ran directly to the aging house. Together they slipped inside, where it was warmer. The ricks had been stacked ten rows high with full barrels, and there were still thousands of spots to be filled. Moonlight entered the spaced windows, although Polly navigated the maze-like rows as if she'd designed them herself. She pulled William to a fixed spot in the far back corner where the boards had been upturned. Pillows and blankets had been positioned in a pallet, walled in on two sides by empty barrels and a third side by the rick house wall.

The smell of the angels' share, especially from the open floor-boards, was potent enough to taste, the air thick with vanilla, caramel, and corn. Polly pulled William down to the pallet. William's ribs hurt with every movement, but he didn't care. He lifted the blankets, and together they slid beneath the warmth.

TWENTY-SEVEN

Polly looked beautiful while she slept. William waited for the sun to rise, a sliver through the window and then a thick swath of light across Polly's face. He traced her jawline with his fingers and her eyes fluttered.

Birds sang from the trees. The angels' share had a different smell in the morning, more crisp than thick, and the aroma made him hungry. He asked Polly to listen, to see if they could hear the barrels. Supposedly they expanded and contracted when the weather changed.

"What time is it?" Polly kissed the corner of his mouth. "Are you afraid your father will find us here?"

He kissed her forehead. "Are you?"

The dog barked and a man's deep voice sounded from the potter's field. "Dooly McDowell! Come out and take what's owed."

Bullets cleaved the air, rapid fire, burrowing into wood and pinging metal, tin, and stone. Windows shattered all over the distillery. People screamed; Cat barked and barked.

William jumped from the floor and looked over the lip of the window to see Tommy the Bat at Asher Keating's grave, facing the main house and firing a tommy gun with abandon. Three goons stood behind him, firing machine guns every which way. Bullets whizzed back at them from the main house. The screaming intensified as people ran from the onslaught; as the crowd fled, the deer that had been watching from the woods darted *toward* the chaos, frantically sprinting across the potter's field. Then dozens of holes punctured the side of the aging house. Glass and wood flew inward. Bullets punctured barrels and bourbon sprayed across the floorboards.

"Polly?" William shouted. "Are you hit? Are you okay?"

"I'm okay!" Polly pulled the blanket up to her neck and hunkered down.

William scrounged for his shoes and threw them on untied.

"William, what are you doing?"

"I'll know in a minute." He put on his hat and took off running. He wished he'd had a gun on him, or a knife. He saw a police officer bleeding in the grass, alongside two dying deer.

"Dooly McDowell!"

Tommy Borduchi had disappeared around the corner of the house, calling out Dooly McDowell's name. William realized all four cops were down. So were two of Tommy's men, and three of Barley's were in the grass near the house.

William made it to the locked back door. A deer scooted past and disappeared around the corner of the house. He banged on the window as shots fired from the front of the house.

"Dooly McDowell!"

A barrage of shots was fired. Someone yelled in pain; his mother screamed. William punched a hole through the lowest pane, shattering the glass and cutting his arm. He reached in up to his armpit and unlocked the door as more bullets rang through the house. He entered, lowered himself to a duck-walk, and scrambled into the dining room. The walls were shot to plaster and dust. In the living room he saw Samantha crouched next to the fireplace, guarding Annie. Johnny was on the floor, covering his ears. Barley moaned and leaked blood.

William's heart was in his throat. He was exposed between the dining and living rooms without a weapon. The front door was creaking on one hinge, wide open, giving view of Barley's fourth guard riddled with bullets and dead on the porch. Tommy dropped his machine gun, removed a baseball bat from his coat, and approached Barley.

"Stop!" William screamed.

Barley, who was alive enough to roll on his back, hissed at William, "Run."

William didn't run. "Some things just already are. My brother. He said some things aren't learned. They just already are. Sometimes the bad stuff gets in. You cut yourself. You do it to let the bad stuff out, so you don't burst. But still it comes."

Tommy laughed. "Says the palooka standing unarmed in my face." Polly entered the kitchen. William saw her from the corner of his eye, and in that glance he also saw Barley's rifle leaning against the dining room table. A deer scurried through the open door, its hooves *tick-tack*ing across the hardwood in a panicked dance. Tommy watched the deer.

William used the distraction to grab the Machete. "Take another step, Mr. Borduchi, and I'll blow your head off."

"You don't have the sand, boy." Tommy insolently took a step forward.

"Devil's done taken his share from this family."

The bullet bored a hole through the middle of Tommy.

—————

Polly was the first to check on Barley. Samantha commanded Annie to stay put. Then she hurried over to her husband and wept as Johnny made it to his feet, crying, his face covered in white plaster dust. "We have to pray, William," he said frantically. He started toward the front door where the panicked deer had just fled.

Barley grabbed Johnny's ankle. "No, son. Don't."

And then it dawned on William. It was a miracle that no one else had been hit. Barley was ready to die. He'd known. That was why he visited all of their rooms last night. But knowing this didn't make it any easier to watch his father bleed to death. William bit his lip, fought the rage that was welling up inside him. He'd only begun to know his father.

He removed his shirt, tore strips from it, and attempted to stymie the blood flow.

"William, don't," Barley said. "Let me go."

Cat walked in covered in dirt and blood. He licked Barley's hand.

"William." It was Polly. He tuned her out.

He turned toward Tommy Borduchi, who lay half-strewn across the sill of the bay window. William pulled the bat from his slack grip. He hoisted it above his right shoulder and brought it down. Annie started screaming. Her voice stopped him cold.

He dropped the bat, wiped his face. "Don't look, Sugar Cakes. Don't look. Everything's going to be jake."

Samantha stopped crying. She gripped Barley's hands in her own and kissed them. Her lips had blood and tears on them.

"I see you," Barley said softly.

Samantha nodded, squeezed his hands.

William knelt beside Barley.

"Nice shot, William." Barley's chest rose and settled through gurgled breaths. "William." Barley choked on blood. "Tell Wildemere . . . he's forgiven."

William's voice caught, but he stayed strong. "I'll do that, Father."

Contentment washed over Barley. His eyes gleamed and a tear trickled from his right eye. "Henry . . ." Barley's lips parted and his eyes opened wider.

Samantha sobbed and so did Johnny. William reached out, closed Barley's eyes. He closed his father's mouth. He gripped Polly's hand. Together they pulled Samantha and Johnny into the fold along with Annie.

Just the way Barley would have wanted it.

TWENTY-EIGHT

November 26, 1934

Dear William McFee,

My condolences on the tragic death of your father. I pray your family is able to move on from such unspeakable horror. I do my utmost to keep such news from my patients. They have experienced tragedies of their own and need not be reminded of the evils outside our walls. But, as water often finds ways through cracks, so does the news. Maryanne Keating has learned of what happened at your distillery and has begged to send you a letter. I understand the crowds have diminished, and she hopes that her son can finally have peace. Maryanne's behavior has improved of late. Although she still sometimes has illusions of grandeur, she has been much sounder of mind since your visit, and she prays that the enclosed finds you, and finds you well, after all that has occurred.

Sincerely,

Dr. Sebastian Givens

Superintendent, Central
Kentucky Asylum for the
Insane

I was at sea for twelve days, aboard the RMS *Celtic* of the
White Star Line. From Liverpool to New York with a call at
Queenstown.

Steerage was full with over four hundred foreigners.
Women without escorts were stowed on the sides of the
ship, like pockets, divided into rooms that held up to sixteen
people, with a common meal room. The air was soured with
body odors. There was no repository aside from the corner of
the berth. No sick cans. Washrooms were too few and over-
crowded. The bunks were iron with straw mattresses, the
blankets made of horsehair, and we each had a tin plate and
pannikin, a knife, and a fork or a spoon. I was the only one
with child.

We all set about fixing our bunks in silence, and I noticed
that most of the women had something for seasickness: bottles
of foul-smelling liquids and medicines, lime drops, apples, and
raw onions. I brought nothing but my small bundle of clothing and the growing bundle inside my belly. I rubbed it when
the boat tossed and turned. A German woman asked if it was
for good luck that I rubbed my belly, and I nodded. A Finnish
woman asked if a genie was going to come out. All across steerage hooligans had begun their drunken rowdiness. People
danced and made love while flutes and accordions played and
dancers did the jig. The atmosphere turned to misery as we
ventured deeper out into the Atlantic. A northwester tossed

the boat across the clumpy sea. I kept to myself, speaking only to the baby inside me, numbing my fears with sips from the flask of whiskey in my pocket.

On day three the stewards rounded up steerage for vaccination. I waited for three hours in line. Everyone was tired and hot, and we'd yet to eat that day. Babies cried, and so many complained in a variety of languages. One child in particular, in the arms of his overwhelmed mother, screamed so loudly, and it was incessant. A Welshman threatened to shut the boy up himself if the mother would not, but the boy just kept crying. His eyes were directly on me, on my belly. The mother soon noticed it as well and walked the baby back to me, allowing the ones in front of me to pass her. "Go on," I told her. She stepped closer, cautiously, for her screaming baby was now reaching for my belly. His tiny hand brushed me and his crying calmed. He began to pet me, so gently that his touch gave me comfort as well. He kept his hand on my belly until it was his turn for inspection, and by then he'd calmed enough for his thankful mother to lure him away from me. That evening, the same woman who'd asked me if I had a genie inside me made a comment about my baby being special. I nodded in agreement. She asked if I thought it was a boy or a girl. I told her it was a boy. She asked how I knew. I told her it felt like a boy. She asked me if I had other children. I told her no, this was my first. She left me alone, although she watched me from across the room for the rest of the voyage.

Sparing the horrifying details of nearly two weeks in steerage with drunken fools and filth, we eventually docked at the East River pier, and I was fortunate enough to witness the arrival from the deck's railing, with a cool washrag against my forehead. I'd been having contractions for hours, and my fellow passengers had enough heart to give me space—there was a noticeable upturn in mood as we'd approached the shoreline.

The first- and second-class passengers passed Customs on the boat and were immediately allowed down the gangway, but third class and steerage were roped back and held on the boat for another hour as we gathered our citizen's papers. For two hours we waited on the pier for the barge to take us to Ellis Island for our medical and legal inspections. There we baked in the sun while Americans swore at us and told us to go back home.

An Italian man asked me where the father was, and his words made me melancholy. Was I doing the right thing running from home? I pondered the question, just as I had before leaving Dublin, leaving behind a family who loved me, I once thought, unconditionally—until they called me a harlot. How could I not know the father? My own father never wanted to see me again. He had wholesome daughters to take care of, and if I was old enough to be with child, I was old enough to be out on my own. My mother was of the opinion that I should be sent to the asylum. She called me a blasphemer and said the Devil in me needed to be cast out before any more harm could be done to my tender brain. Of all the words they'd thrown at me, oddly enough, it was the word *tender* that made me want to leave and never come back. Up until then it had been a pleasant word, but then it became a closing door, a feared future. Perhaps in another country I would be understood, and welcomed. I didn't ask for this.

On that pier, while mean-spirited men and women shouted slurs, it was the voices of my mother and father that

I heard. They'd followed me across the Atlantic and they will follow me until the end of my days, for they follow me still. I entertained thoughts of suicide—I'd nearly tried it a half dozen times in the first five months, before I'd begun to show. The truth was I never pressed the knife deep enough. I never swallowed enough to do the job. The noose was not tied correctly when the chair toppled.

I thought about drowning myself in the river, and possibly would have had the deer not tapped across the pier with its nose perked to the river and its eyes on me. It watched as the first group of us loaded onto a barge. It watched as we drifted away, and then all of a sudden it got a running start and leapt. Some people screamed, some laughed, but everyone backed away to give it space. The deer never came close to me as I sat on the grungy floor, but it watched; it watched me until we docked at Ellis Island, and then it followed me as two kind gentlemen helped me walk to steady land again. Lines formed toward the building. The deer stayed outside near the water, skittish as immigrants passed it by.

Jesus was born in a manger, I told myself, hobbling into the Great Hall, where we were grouped and tagged. There were animals present to witness His birth. Doctors scanned quickly for anemia, varicose veins, or goiters, and when they noticed my obvious discomfort, they pulled me out of the line. Two things happened at that instant. The deer ran through the open door and into the Great Hall, and I gave birth, right there on the floor of the Registry Room, as a thousand immigrants watched. There was no crying. None at all. But my boy was alive. His little eyes watched over the room. I named him Asher. I'd decided on the Hebrew name before I'd boarded the steamship. It means "happy, lucky, blessed." I hoped to be all of those things when he was born, and in that moment my hopes came true, for I'd never been so happy, never felt so lucky, never felt so blessed. I cried, however, because I knew I now had a future.

I kissed Asher's forehead. I forgave my family for not believing me, for they understood not what was needed from them. Had that nosy Italian man asked me at that moment about the absence of the father, I would have proudly told him to look into my son's eyes, and there you will find the Father, because his Father is everywhere, and in everything, and the voice that had come to me in my dreams was as real as the baby who never cried.

AFTER

November 1940

Annie McFee said Johnny would look handsome in an army uniform. But Samantha had begged her wayward son not to enlist. William had known since '39 that his brother would try to go; he said he wanted to kill Nazis like his father had killed Krauts.

Samantha tied a red balloon to a low tree limb in the family cemetery. Today was both a sad and joyous occasion. Johnny was leaving for basic training in the morning. To send him off properly they were tasting the first batches of Old Sam. It had aged six years.

A fresh bouquet of flowers leaned against Barley McFee's headstone. The surrounding trees were decorated patriotically with red, white, and blue balloons.

"Will Johnny go to war?" Annie stood from the bench. She'd just finished telling stories about Henry and Barley.

William tapped a blue one, bouncing it into the red and

295

white balloons next to it, and watched as the cluster swayed in the breeze. He longed for the days when he was able to carry his little sister around, but now, at twelve, she was nearly as tall as their mother. "Well, not yet," he said. "But he is enlisting. To protect us."

"From Nazis?"

"From whoever threatens us," William answered. He walked with Annie toward the front of the house. More red, white, and blue balloons floated from the porch columns; the paint was starting to flake again, and William made a mental note to repaint it soon.

He added, "Though I don't see how we can stay out of this one."

William dreaded the tax increase should they go to war. The country always raised taxes on the aging houses to pay for the wars, and that burden would fall on his shoulders.

"He'll kill a lot of them," Annie said confidently. She was an aunt now, twice, in fact—William and Polly had a three-year-old named Sam and a one-year-old named Mary.

William offered his hand. Annie gripped it, and together they walked across the driveway toward the potter's field. She was too old to carry, but she still liked to hold her brother's hand. They'd become even closer after their father's death.

William made sure not to walk too fast. Two years after the Potter's Field Massacre—which had left twenty dead—Annie began to acquire a subtle hitch in her walk. It never worsened to more than a limp and was rarely spoken of because Samantha refused to acknowledge it. *"She walks fine, William,"* Samantha insisted. *"Stop your gumshoeing."*

The potter's field was overgrown with weeds now, and most

of the crosses had collapsed with the seasons. A new potter's field had sprung up five miles down the road. Only Asher's grave was cut and tended to regularly, which was what Barley would have wanted, according to Johnny; so he was the one who tended to it.

For months after the tragedy, people continued to visit Asher's grave, but by the next year visitors had slowed to a trickle, and then finally to an infrequent knock on the door. Although the grave site had lost its luster, ten churches had moved into Twisted Tree, and the main strip upon which they'd settled was referred to as the Highway to Heaven.

The distillery was thriving with a full slate of workers now. Ronald's Ghost was wildly popular, as was the limited two-year-aged bourbon they'd released as Barley McFee.

Still, William often missed the excitement of the Potter's Field Christ. Six years had passed since the burial, and now, to most in the country, Asher Keating was a distant memory. But not to William, and not to the McFees, and not to a good portion of the folks in Twisted Tree, whose town had been revived in part because of Asher Keating.

William had drawn national acclaim with his coverage of the 1937 flood, but it became the last serious journalistic work he would do. As master distiller, he had made the distillery his life. To fulfill the occasional urge to report the news, he wrote a weekly column for the *Courier-Journal*. It was about bourbon distilling.

He did miss the hope Asher's stories had brought forth. *"Asher Keating did his job,"* Polly told William. *"He was a reminder. He was fuel. Let him rest."*

William agreed that Asher had been fuel, but he had burned out too early. The country had moved from the Depression to the uncertainty of another global war. Asher's stories could be rekindled, could prove useful to morale. But he didn't want the attention brought back to his family, so he ultimately decided to let Asher rest.

Annie still prayed in thanks every day and often left flowers on Asher's grave. The blackened cross was still intact. Annie had tied balloons to it in the morning. They bounced together as the two approached the aging house, where the party was to begin.

Backdropped by thousands of golden trees, Johnny opened the door and hung halfway out into the sunlight. "Come on, you two. Let's not wait until it gets aged to seven!"

William gave Johnny a hug; his brother clapped his back. "Want to join me, old man?"

William laughed it off. The truth of it was, Johnny had yet to, as Samantha said, find himself. He'd gone through a half dozen jobs in the two years since he'd turned eighteen, and three times that many girlfriends. He was lost and needed a road map.

Polly walked her husband over to the barrel Mr. Browder had tagged as "the one." He hadn't cut the bourbon down to proof yet, so William's first taste was only one of ceremony.

William nosed the glass and smelled teases of fruit, vanilla, and caramel. "To Barley McFee, and Sam, before him," William said, savoring the first sip, a smooth wave of flavor. "To Johnny. May the Lord keep him safe in his future endeavors for our country."

Johnny took the glass and then a sip before he handed it to Annie. She held her nose and took a sip. She stuck her tongue out, which made everyone laugh. Annie gladly handed the glass to her mother, who was motioning for a little dusty-haired boy of five to come over from one of the rows of barrels—William's youngest and most unexpected sibling.

"Barley," Samantha said. "Come on, boy. You're just like your father."

The little boy sat on Samantha's lap as she took a drink, savoring it with her eyes closed.

"I want a drink," Barley Junior said.

His mother gave him a smell.

Barley Junior rolled his eyes and pretended to collapse on the floor. They all laughed and then smiled when the boy broke out into a quick little dance. Just like Henry would have done, although without the God-given talent. And then Barley Junior ran off to whatever he was doing in between the barrel rows before his mother had called him over.

William and Annie watched their little brother as he pretended to write on a notepad. "He's taking inventory," William guessed.

The surprise pregnancy had helped Samantha survive Barley's death. *"It had to have happened after that date,"* Johnny said after they'd found out their mother, at forty, was pregnant. *"Probably so,"* William told him.

Annie watched Barley Junior. "He *is* a little miracle," she said to William.

"The kind I can more easily wrap my head around." William saw daily the uncanny resemblance between Barley Junior and Henry. They could have been mistaken for twins. Barley Junior's feet moved subtly as he took inventory of the barrels, shuffling to a beat only he could hear.

Annie leaned her head on William's shoulder. "Remember what I used to ask you about Henry?"

William nodded against the top of her head.

Still watching Barley Junior, Annie said, "I always knew that he'd come back."

HISTORICAL NOTE

I suppose I'd categorize *The Angels' Share* as commercial fiction set during historical times, rather than straight historical fiction, because the town of Twisted Tree doesn't exist, except in my mind, and now hopefully in yours as well. But it does represent what the old distillery towns could have been like—the lifeblood of the town, in many cases—prospering for years and then declining suddenly because of Prohibition. So it is true that these towns experienced their own type of depression a decade before the Great Depression gripped the country, and once Prohibition was repealed, most of the distilleries never bounced back. In order to become bourbon, whiskey has to age, so the distilleries that did start running again couldn't bear the fruit of their labors until years down the road, unless they decided to sell the clear, unaged corn whiskey right off the still, which many did until the bourbon whiskey aged.

One bourbon to survive Prohibition was Old Forester—originally Forrester with two *r*'s—and it was one of only a handful allowed to be made for medicinal purposes. *Medicinal* was a very loose term, and during Prohibition, whiskey was prescribed for just about every ailment, even as minor as the common cold, especially for those wealthy enough to pad the doctors' and pharmacists' pockets with some cabbage. In other words, it was not hard for the well-to-do to obtain liquor; while, on the other hand, the rest had to attempt to make their own—which sometimes resulted in sickness or death—or they had to find their way into whatever avenue they could of the ever-increasing world of speakeasies and bootlegging that soon gave way to organized crime. Thank you, Volstead Act, for creating all those gangsters in the twenties and thirties!

As far as bourbon is concerned, there are rules that make it so. There's the old adage: "All bourbon is whiskey, but not all whiskey is bourbon." These bourbon rules were not yet regulated during the time of this story, but here they are: First, it must be made in the United States. It certainly doesn't have to be made in Kentucky, although that state does produce 95 percent of the world's bourbon supply, and that percentage was still accurate during the time of this story. Kentucky has an abundance of white oak trees—what some call the whiskey trees—as well as a lot of limestone to naturally filter the water used for distilling. Louisville, specifically, consistently ranks at the top of the list for some of the best tap water in the country. Second, the aging must take place in a new, charred oak barrel. If it ain't new and charred, it ain't bourbon. Oftentimes Scotch will be aged in used bourbon barrels from Kentucky. Third, the mash bill—basically the ingredients—must be at least 51 percent corn, with some distilleries pushing up to 70 percent or more. The rest is made of rye and barley. Fourth, the whiskey can't enter the barrel at higher than 125 proof—it has to be watered down—and it can't be bottled at less than 80 proof. Fifth, and lastly, nothing can be added except for water, and this would only be to decrease the proof. If you've got some kind of flavored whiskey, or anything with color and flavor, it's not bourbon. Bourbon gets all of its coloring and flavor naturally from the charred oak wood as it expands and contracts during the aging process.

The first bourbon distillery I ever visited was Jim Beam in Clermont, Kentucky. The campus, like every distillery I've toured since, is quaint and beautiful, and as soon as I stepped foot inside one of their aging houses to see rows upon stacked rows of barrels aging on ricks, I knew I had to write a story about bourbon, and more specifically about what I smelled inside the aging house: the thick, buttery aroma of vanilla and butterscotch and caramel and fruit—I could go on—of what I learned was called the angels' share. The whiskey that evaporates through the barrel staves as it ages, the offering to the angels! Some believed, especially back in the day when fires were more prevalent, that the angels, after receiving their share, in turn kept the distilleries safe from fire. Some distilleries unfortunately still caught fire, and when a distillery burned, there was no putting it out. They usually burned to the ground. Jim Beam actually has a bourbon now called Devil's Cut, which comes from liquid extracted from the used barrels, the theory being that if the angels get their share, the Devil might as well get his cut too, which gave me the idea for Old Sam McFee pouring an offering off the still into the well so the Devil would also get his share.

Last year alone, over eight hundred thousand people visited the Kentucky bourbon distilleries in what is now widely known as the Bourbon Trail, and my wife and I, along with some eager friends, are knocking them off one by one, collecting bottles and sampling and taking in every little nuance of these hidden gems. There is also a growing craft tour of smaller distilleries that are equally as pleasing to the palate.

We are right smack-dab in the middle of a bourbon boom that stretches the globe with distribution, a Golden Age so to speak, and there are now more barrels of bourbon aging in Kentucky than people. Bourbon is not just a drink anymore; it's now a culture and a growing identity. So if you, loyal reader, haven't had the chance to visit these distilleries and take in the smell of the angels' share, I hope that one day you will.

As mentioned before, Twisted Tree is a fictional place, but I'd like to take a few words to mention the aspects of the story that were rooted in history. Leaning on what I've seen from my many bourbon tours, I had to blur my eyes and imagine what the distilleries could have been like back then. They didn't have gift shops and T-shirts as they do now, but I'd like to think they were very similar to how I described Old Sam McFee in the book, secluded and surrounded by trees and limestone water and ripe with the fresh smell of mash.

Unfortunately, the Klan was very real. Although much smaller in the 1930s than it had grown during the mid-1920s when it became one of their main priorities as Prohibitionists to break up speakeasies and dismantle anything to do with rum running and evil spirits—along with perpetuating the hate we've come to associate with the Klan—the KKK was still a force in the South during the time of this story.

The coke ovens where Polly sometimes stayed were real, and after they were no longer used, the homeless did move in and the police would move them back out.

Rose Island was a real place, like a modern-day amusement

park, with all the fun things mentioned in the book, even down to the famous black bear in their zoo named Teddy Roosevelt. Rose Island now looks like a ghost haven, but at one time was a wonderful place for families to spend their day. To my knowledge, no shady dealings between gangsters and bootleggers took place there, but who really knows?

The *Courier-Journal* building where William takes his stories was a real place, as were most of the mentions of Louisville back then.

The Lakeland Lunatic Asylum, where Asher Keating's mother stayed, was a real institution and looked as described in the book. It was torn down decades ago and replaced by a prison.

Everything of historical significance in the book, from Prohibition and bootlegging, to the war and the Great Depression, to the Roaring Twenties and the unique language used then, is as accurate as I could make it. Obviously when dealing with history and fiction, sometimes facts and details slip through, but my goal was to provide the best overall impression of the times as I could, and hopefully I did that.

Lastly, homelessness resides at the heart of *The Angels' Share*, and no time was it more prevalent than during the Great Depression, when so many lost all they had and finding work proved difficult. It saddens me to think of the number of homeless in the world, and homeless veterans especially, men and women who fought for their country but somehow slipped into obscurity and go unremembered in death, as if their lives didn't matter. That's when I came up with the character of Asher Keating, a homeless veteran buried in a field with others cast aside and forgotten. I thought, *What if this one did matter, a lot, and to a lot of people, despite the fact that he was homeless and possibly mentally ill?*

What if he mattered so much that those who knew him thought him special, someone who had little but gave much and changed lives for the better? A man, even though dead for the entire story, who could brighten days with memories of how he lived his life, with generosity and compassion for all?

And so the story of the Potter's Field Christ was born.

I hope you enjoyed reading it as much as I enjoyed writing it.

Until next time.

James Markert
May 17, 2016

ACKNOWLEDGMENTS

An author may get the praise and his name on the front cover, but no book can be written without the guidance and support of others. Writing a novel truly is a team effort. Writing the acknowledgments is the most stressful part of a novel for me, because I'm paranoid I'll leave someone out. So for all those I'm leaving out, thank you so much! I would like to thank my wonderful parents for raising me in a loving household where creativity thrived and the arts were as regular as the seasons— that upbringing will forever be my muse. To my earliest first-draft readers, Craig Kremer, Tim Burke, Lloyd Holm, Jeff Bunch, Tom McGraw, Amy Stock, and Carrie Coe; to my siblings, David, Joseph, and Michelle, for their unflinching support; to my cousin John Markert for being a constant sounding board. Thank you to my friends and support system at St. Edward, and to all of my tennis families and friends in Indiana, Blairwood, and Louisville Tennis Club, especially Larry Kline for his friendship and support over the past twenty years. To Gill Holland for your early praise and enthusiasm for this novel; you got the ball rolling for sure, so thank you. I consulted several books in researching this novel, and I'd like to give those authors and titles a quick mention: *Kentucky Bourbon Country* by Susan Reigler, *Bourbon in Kentucky* by Chester Zoeller, *Prohibition: Thirteen Years That Changed America* by Edward Behr, *Boardwalk Empire* by Nelson Johnson, *The Great Depression: America in the 1930s* by T. H. Watkins, and the great book *The Encyclopedia of Louisville*, edited by John E. Kleber.

Any mistakes in the novel are mine.

I'd like to thank one of my high school English teachers who has passed away—Roger Eppinger—for having us read Stephen King our senior year instead of the so-called classics. You got kids to read, and more important you helped nurture *my* love for reading, and the rest, as they say, is history. After a few drafts of this novel, I was confused and felt like I was swimming upstream with no paddle, and then my brilliant agent sent Allison McCabe to the rescue. Allison, your editorial advice not only helped save the novel but gave me the confidence to plow on with what will hopefully be a long, fruitful career of making stuff up. You helped pull from the muck the exact voice and tone I was striving for, and I look forward to collaborating on future projects. To all of my new friends at Thomas Nelson/HarperCollins, I can't wait for this ride to begin: Becky Philpott for championing this thing from the start; Daisy Hutton for welcoming me aboard; Karli Jackson for your keen editing eye and for molding the final product into perfect shape; Becky Monds, Jodi Hughes, and Kristen Golden for helping this book shine brighter; Julee Schwarzburg for the line editing and expert advice; and all those who have contributed throughout the process from editing to marketing to distribution—thank you!

All writers think they have the best agent, but I really do. Thank you, Dan Lazar from Writers House, for believing and never giving up on me. You were so correct, the second book is tough. But we did it, and now I'm ready to start kicking out books at a rate James Patterson and Stephen King would be proud of! And to Torie Doherty-Monroe at Writers House for reading those early drafts of *The Angels' Share*—your notes proved helpful as always.

My biggest support, no doubt, comes from Tracy, my wife of seventeen years and counting. She has never once given a hint that she didn't believe in what I'm doing, however financially inconsistent it may be. Thank you for always believing in me and our dream, and never, verbally at least, telling me to give up and get a real job. And oh, "I think this book is finally 'The One'!"

And lastly, thank you, loyal reader, for doing what you do.

DISCUSSION QUESTIONS

1. At the beginning of the novel, William's relationship with his father is not especially deep. How does their relationship as father and son evolve throughout the story?

2. The concept of miracles runs throughout *The Angels' Share*. What events could be considered miracles? Which one is the most essential to the outcome of the story?

3. How do hope and redemption play a role in the novel, specifically with Barley and his past?

4. Which character changes the most from the beginning to the end of the novel? How and why?

5. Asher, despite not being alive for the entirety of the novel, is the force that pushes the narrative. Discuss Asher Keating. Was he a normal man? Was he born special, like a prodigy? Or could he have been something more?

6. Prohibition may have caused more problems than it solved, and organized crime was a result of it. What role did Prohibition play in the plot of the novel?

7. What influences did Asher's life have on the major characters of the novel? William? Annie? Samantha? Barley? Johnny? Mr. Browder? Tommy the Bat?

8. Discuss the concept of nature versus nurture, with Tommy the Bat and his nun twin sister as a starting point.

ABOUT THE AUTHOR

Photo by John Markert

James Markert lives with his wife and two children in Louisville, Kentucky. He has a history degree from the University of Louisville and won an IPPY Award for *The Requiem Rose*, which was later published as *A White Wind Blew*. *The Angels' Share* is his second novel, and he is currently writing his next historical novel. He is the writer and co-producer of the feature film and tennis comedy *2nd Serve*. James is also a USPTA tennis pro and has coached dozens of kids who've gone on to play college tennis in top conferences like the Big 10, the Big East, and the ACC. Learn more at jamesmarkertbooks.com.

Facebook: James Markert
Twitter: @JamesMarkert